CODE OF HONOR

Also by Alan Gratz

Prisoner B-3087

ALAN GRATZ

CODE OF HONOR

SCHOLASTIC PRESS / NEW YORK

Library of Congress Cataloging-in-Publication Data

Gratz, Alan, 1972- author.
Code of honor / Alan Gratz. — First edition.
pages cm
Summary: When Iranian-American Kamran Smith learns that his big brother, Darius, has been labeled a terrorist, he sets out to piece together the codes and clues that will save his brother's life and his country from a deadly terrorist attack.
ISBN 978-0-545-69519-0 (jacketed hardcover) 1. Brothers—Juvenile fiction. 2. Terrorists—Juvenile fiction. 3. Code and cipher stories. 4. Terrorism—Juvenile fiction. 5. Iranian Americans—Juvenile fiction. 6. Muslims—Juvenile fiction. 7. Terrorists—Fiction. [1. Brothers—Fiction 2. Ciphers—Fiction. 3. Terrorism—Fiction. 4. Iranian Americans—Fiction. 5. Muslims—Fiction.] I. Title.
PZ7.G77224Co 2015
[Fic]—dc23
2014046797

10 9 8 7 6 5 4 3 2 1   15 16 17 18 19

Printed in the U.S.A.   23
First edition, September 2015
Book design by Nina Goffi

For Donald, the only real spy I know

A CRASH LIKE A LINEBACKER COLLIDING WITH A quarterback woke me, and I shot straight up in bed. I blinked at the clock beside me, trying to make sense of the world. Red numbers glowed in the darkness. *Three twenty-three.* It was three twenty-three in the morning. Why was I awake at three twenty-three in the morning? Had I dreamed the crashing sound?

"Kamran?" my mother called from down the hall. "Kamran? Was that you? Are you all right?"

Thunder. No—footsteps. Feet pounding down the hall. Someone was coming for me. Half-remembered childhood nightmares seized me, and I scrambled backward across the bed in a panic, trying to get away from Voldemort, the Joker, the aliens, the demons. I fell on the floor with a thump, the bedcovers coming with me. My legs were tangled in them. I couldn't kick free.

And then they were there. Dark shapes surged into my room, black on black silhouettes with hulking shoulders and big round eyes that flashed. My fear made me five again. I curled up against the side of the bed like I was playing hide-and-seek with my older brother, Darius, hoping he wouldn't see me. But the demons knew where I was. They homed in on me like guided missiles.

Rough hands grabbed me. Hauled me to my feet. Threw me face-first on the bed. Somewhere, remotely, I heard my mother scream, heard my father cry out. The demons had come for them, too.

"Mom! Dad!" I cried. I kicked and squirmed, trying to get away, but my arms were wrenched behind me and bound with a plastic zip tie that cut into my wrists. The hands pulled me up again, and I read the words on one of my captors' uniforms:

POLICE

HOMELAND SECURITY

Reality finally overrode my half-awake nightmares. "No. No! Darius is innocent!" I cried. "He's not a terrorist! You don't understand! They're making him do everything!"

The DHS agents wrangled a thick bag over my head, and the already dark room went completely black.

"No! Please! Don't!" I yelled. The black bag was close. Suffocating. My hot breath was damp on my face, and I started to panic. "You can't do this! I was born in America! I'm an American citizen!"

The DHS agents ignored my protests. I kicked and thrashed as they dragged me from my room, down the hall, and out through the front door.

A few days ago, all I had cared about was winning the homecoming game. Getting into college. Going on a date with Julia Gary. Normal high school senior stuff. A few days ago, I had been king of the world.

Now I was a prisoner of the United States of America.

CHAPTER ONE

A FEW DAYS AGO

"LADIES AND GENTLEMEN, I GIVE YOU EAST PHOENIX High School's homecoming king and queen: Kamran Smith and Julia Gary!"

The crowd clapped and cheered, and Julia and I descended the steps to the dance floor. Julia clung to my arm like she was never going to let me go, and I grinned at her.

I spied my best friend, Adam Collier, in the crowd. He gave me a deep, flourishing bow like some duke at court, and I laughed. Even though Adam and I had joked around about the homecoming dance, I had to admit that being crowned king—especially alongside Julia—felt pretty amazing.

When Julia and I got to the middle of the dance floor for our spotlight dance, the DJ played that old Green Day song "Time of Your Life." I put my arms around Julia's waist and she leaned into me, laying her head on my chest.

"I am, you know," I told Julia, tucking a lock of blond hair behind her ear. "Having the time of my life. With you." I didn't even care if it sounded cheesy. I meant every word.

Julia stood on her toes to kiss me, which made my head tingle, like always. I loved Julia. There. I said it. I maybe hadn't said it *out loud* to her yet, but she had to know it. Julia was smart, funny, and *way* cute. We'd been dating for two months, and I didn't know what we were going to do when I left Arizona for West Point next year. But this was definitely not the night to think about that.

The DJ slid into a bouncing hip-hop song, and kids streamed onto the dance floor, hopping and waving their arms. Adam and some of my other football teammates and their dates surrounded us, shouting their congratulations.

"Double congrats," Adam said, punching my arm. He glanced around at our teammates. "Did y'all know there was a college scout at the game tonight? From the University of Colorado. Pac-12! That's big time. And Kamran put on a *show* for him!"

I shrugged and blushed. I hadn't told anybody else about the scout, not even Julia, because I didn't want to make a big deal out of it. I was committed to going to West Point and playing for Army anyway. But it had still made me play harder, knowing the scout was there in the stands. I'd had the best game of my high school career, scoring three touchdowns.

"I wouldn't have run for all those yards without the offensive line stepping up," I said. "That last touchdown was me just following Antonio into the end zone."

Adam scoffed. "Dude, you're too modest. This guy's going to the Super Bowl one day," he told everybody.

"Yeah, um, I don't think so."

"No, I mean it," Adam said. He pulled out his phone and brought up a photo. Fanned out on a table were four oversize silver tickets, each with a picture of the Vince Lombardi Trophy and SUPER BOWL XLIX written across the top. "We're going to the Super Bowl, amigo!"

If anything could make me stop dancing with Julia, it was that. I took the phone from Adam and stared at the screen. I couldn't believe what I was seeing. *"He got them?"*

This year's Super Bowl was going to be in Arizona, right across town in Glendale. Adam's dad was a big shot at a Phoenix bank, and he'd put in for some of the tickets the company got for being corporate sponsors. But Adam and I had never thought Mr. Collier would actually get them.

Adam beamed. "Yep. One for my dad, one for my mom, one for me, and one for *you*."

I shook my head, still staring at the tickets. Beside me, Julia squeezed my arm. She knew how much I wanted this. But then I saw the price on one of the tickets and my eyeballs almost popped out of my head. Each ticket was *$700*. I was looking at $2,800 worth of football tickets—way more if you considered what you could get for scalping them once the Super Bowl teams were settled.

I handed the phone back, feeling sick to my stomach. "I can't," I told Adam. It just about killed me to say it. But my dad was an assistant professor at Arizona State, and my mom worked at a horse ranch out in Apache Junction. There was no way I could afford a ticket to the Super Bowl.

"It's taken care of, bro," Adam said. "Compliments of the family Collier." Adam was an only child. I'd been like a brother to him most of my life, but still . . .

"No, I can't, really," I said again.

"Will you get this idiot out of here before he says no to a free ticket to the Super Bowl again?" Adam asked Julia.

"Gladly," she said. She pulled me over to the snack table, ladling punch into cups for each of us. We sipped our drinks, my mind still spinning from Adam's offer.

"You should totally go," Julia told me, a smile in her voice. "Don't feel guilty about it."

I chuckled, grateful that she knew me so well. I put my arm around her and leaned down to kiss her again.

."Wooo! Yeah! Kissy-kissy!" an obnoxious voice yelled over the music. I turned around, thinking somebody was making fun of us. But it was a gang of senior boys giving an underclassman and his date a hard time. The kid who'd shouted was a senior named Jeremy Vacca. We'd had a few classes together over the years. He was the kind of guy who wore backward baseball caps and pants that sagged three inches below the waistline of his underwear. I'd always thought he was kind of a jerk, but he'd never bothered me, so I never paid much attention to him.

"Oh God," Julia said, nodding toward the underclassmen. "Seamus Laurie and Anne Henry."

"Who, the little guys? You know them?"

The girl, Anne, was petite and red-haired, wearing a modest white dress with a big pink bow on the back. Seamus was short and gangly, with a huge ball of curly brown hair that circled his head like a space helmet. He was exactly the type of guy who attracted bullies, and he hadn't helped matters by overdressing for the homecoming dance. He wore a powder-blue tuxedo with a white ruffly shirt.

"They're in the fall play with me," Julia said. "They're super sweet."

Jeremy flicked a finger at Seamus's ruffled shirt. "Nice tuxedo, dorkwad! You two look like you're going to a dork wedding. You don't have to marry her, you know." Jeremy shoved Seamus aside. "Can I cut in?" He grabbed Anne around the waist, laughing in her face.

Anne scowled and tried to twist away from Jeremy, but Seamus only stared helplessly at the ground. God, had I ever been that small?

I couldn't watch any more. I pulled away from Julia and pushed in between Jeremy and Anne. "All right, Vacca, you've had your fun," I said. "Why don't you leave them alone?"

Jeremy took a step back, looking at me like I was something his dog had barfed up on the carpet.

"And why don't you mind your own business . . ." he said. "*Towel head.*"

CHAPTER TWO

TIME SLOWED TO A STOP. IT WAS LIKE WATCHING A football game on TV, when they freeze-frame the action to show you whether a guy's feet went out of bounds or not. All the other students around us stopped dancing.

"I'm sorry," I said. "*What did you just call me?*"

Jeremy looked me in the eye. "I called you a towel head, *towel head.*"

I blinked. Adam appeared next to me, and we exchanged an incredulous glance. I was no 100-pound freshman Jeremy Vacca could push around. I was five foot eight, 155 pounds, almost all of which was muscle. I could wipe the floor with this guy. I knew it, Adam knew it, Julia knew it, everybody in the crowd gathering around us knew it. Even Jeremy knew it. So what made him think he could start calling me names and get away with it?

"What'd I ever do to you?" I asked him. I really wanted to know.

"It's what you and your kind are doing to my *country*, camel jockey." Jeremy turned to his buddies, and they snickered.

Adam launched himself at the guy, but I threw out an arm to hold him back. I pretended it didn't bother me, that I didn't care what some idiot like Jeremy thought. But the truth was, it hurt like a sucker punch to the stomach. I'd heard it all before, of course. Towel head, camel jockey, sand monkey, rag head, and a couple worse ones I won't repeat. My dad's white, but my mom's Iranian. Me? I couldn't look more Middle Eastern, even though I was born right here in Phoenix. I've got thick black curly hair, heavy black eyebrows, a strong nose, olive skin.

When I was six years old, there were these older kids on my block, Steve and Ben Hollis. One day I went over to their house and they started calling me names, like Jeremy here. I'd never heard those names before, and I had no idea what they meant. I don't think Steve and Ben did either, really—they'd probably just heard some adult somewhere ranting about people who looked like me, and they were trying it out. But I knew the words were mean. I knew that they were insulting me. Laughing at me. I ran home in tears. When Darius found out, he went over to their house and beat the snot out of them. He got in big trouble with my parents for doing it. I was grateful, but still kind of stunned. It was the first time I'd realized how hard it was going to be, growing up Persian American. To this day, that kind of name-calling always hits me so suddenly, so hard, it makes me feel like I'm six again, running home in tears to Darius. Every. Single. Time.

Adam still wanted me to let him get at Jeremy, but I shook him off. I fought my own battles now.

"What's your problem?" I asked Jeremy.

Jeremy shouted so the crowd all around us could hear him over the music. "My *problem* is that our homecoming king is the brother of a *terrorist!*"

I laughed out loud. Darius? A terrorist? Adam and the other guys around me chuckled, too.

"You got the wrong guy, Vacca. My brother graduated from West Point. The United States Military Academy? Maybe you've heard of it. He's an Army Ranger. You know what you have to go through to become a Ranger? Soldiers *die* training to be Rangers." I felt the pride fill my chest as I thought of Darius. "He's in Afghanistan right now with the Third Ranger Battalion Special Ops, protecting *your butt* from terrorists."

"Kissing terrorist butt, more like," Jeremy said. "Maybe if you'd been home watching the news before the dance, not being a big sportsball hero, you would have heard: your brother's a traitor to his country. A *terrorist*." Jeremy turned to his friends. "Once an Arab, always an Arab, you know?"

I threw myself at him. I rammed Jeremy hard enough to drive him out into the middle of the dance floor, where a circle opened up for us like it had for my first dance with Julia. I punched Jeremy in the stomach, got a glancing blow in on his face, but he didn't go down. He wrapped an arm around my head and tried to punch me. All around us, people were yelling and cheering, the music was thumping, the colored lights were flashing. Jeremy's friends jumped me, pulling me away, punching and kicking me, and then Adam and the rest of the football team were there throwing punches, and the crowd was chanting *fight, fight, fight*, and I was punching back, hitting anything that moved, and then Mr. Philpot was there pulling us all apart, and Mr. Marks, and Señor Serrano, and then it was over.

CHAPTER THREE

TEN MINUTES LATER, I SAT OUTSIDE THE PRINCIPAL'S office with Adam and a couple of my teammates. Julia had gone off in search of some more ice for my split lip, which was hurting really bad. Jeremy and his friends were inside the office now, getting chewed out so loud we could hear Mrs. DeRosa through the wall. Jeremy was definitely in trouble for saying the things he had, but we were *all* probably going to be suspended for fighting.

I didn't care. It was worth it to defend Darius. He and I had a code. A code of honor. We looked out for each other, no matter what. Just like me and Adam. I nodded to my friend in silent thanks for sticking up for me, and he nodded back. Nothing more needed to be said.

The door to the main office opened, and my stomach sank at the sight of a familiar face.

"Oh, man," I muttered. "They called my *mom*?"

Mom was wearing her work clothes: blue jeans, yellow Western-style shirt, cowboy boots, white Stetson hat. I had the fleeting thought that Jeremy would no doubt be disappointed to learn my mother didn't wear a head scarf.

I slumped down in my chair. I didn't need my *mom* to come pick me up from school—especially from the homecoming dance. What was I, twelve? I was a senior in high school! I had my own car, for crying out loud. One of my teammates snickered, and I knew I was never going to live this down. Some homecoming king I was.

"There you are, Kamran joon," Mom said. She used the Persian word for "dear" whenever she was worried about me or Darius.

"Listen, Mom, I can explain," I said, trying to head things off before she blew up at me.

Mom frowned at my bruised face. "Kamran, have you been fighting?"

"It's not his fault, Mrs. Smith," Adam said. "This idiot was saying really stupid stuff about him and Darius."

Mom looked up sharply at the mention of Darius's name.

"You didn't know I'd been in a fight? The school didn't call you?" I asked.

Something was wrong here. Something big. Suddenly I realized Mom wouldn't usually be in her work clothes this late at night. She would have changed to come with Dad and watch me in the football game. And now that I thought about it, I hadn't seen them at the game at all. I'd been so focused on the scout, I hadn't looked for my parents in the stands. Had they even been there? They never missed a game. But if they weren't at the game, what were they doing?

Jeremy's sneering voice came back to me. *Maybe if you'd been home watching the news before the dance, not being a big sportsball hero, you would have heard: your brother's a traitor to his country.* My head spun. I felt like my whole body was sinking right through the seat of my chair, the floor swallowing me up.

"Mom," I said. "Mom, what's going on?"

Mom looked like she was about to cry, and then I realized— she *had* been crying.

"Kamran, you have to come home right away," she said. "It's your brother."

CHAPTER FOUR

MOM GRIPPED THE STEERING WHEEL OF HER Suburban so hard I thought it was going to snap off in her hands. We'd left my car at the school so I could ride home with her. She'd already spoken to Mrs. DeRosa, though I had no idea about what. I didn't know anything.

"Mom, what is it? What's going on?" I demanded. "Is Darius okay?" My greatest fear was that Darius was hurt—or worse.

A light turned red ahead of us, and Mom stopped the car so suddenly I was thrown against my seat belt.

"There's this report. On the news," Mom said at last. "An attack on the US embassy in Turkey. And there's someone in the video—someone who looks like your brother."

"What, defending the embassy?" None of this made any sense. Darius wasn't assigned to any embassy. He was deployed in Afghanistan.

"No," Mom said. "Attacking it."

"*What?*" I felt a jolt of shock. "But—no! It's not Darius. It can't be! This is crazy! Why would he attack a US embassy? How could he be in Turkey?"

"I don't know," Mom said. The light turned green and she gunned the car, throwing me back against the seat. "Someone from the paper called us while we were getting ready to come to the game. We had no idea what they were talking about. The Estellas across the street called and told us to turn on the news. That's when we saw the video."

"Is it him?" I asked. "It can't be him."

"I don't know," Mom said again, still squeezing the steering wheel. "It's hard to tell."

"What does the army say? They have to know if he's in Turkey, right?"

"We haven't heard from them. Your father's been trying to call them."

"This is nuts!" I said. I wished for the millionth time that my parents had bought me a smartphone, but all I had was a flip phone that could barely text. Same with Mom. I turned on the radio instead, surfing for something, anything about Darius. It was all just pop stations until I flipped over to the AM dial and found a political shock jock ranting about it.

"So this soldier—no, that's not fair to real American soldiers," the guy was saying, "this man, this *Muslim*, he goes to West Point and learns everything America has to teach him about tactics and military history and advanced warfare, then gets himself sent to Afghanistan so he can go AWOL and share everything he knows with al-Qaeda! So I guess that's what the US Army does now: train Islamic extremists how to fight and then pay their way overseas so they can become terrorists. Our first problem here is allowing *Muslims* to join the army—"

"Turn it off," Mom said.

"But—"

"*Turn it off.*"

I punched the radio off and sat back in my seat with a huff. The guy was full of it, but I wanted to hear any news I could about Darius. The idea that Darius went to West Point so he could learn all kinds of stuff for al-Qaeda was ridiculous. As I stared out the window, I remembered that day, almost seven years ago now, when we'd gotten up at the crack of dawn to drive Darius to his first day at the United States Military Academy.

The four of us—me, Darius, Mom, and Dad—had stayed overnight at a motel just outside West Point, New York, after flying in the day before. I was still jet-lagged and could hardly drag myself out of bed, but Darius looked like he'd been up all night. He was so excited and so nervous he couldn't eat a thing at breakfast, and he hardly said two words to us on the drive over.

We filed into Eisenhower Hall, where an older cadet told us about how hard the next seven weeks of cadet basic training were going to be. "Beast Barracks," he called it. I looked up at Darius. He sat hunched over in his seat, his arms folded across his stomach like the time when he was trying not to be sick on a roller coaster at Castles-n-Coasters.

"Are you gonna puke?" I whispered.

"No. Shut up," he told me, but he sure looked like he was going to puke. I scooted a little closer to Mom.

The cadet checked his watch. "You now have ninety seconds to say good-bye to your loved ones," he announced.

There were gasps and cries of alarm, and mine was one of them. I knew why we were there, of course: Darius was going off to college. A very special kind of college, where we wouldn't see him again until he got leave at Christmas. But the reality hadn't set in until that moment, when they told us we only had a minute and a half to say good-bye. Darius had been my constant companion—my sometimes playmate, sometimes confidant, sometimes adversary, and full-time best friend—and now he was going away forever. Or close enough to forever.

Little kid that I was, I burst into tears.

Mom was in tears as well, hugging Darius, and I shamelessly threw my arms around him, too. I sobbed and wouldn't let him go, even when older cadets started calling for the newbies to come away with them.

"Hey, you're going to be okay," Darius told me, hugging me back.

"Don't go," I told him. "I don't want you to go."

"I'll see you again soon," he promised. "And when I do, I'll be a real soldier."

"I don't want you to be a real soldier. I want you to stay at home with me."

The older cadets called out again.

"I have to go, Kamran," Darius said, pulling away. "You have to be the strongest of the strong, the bravest of the brave. You can do that, can't you?"

I shook my head, still sobbing.

"Yes, you can," Darius said. "I know you can."

Darius gave Mom and Dad one last hug and hurried off, wiping at his eyes. I watched him until he disappeared down a hallway with the thousand or so other new cadets.

The rest of the day was dreadfully boring for a fifth grader. Speeches from officers, a tour of the academy, lunch in the cafeteria. I walked around feeling like a hollow shell of myself, as if the best, most important part of me had been scooped out with a spoon.

We saw Darius again that day only once, at the oath ceremony. We sat in bleachers while the new cadets marched across the quad to the trumpets and drums of a military band, every family straining to find their son or daughter in the ranks. We didn't have to stretch to see Darius, though—he was right there in the first row. At least, I was pretty sure it was Darius. While we'd been wandering around the academy grounds, Darius had gone through a transformation. His shoulder-length curly black hair was replaced by a severe crew cut that made him look almost bald, and gone, too, were his jeans, T-shirt, and sneakers, replaced with a white button-down short-sleeved shirt, black shoes, and gray pants with a thick black line down the sides.

Darius and the other new cadets stopped with parade-ground precision, then repeated the military academy's oath back to a senior officer: "I do solemnly swear that I will support the Constitution of the United States, and bear true allegiance to the National Government; that I will maintain and defend the sovereignty of the United States, paramount to any and all allegiance, sovereignty, or fealty I may owe to any State or Country whatsoever."

Seeing Darius there reciting the oath, head shaved, face serious, so proud that he was practically about to pop a button on his new army-issue shirt, everything changed for me. All day I had wished he would come back home with us, but right there, in that moment, I understood why he would leave sunny Arizona and fly across the country to this cold gray place. Why he would abandon his friends. His family. *Me.* Darius was going to be a part of something much greater than himself, something with tradition, with *meaning.* An extension of everything Mom had taught us about being Persian. Darius was joining a new family. He was going to be a United States soldier.

That was the day I decided I was going to go to West Point and be a soldier, too.

"He swore an oath," I said, my forehead against the car window.

"What?" Mom asked.

"Darius swore an oath to defend the United States," I said. "He wouldn't go back on that."

Mom turned onto our street and pulled up short. An army of local TV trucks and camera crews was parked outside our house, waiting for us.

CHAPTER FIVE

"HAVE YOU HEARD FROM DARIUS?"

"What has the army told you?"

"Is Darius a traitor?"

Reporters with microphones and cameras swarmed our car, yelling questions through the window.

"Are you Muslims? Is Darius a Muslim?"

"Have you seen the footage yet? Is it Darius?"

Mom honked and gunned the engine, and the reporters jumped out of the way as she sped into the driveway.

"Go straight inside," Mom told me. "Don't say anything to them. Don't even look at them."

Butterflies filled my chest and my pulse quickened. Mom pulled the keys out of the ignition, and I leaped out of the car and ran for the front door.

"Kamran, wait!" someone yelled. "Tell us about your brother!"

I kept my head down and kept running.

"Stay off our property," Mom yelled at the reporters. She hurried inside after me, slamming the door.

Dad had the TV on CNN, watching the news coverage. He stood when we came in, going immediately to Mom to give her a hug. I went right to the TV. Headlines scrolled across the bottom of the screen, but they were on a commercial break. I never watched CNN. I didn't even know what channel it was on. The only news I ever watched was sports news on ESPN.

"What are they saying?" I asked. "What's going on?"

"Nothing new," Dad said. "It might be Darius, it might just be someone wearing his uniform."

Dad and I shared a glance. The only way someone else could be wearing Darius's uniform was if they had taken it off him, which meant Darius was captured.

Or dead.

So either Darius was now a terrorist, or he was captured or dead. I didn't know which was worse.

"Welcome back," said CNN's Wolf Blitzer. He stood in front of a bank of huge televisions, all showing different videos of gunfire and explosions around a sandstone-white building flying the US flag. "We return now to the attack on the United States embassy in Turkey, where fifty-three people are known to be dead, including twenty-two civilians. And most disturbing of all, leading the attack appears to be US Army Ranger Captain Darius Smith. Or perhaps not. With me now is the former director of the US National Counterterrorism Center, Trip Conrad. Mr. Conrad—"

CNN put a picture of Darius up on the screen, a posed photograph of him in his uniform, looking as handsome and serious as ever. Then they split the screen and showed a still from a video taken in the embassy; in the background, a guy stood waving his finger in the air. He was the same height as Darius, but I couldn't make out his face.

It was surreal, listening to Wolf Blitzer talk about my brother. Saying where he grew up, what his grades were like at West Point, going over his acceptance into the Army Rangers, his assignments in the Middle East. It was as weird as if Emily Reed, my favorite correspondent on ESPN (and not just because she happened to be so pretty), had been talking about my performance in the homecoming game on SportsCenter.

The house phone rang. I reached for it, but Dad waved me away and answered it himself. "Hello? No. *No*, we have no comment at this time. Please don't call again." He clicked off the phone and tossed it on the couch. "They won't stop calling. But I have to keep answering in case it's the army."

"Mr. Conrad, I'm going to have to stop you there," Wolf Blitzer said on TV. "I'm told we have a startling new video just released by al-Qaeda that definitively includes US Army Captain Darius Smith. Let's bring you that video now."

Mom and Dad and I huddled around the television set as Darius appeared, seated behind a desk in front of a black curtain. A wave of shock hit me. It *was* Darius. My brother. But just like that first day at West Point when he'd appeared transformed, now he was transformed all over again.

Darius was still wearing his army fatigues, but he'd grown a scraggly little beard and wore a white head scarf around his curly hair. Mom let out a gasp, and Dad put his arm around her. I felt the room start to spin all over again.

"My name is Darius Smith," Darius told the camera, "and I take full responsibility for today's al-Qaeda attack on the US embassy in Turkey."

My mother sobbed once, and my father closed his eyes. I shook my head, silently pleading with Darius not to say this. Not to do this. But he kept going.

"I was once asked to commit atrocities against the Muslim people by the United States government," Darius said, reading from a piece of paper. "I now choose to lead those same innocent victims in the fight against American tyranny. Today's strike on the US embassy is merely the first in a series of planned attacks against the United States to punish the infidels for their crimes against Islam."

Once, when we were little, Darius and I were watching a movie about aliens, and I was scared. I covered my eyes and told Darius to tell me when the things were off the screen. I waited, terrified that if I peeked through my fingers, I'd see one and have nightmares for weeks. Finally, Darius told me it was all right to look.

The aliens were still there.

I'd screamed, and Darius had laughed and laughed. He'd done it on purpose, just to mess with me. I was so mad I grabbed one of the sofa cushions to beat him over the head, but then I got so scared I hid behind it instead.

I felt like that now. I couldn't decide whether I was more frightened or mad. I started trembling. "No. No!" I yelled at the Darius on TV. The tie I'd worn to the dance felt like it was suffocating me, and I tore it off and threw it to the floor. Darius kept talking about infidels, jihad, martyrs, al-Qaeda—but I wasn't listening anymore. All I could hear was the sound of my own blood thumping in my ears, my breath coming short and fast, my mother crying quietly beside me.

Whatever else Darius had to say didn't matter anyway. All that mattered now was that our lives were never, ever going to be the same.

CHAPTER SIX

FOR THE FIRST TIME SINCE KINDERGARTEN, I WAS officially afraid to go to school.

I stood at the bottom of the steps that led to the front doors of my high school, letting the other students flow around me. A few of them didn't know who I was. Freshmen, mostly. Kids who didn't care about football or homecoming or any of that stuff. Kids whose parents didn't watch the news.

The rest of them knew exactly who I was, and all about what Darius had done. Or *said* he had done.

I hadn't slept at all Friday night, going over the video of Darius in my mind. The more I'd thought about it, the more I'd realized that Darius's speech was textbook terrorist screed—which is why I was sure it was written for him by somebody else. Somebody who made him read it. Or brainwashed him into reading it. There was no way Darius had willingly abandoned the army to join al-Qaeda. I was sure of it. Even if he cared much about Islam—and our family had never been religious at all—Persians were Shi'a Muslims. Al-Qaeda were Sunni Muslims. There's no way he would want to join al-Qaeda, and there's no way al-Qaeda would let him.

I tried to tell my parents my theory, but they'd been too numbed by shock and sadness to listen. And that first video of Darius had been followed by another on Saturday. And another on Sunday. Darius training al-Qaeda troops. Darius calling on American Muslims to take up arms against their country. With each new video, the case against him mounted.

And from the looks the other students were giving me on Monday morning, he'd already been found guilty. And I was guilty by association.

My hands clenched into fists. My heart raced. My face got hot. A flood of emotion overcame me, a mishmash of feelings I thought I'd already dealt with during the roller coaster of a weekend. I wanted to run away and hide. I wanted to scream. I wanted to cry. I wanted to punch something. I wanted to punch some*body*.

What I *didn't* want to do was climb those steps to school. But I did. I was *not* going to let those looks stop me from living my life.

Inside, it was worse. The crowd in the hall parted from me like they were a stream of water and I was a drop of oil. Conversations stopped. Eyes followed me. Silence stalked me. I'd been stared at like this before, but never so blatantly. It happened sometimes when I was out in public, someplace where nobody knew who I was. I'd be with Darius at Metrocenter Mall and people—adults, mostly—would give us these side glances. They'd look us up and down, suspicion in their eyes. They didn't think we noticed, but we did. I did, at least. More than seeing it, I could *feel* it. Feel the way people watched me as I browsed the game store and stood in line at Orange Julius. As soon as I got comfortable, as soon as I forgot that I happened to have the same nose and skin and hair as some monster who'd once hijacked a plane, a suspicious glance would remind me all over again. These people had no idea I'd grown up in a suburb of Phoenix like any other American kid, playing Xbox and eating Cheetos. Or they didn't care. They feared me—*hated* me—just because my skin was brown.

But it had never been that way at my school. This was my turf. My kingdom.

Just the short walk to my locker twisted my guts into a tangle of spaghetti. I didn't know how I was going to survive a whole day of this. I looked for Adam. He'd texted me a little over the weekend, stuff like HEY. U OK?, but mostly he had given me space while my family and I dealt with each new horror that appeared on CNN. The one person I hadn't been able to talk to was Julia, and when I spotted her down the hall, surrounded by her girlfriends, I practically ran over to her. If I needed anybody's support now, it was hers.

"Hey! Julia!" I called.

Julia's friends gave her a quick glance and then peeled off. I leaned down to kiss her and she turned away, making me kiss her cheek instead of her lips. I frowned.

"I tried calling you and texting you all weekend," I said, fighting down a pang of worry.

"I was busy with the play," she said, still not looking at me.

Something was definitely up. Could it be about Darius? But Julia *knew* me. She knew Darius! I pushed on, trying to make things right by ignoring the tension between us. "How'd rehearsals go?"

"Fine," Julia said.

"Did you get that one scene right? The one you'd been working on?"

"Yes," she said. And then: "I have to get to homeroom."

"Julia, wait," I said, catching up with her before she could run off. "What's going on?"

She looked up at me at last, her lips thin, her blue eyes filled with hurt and sorrow. But there was something else in her expression.

Fear.

I staggered back, as startled as if she'd slapped me.

"Julia—"

"Please don't call me anymore for a little while," she said, her voice small, the opposite of her usual confident tone.

"Are you—are you breaking up with me?" I asked. I blinked, feeling light-headed. "You can't break up with me," I said. "*I love you.*"

Julia swallowed a sob and turned away, a hand to her mouth.

"Julia!" I called, my voice cracking, but she was gone. I realized suddenly that we'd had an audience—a bunch of kids who'd been pretending not to watch the homecoming queen dump the king. My face was hot with embarrassment as tears welled up in my eyes. I couldn't let them see me cry, too. I pushed through the gawkers into the boys' bathroom and huddled over the sink.

I wiped away a tear with the back of my hand. My chest burned like my heart had been ripped out. I didn't know how to handle this. I'd never been dumped before. I'd never told a girl I loved her before. Now both had happened on the same day.

Out in the hall, the bell rang. I was going to be late to homeroom, but I didn't care. I ran the water and splashed some on my face, trying to hide the tearstains. I wanted to crawl into a corner and fold in on myself until I disappeared. *Julia had broken up with me.* But what really haunted me was that look in her eyes.

Julia was afraid of me.

I looked in the mirror, trying to see what she had seen there. Trying to see the monster everybody else saw, the terrorist. But all I saw was me.

CHAPTER SEVEN

"TWENTY-TWO! TWENTY-TWO! BLUE SEVENTEEN!" Francisco called.

I stood behind him, watching the defense shift. We were an hour and a half into another grueling practice. The air was dry and dusty, and the Arizona sun was blazing, even though it was November. Sweat poured down my face inside my helmet. This was hard, but it was nothing compared to what I'd been through at school that day. The glances. The whispers. The fear.

Julia's face came back to me again. *That look*. That look that squeezed my heart and wrenched my gut.

It was a look I'd seen all day in the faces of my classmates. All except Adam, who'd been the only one to talk to me, to sit with me at lunch. Everyone else seemed to believe that I was some radical Islamic terrorist.

I didn't have anything against Islam. My mom's younger brother, my uncle Rahim, he was more religious than my mom was. He took me and Darius to a mosque when we were little, and I remember the men on their prayer mats, bowing and muttering their prayers. But my family wasn't religious. We celebrated Christmas, not Ramadan, but mostly because we liked giving each other presents. We didn't go to any church, Christian or Muslim.

But nobody cared about facts. They'd already decided I was Muslim, and that I was going to turn on America, just like my brother had.

I steamed underneath my football helmet. I had seven more months left until graduation, and then I would be off to West

Point, and they would never have to see my "Arab" face ever again. I shook my head. Persians weren't even Arabs. They were two different things. But like I said, nobody cared about facts.

"Set! Hut!" Francisco called.

The ball snapped. Francisco dropped back to pass. I blinked. Tried to remember where I was, what I was supposed to be doing. I stepped up a second too late to block.

WHAM. Omar, the linebacker, absolutely plastered me, knocking me off my feet. It took me a few seconds to get my wind back and sit up, and by that time Francisco had already thrown the ball downfield and the play was over.

I shook my head, trying to see straight again. That knock from Omar had been a cold reboot to my system. We weren't supposed to hit that hard in practice, but I knew it was more my fault than Omar's. My mind was everywhere else but here: Wolf Blitzer's face on TV; Julia's face in the school hallway; Darius's face, reading a terrorist screed halfway around the world.

Coach Reynolds blew his whistle, and I pulled myself to my feet. Nobody offered to help me up.

"Smith!" Coach shouted at me. "No doubts. No second guesses. No *distractions*. Right?"

Easy for him to say. I nodded to let him know I'd gotten the message and came back to the huddle. *Fine,* I thought, half listening as Francisco called the next play. School was going to be tough, practice was going to be tough, *life* was going to be tough from here on out, but I could be tough, too. I'd been tough all my life. I'd had to be, to keep up with Darius. He was eight years older than me, and eight years is a long time in kid years. He was a giant to me. We'd played together a lot, the way brothers do, but there were other kids Darius's age in the neighborhood, and he liked playing with them, too. Especially football. I was way smaller than Darius and all his friends, and they never wanted me in their games.

"Go home, Kamran," Darius told me one day when they were picking teams.

"I want to play, too!" I whined.

"You can watch from the tree," he said.

"I don't want to watch! I want to play!"

"You're too little."

"I am not!" I started to cry and pitch a fit. "If you don't let me play, I'll tell Mom and Dad!"

The other kids rolled their eyes and begged Darius to come on and start playing, but I turned the crying up to eleven. Darius huffed and dragged me away by the arm.

"Stop being a baby," he told me when we were away from the other boys.

"I'm not a baby," I protested.

"Then stop acting like one."

I sniffled and dragged the back of my hand across my nose. "I want to play."

"You're too little, Kamran."

"I don't care."

Darius huffed again. "Okay. Fine. You want to play? You can play. But if you get knocked down, you can't cry. You don't get the ball, you can't whine. You get scraped up, you walk it off. You understand? If you're going to play with the big kids, you can't be a baby. You have to be tough."

"The strongest of the strong," I told him, still sniffling. "The bravest of the brave."

He frowned like he didn't think I could do it, which only made me want to show him all the more. To prove I could be tough enough.

That day, everything happened that Darius said would happen: I got knocked down, scraped up, and I never once got the ball. But I did what I promised: I bit back tears, I kept my mouth shut, I wiped off the blood and kept playing. And the next day, I came back. And the next day, and the next. And pretty soon they were giving me the ball, really including me in plays. Then one day I wasn't the last picked for a team. Those games with the big kids were how I got to be so good at football. Those games had made me better, tougher, and I was going to need that toughness now. Every last bit of it.

The center hiked the ball. Francisco dropped back. Omar came right at me. This time I was ready. I met him with my shoulder, knocking him away. He bounced back at me, pushing, shoving. I could barely get an arm in to block him. He bumped me, rammed me, elbowed me. It was like he wasn't even trying to get past me. He was just roughing me up, like the big kids had done to me that first game back in the neighborhood.

I felt all the frustration of the whole day wash over me, and I lost it. The whistle blew, and I got right in Omar's face, ready to fight.

CHAPTER EIGHT

"WHAT'S YOUR PROBLEM?" I YELLED.

Omar shrugged like he hadn't done anything wrong. I shoved him, and he shoved me back. I swung a fist at him, trying to score a hit around his pads, and soon we were punching and kicking at each other.

Coach Reynolds ran over, blowing his whistle and pulled us apart.

"Enough—enough!" he told us. "What's going on here?"

"He went crazy!" Omar said. "He started shoving me, and then he took a swing at me."

"Because *you* attacked *me*," I said. I threw myself at Omar again, but Adam grabbed me and held me back.

"You!" Coach Reynolds told me. "Go cool off. The rest of you line up again."

I kept trying to get at Omar, but Adam spun me away.

"Hey—hey!" he said. "Kamran, hey. Listen to me. Omar was just rushing the passer."

I blinked. I was still breathing hard, my rage making fists of my hands. I twisted to look over Adam's shoulder, to see if Omar and his buddies were talking about me. Adam tugged my helmet back around.

"Kamran, he was just doing the same thing he always does. I saw him. Let it go," Adam said. "Don't be so sensitive."

I turned on Adam. He was tall and gangly, his Adam's apple sticking out beneath the chin strap of his helmet. "Don't be so *sensitive*?" I said, my voice rising. "Maybe you didn't notice the way everybody treated me today, like I had a *bomb* strapped to my chest."

Adam was quiet. All day, we'd studiously avoided the subject of Darius, talking about stuff like the Super Bowl and math homework instead. But I couldn't pretend to ignore the truth anymore. People hated me. Feared me.

"Look, Kamran," Adam finally said, "you can't blame people for reacting like that."

"*I can't?* Not even my teammates? Not even my *girlfriend*? They think Darius is a terrorist. They think *I'm* a terrorist."

"That part's stupid," Adam admitted. "But, Kamran, you have to understand how everybody else sees your brother. He basically went on TV and said 'I'm a terrorist.' "

"But he's not! He can't be. *You* know that. We've been friends since third grade. You know Darius."

"I thought I did," Adam said quietly.

His words hurt worse than anything Omar had done. I shoved Adam in the shoulder pads, making him stumble. "Take it back," I told him. He shoved me, hard, and we faced off, a clock's tick from throwing punches like Omar and I had.

"*Darius. Isn't. A terrorist,*" I told Adam, my voice low.

"Who are you trying to convince? Me or *you*?" Adam shot back.

That one hit too close to home. All the doubts I'd been fighting crowded into my head, and my face burned with guilt and shame under my helmet.

I pushed Adam away. "You know what? Keep the Super Bowl ticket. You can take Omar. Or better yet, take Julia. I hear she's free."

"Kamran—" Adam called, but I was already on my way to the locker room. I was done.

Coach Reynolds would be mad at me, probably bench me for the start of the next game, but I would deal with that later. Right then I just wanted to get out of there. Go home and disappear into my room and never come out again.

I slammed my helmet on its shelf and yanked off my pads. In all my life, no matter where I'd been or what else was happening, the football field had been sacred ground. When I put that helmet on, I wasn't a terrorist, or whatever else people secretly thought of me. I was Smith, number 13, running back. I was part of a team, judged only on my efforts and accomplishments. People cheered for me on the football field. Held up signs encouraging me on. Now I felt like even this last place of refuge was gone.

I showered, changed, and got out of there before anyone came back to the locker room. I didn't want to see anybody. Especially not Adam. He and I had been best friends since elementary school, and he'd known Darius that entire time. Darius used to throw the football for us in the backyard. Used to play video games with me and Adam after school. If Adam didn't believe in Darius, we couldn't be friends anymore.

First Julia. Now Adam. I was totally on my own.

When I drove up to my house, I wasn't surprised to see the row of TV vans up and down my street. But there was something else there, too. Something new. A black armored car with HOMELAND SECURITY written on the side was parked in my front yard. It looked like something from Darius's pictures from Afghanistan. A tank on wheels. And all around it were white delivery vans marked DHS, and big black SUVs with flashing red and blue lights.

The Department of Homeland Security had come to visit.

CHAPTER NINE

PEOPLE IN BUSINESS SUITS AND WHITE ZIP-UP hazmat gear moved in and out of my house. I couldn't get anywhere close to my own driveway, so I parked down the street and walked up. A policeman stopped me at a barricade.

"I live here," I told him. He told me to wait while he radioed it in. I felt a bead of sweat roll down the center of my back. My pulse quickened and my breath came short. If you'd hooked me up to a lie detector right then, I couldn't even have said my name was Kamran Smith without the needle jiggling all over the place. I felt like a criminal and I hadn't even done anything. Across the street, the Estella kids stared at me from their driveway.

Two government agents in suits came out. They asked me to unzip my gym bag and my book bag so they could look inside with flashlights.

"What's going on?" I demanded, but they didn't answer. Why wouldn't anybody tell me anything? Why did I have to be searched before I could even go inside my own house?

When they were sure my American history textbook wasn't a bomb, the two agents walked me inside. Mom and Dad stood in the living room talking to two more agents in suits while the astronaut-looking hazmat people took apart the kitchen.

"*What's going on?*" I asked again.

"They're searching the house," Dad told me.

"For what?" I looked down the hall. There were hazmat guys *in my room*, going through my stuff! "Wait. You can't do that," I said, heading down the hall.

An armed policeman stopped me and corralled me back with my parents.

"I assure you, we can," said one of the agents. She was a large white woman in a gray skirt and jacket. Her partner, an African American guy in an almost matching gray suit, showed me his DHS badge.

"We're from the Department of Homeland Security," the woman said.

"Yeah. I saw your *tank* parked on the lawn."

"Kamran," Mom said.

"What? It's like Operation New Dawn out there," I said.

"What do you know about Operation New Dawn?" the male agent asked me.

"I know my brother, Darius, was taking part in it as a *US Army Ranger* until he was captured and brainwashed by al-Qaeda!"

"Kamran, don't," Dad said.

"Dad, they're taking our house apart like we're terrorists! We're American citizens!"

"We've been authorized to conduct a search of these premises," the woman said. "A similar search has already been conducted at your brother's apartment near Fort Benning. We'll be wanting to talk each of you, individually at first, and then together."

"Darius isn't a terrorist!" I yelled. All the hazmat people stopped and turned to look at me, but nobody said a word. It was creepy. I took a step back. "I'm telling you, he's *not*."

"Kamran, don't make this worse than it already is," Dad said.

"Worse? *Worse!?* How could it be worse?"

"Kamran, just do what your father says and have a seat on the couch," said the woman.

"I don't want to sit on the couch," I said.

"It wasn't a suggestion," the woman told me.

I clenched my teeth, my face hot. Who was this stranger to tell me what to do?

Mom put a hand on my arm. "Kamran, sit with me."

Mom had always been able to calm me down when I got like this. When I wanted to argue and fight. I let her pull me to the couch, and the woman from the DHS went away. The guards in black SWAT uniforms stayed.

I watched as a DHS agent went through our DVDs in the living room, like there might be something hidden inside the *Iron Man* case. Down the hall, I heard somebody taking the lid off the toilet in the bathroom I'd once shared with Darius.

My stomach clenched, and I fought the urge to yell again. *This wasn't fair.* None of it. Mom and Dad and I hadn't done anything wrong. And we were just supposed to sit here and take it, like I was supposed to just take the stares of my fellow students, the betrayals of my friends. I shook with rage. I hated the DHS, I hated the press. I hated the people at the mall, the kids at school. I hated my mom and dad for sitting by, I hated Adam and Julia for turning on me, I hated Darius for doing this to me.

Darius.

All the tension went out of my arms and legs, like when you get off a roller coaster and can't walk right for the next few minutes. It was true: *I hated Darius.* It was Darius's fault all this was happening. It was Darius's fault my life was ruined.

The agents came back over to where Mom, Dad, and I were sitting, and they questioned us. Had Darius ever expressed anger at the United States government? Had he ever expressed sympathy toward al-Qaeda? Had he shown unusual interest in

Sunni Islam? In Sharia law? Who were his friends? His acquaintances? Had we heard from him in the last few weeks? Letters? Phone calls? Emails?

Mom and Dad answered most of the questions, but when the agents looked to me, I answered robotically, keeping my anger at Darius buried deep inside. When it was clear they weren't going to get anything else from us, everyone departed, leaving behind more TV camera crews and an overturned house.

Mom and Dad went to work silently cleaning up the living room and kitchen. I went down the hall to see what they'd done to my room.

CHAPTER TEN

I WALKED INTO A WRECK. MY CLOTHING DRAWERS
had been rifled through. My comic books were all pulled out.
My bedsheets removed, the mattress flipped. Everything in my
desk drawers had been dumped out. They had gone through
every book on my shelves, every bag of football equipment, every
CD and DVD case. The posters on my walls had all been taken
down, my closet emptied. Homeland Security had left no pile
of dirty clothes unturned.

I lay down on my stripped bed, trying not to cry. It felt
like thieves had broken into our house. Like my belongings
weren't really mine anymore. And they weren't. Not if the
DHS could come in anytime they wanted to and mess with
everything.

As much as I hated him right then, I wished Darius were
there. He was the person I'd always turn to when bad things
happened. Even before Adam. Darius had always given the best
advice.

*But you never told me what to do when you were the prob-
lem, Darius.*

I rapped on the wall between my room and Darius's room
with my knuckle, using the old signals we'd used as kids to
communicate with each other when we were supposed to be
asleep. A certain series of knocks from Darius meant Mom and
Dad were watching TV, so it was safe for me to come to his
room. I'd sneak over and Darius would invent stories for me,
using his G.I. Joe action figures as stand-ins for Rostam and
Siyavash, heroes from Persian mythology.

Come over, I tapped. *Come over.*

Come back, Darius. I need you.

I knew, of course, that my brother wasn't going to answer. I got up and went next door to his room. Homeland Security had gone through it, too, of course. It didn't look as bad— Darius had moved out when he graduated from West Point, so there wasn't as much to mess up. Still, I put all his school trophies and medals and pictures back in place, rearranged all his model tanks and airplanes the way he liked them.

And then I found the Code.

It was buried under some of the things they'd dumped out of his desk. A piece of loose-leaf notebook paper with Darius's thirteen-year-old scrawl on it, mounted on a faded sheet of blue construction paper. THE CODE OF HONOR, it said at the top, and underneath were written the seven rules we thought all heroes should live by:

1) Be the strongest of the strong.

2) Be the bravest of the brave.

3) Help the helpless.

4) Always tell the truth.

5) Be loyal.

6) Never give up.

7) Kill all monsters.

We were big on killing monsters.

Darius and I had solemnly signed the bottom of the paper in our grade-school cursive. If we could have signed it in blood, we would have.

I read the Code again. It was just kids' stuff. But Darius and I had played by that code for so long that we knew it by heart. We'd *lived* it, believed in it so much that it had become part of us. Like those people who grow up and list "Jedi" on census forms where it asks what religion they are. Our Code of Honor had been a kind of faith. I knew Darius would rather die than break it.

This was Darius, here on this piece of paper, in these neat and orderly shelves. Not the shabby, disheveled nutcase ranting on TV. A wave of guilt pushed me down into the chair at Darius's desk. I'd let myself hate Darius, I realized, because deep down, despite all my protests, a small, dark part of me had believed he really *was* a traitor.

I felt sick to my stomach. How could I have ever thought the Darius I knew, the Darius I grew up with, could be that person?

I remembered being five years old. Darius was thirteen. We were on the trails outside the horse ranch where Mom worked, in the shadow of Superstition Mountain.

"Just look at them, Siyavash!" Darius called to me. "They've all been infected!"

I peeked out through a patch of desert sand verbena. The only thing in the dry creek bed below us was a lumpy brown toad sunning itself on a rock, but in my mind's eye I was looking down at millions of zombies staggering around the streets of downtown Phoenix.

"What do we do, Rostam?" I asked, dead serious.

This was our never-ending game: Darius pretended to be Rostam, and I was always his protégé, Siyavash. Mom had read us stories about the heroes, but Darius and I loved making up our own adventures, crazy mash-ups of the old Persian legends and whatever movies and books and cartoons we were into at the time.

"We must be the strongest of the strong. The bravest of the brave," Darius told me. "And we must *kill all monsters*."

Rakhsh, the horse we'd ridden out from the ranch, stretched over us to nibble at the verbena.

"But how? There's so many of them!" I said.

Darius pulled one of those cheap plastic troll dolls with fuzzy hair out of his pocket. "With *this*," he said with equal seriousness. "It's a magic troll statue. It turns all zombies back into real people. All we have to do is get this to the top of the Chase Tower before any of the zombies eat our brains." He turned and got ready to run down into the valley. "Are you ready, Siyavash?" Darius said. "It's you and me against the world."

It's you and me against the world, I thought, staring down at the blue piece of construction paper in Darius's room. I couldn't doubt Darius. Couldn't be mad at him. Not when everybody else in the world thought he was guilty. He needed at least one ally in all this, one person who still believed in his innocence, and that had to be me.

But what do I do, Rostam?

The answers were staring me in the face.

Be strong. Be brave. Be loyal.

Never give up.

I knew then exactly what I was going to do. I was going to clear Darius's name.

CHAPTER ELEVEN

I WENT STRAIGHT TO MY DESK AND PUSHED ALL THE junk the DHS had dumped on it onto the floor. My laptop was underneath. I was going to start by watching all the videos Darius had made. The networks never showed every minute of them. All they cared about were the "juicy" parts—the parts where Darius said stuff they could turn into sound bites. I wanted to see each video in its entirety. Maybe there was something I could use to prove Darius was innocent.

Out of habit, I first clicked the bookmark to see the status of my West Point application. It took forever to apply for the United States Military Academy. You started halfway through your junior year. Testing, questionnaires, Summer Leadership Seminar, candidate fitness assessments, nomination applications, transcripts—all that had to be done before you could officially apply. Then more letters, more fitness assessments, medical exams, interviews, more interviews, more transcripts, school evaluations, and then, if you'd done everything right, if you passed all the tests and interviews and had all the right grades, then *maybe* you'd be one of the thousand people accepted out of the fifteen thousand who apply. I'd been building my application for a year now, and every time I got on my computer, I compulsively clicked through to the webpage where West Point marked all the steps as green or red, depending on what had or hadn't been completed.

Mine should have been almost all green. I was in the home stretch now. Just a few things left I couldn't do until January anyway.

But right there, in the middle of all the green things I'd already done, was a red X that hadn't been there before.

Every candidate for West Point had to have an official nomination from their representative in Congress, one of their two senators, or the vice president of the United States. I had already been nominated by my US representative, Kathryn Barnes, but now that green check had turned into a red X. I clicked on the link to find out why. All it said was "Nomination withdrawn."

It was suddenly hard to breathe. I got up and paced my room, my arms shaking, my eyes unable to focus on anything. Months of letters, interviews, fitness tests, and academic exams, *seven years* of hopes and dreams, and it was all gone. Darius goes on TV claiming responsibility for the attack on a US embassy, and my nomination letter to West Point is withdrawn. Boom. Just like that. Representative Barnes had probably set some sort of speed record rescinding her letter once she'd realized who I was. Couldn't let anybody find out she'd nominated the brother of a terrorist to the United States Military Academy.

I stopped pacing and pressed my forehead to the wall. There was still time to get another recommendation, but who was going to give me one now? Certainly not the vice president of the United States. So that was it. I was out. It was over. No West Point for me. My entire life—everything I'd ever done, everything I'd ever planned—was going down the toilet.

I kicked my empty trash can against the wall.

Mom called down the hall to ask if I was all right.

"Yeah," I yelled back. "I'm just great! Everything's awesome."

I kicked the trash can again to let her know just how

awesome everything was, and she didn't say anything more. I paced for a few minutes longer, trying to calm down. As upset as I was, I knew I couldn't worry about West Point now. It wasn't important. What was important was clearing Darius's name. And mine with it.

CHAPTER TWELVE

THE FIRST VIDEO WAS OF DARIUS AT THE US embassy in Turkey, and there was nothing I hadn't already seen on TV: Darius in the background, wagging his finger in the air as he urged on the insurgents attacking the embassy. No sound. I still didn't understand how Darius had gotten from Afghanistan to Turkey, but it wasn't like he'd showed up in Japan. Turkey wasn't that far from Afghanistan in the grand scheme of things.

I called up the second video. There was a lot more to this one that I hadn't seen, and it was hard to watch. I stared into the eyes of my brother as he looked up from the speech he read. It really seemed like he meant all of it—all the ranting against America and the infidels. The video was twelve minutes long, but it felt like an eternity. No wonder they edited this stuff for television. It went on and on, Darius rambling about previous attacks on Islamic countries, death counts, and his plans for retribution.

"Like Rostam slaying the dragon, we will cut off America's head, the poison flowing from it like a river," Darius said. "Like Rostam in the cave of the Sith Lord, we shall emerge triumphant."

Whoa. Wait. Had Darius just said "Sith Lord"? I paused the video and clicked back a few seconds. There it was again: "Like Rostam in the cave of the Sith Lord, we shall emerge triumphant."

What was Darius talking about? The part about Rostam cutting off a dragon's head, that was real. Or a real myth, at least. It was one of the Seven Trials of Rostam. But the line about Rostam in the cave of a Sith Lord, that was something Darius and I had made up one summer about ten years ago. We'd been obsessed with watching all the Star Wars movies, so we'd started adding lightsabers and spaceships and Jedi to all our Rostam stories. One adventure pitted our hero, Rostam, against Chancellor Palpatine, the dude who becomes the emperor in the old Star Wars movies. In our story, Rostam went to fight him, but he was captured and taken prisoner in a cave by Palpatine's apprentice, Count Dooku.

Captured and taken prisoner in a cave. Rostam *did* emerge triumphant in our story, but only after being captured and taken prisoner! And not just that: Count Dooku had used his Jedi mind tricks on Rostam to brainwash him and make him attack his friends first! Darius, as Rostam, had come after me, as Siyavash, and we had fought a long, convoluted lightsaber duel in the backyard. Rostam was just about to kill his old friend when Siyavash used the Force to hit Rostam in the head with a Nerf boomerang. The knock on the head was enough to bring Rostam to his senses right at the last minute, and together Rostam and Siyavash tracked down Count Dooku and killed him.

That had to be the story Darius was talking about in the video. Rostam in the cave of the Sith Lord. But *I* was the only person who knew that story. I sat back in my chair, stunned. There *was* something in these videos that could clear Darius's name. A secret message only I would understand:

Darius had been taken prisoner by the bad guys, and they were making him fight against his friends.

CHAPTER THIRTEEN

"MOM! DAD! IT'S A CODE! IT'S A CODE! DARIUS SENT me a message in one of the videos!" I called, running down the hall from my room.

Dad came out of his study, a messy stack of papers in his hands. Mom came to the door of the kitchen.

"In the second video," I said breathlessly. "Darius said 'Rostam in the cave of the Sith Lord.' That's from one of our games we played. You know, how we always used to pretend we were Rostam and Siyavash?"

Dad blinked and frowned. "What?"

"In that speech he read on TV. I watched all of it, the parts they didn't put on TV. Darius talked about one of our adventures. One where Rostam got taken prisoner, and—"

"Kamran, I seriously doubt Darius is sending you secret messages," Dad said. "I think what he had to say was pretty clear."

"But—"

Mom shook her head, obviously fighting back tears as she returned to the kitchen.

"This is all bad enough as it is, Kamran," Dad said gently. "Don't make it harder on your mother. On all of us. Not now."

"But Darius is innocent! He's been taken prisoner! He needs our help!"

The phone rang. Again. Dad picked it up, and I saw a flicker of hope pass across his face as he said hello. We were all still hoping the army would call. Say Darius had been recovered. That he was safe. That it was all a huge mistake.

Dad's face immediately fell. It was just another reporter. "No," he said. "No comment. Please don't call again." He hung up and dropped the phone on the couch.

"Dad, I'm serious. Darius was trying to tell me something."

"Kamran, it's been a long day," Dad said. He turned and went back into his office.

I wanted to scream. I picked up the phone and squeezed it. I wanted to throw the phone at the wall and smash it into a thousand pieces. Knock over the lamps. Kick the TV. Break the windows, the door. Anything to get my parents to wake up from this fog they lived in now. I reared back, ready to throw the phone like a football, when I remembered: *the DHS*. I could call the DHS! That lady from the Department of Homeland Security had left her card here somewhere. Told us to call in case Darius tried to get in touch with us. Well, he *had* tried to get in touch with me, hadn't he? In the video.

The woman who'd raided our house less than two hours ago answered the phone on the second ring. "Department of Homeland Security. This is Agent Griggs."

"Um, yeah," I said. "This is Kamran Smith. You left your number and said to call if my brother tried to contact me. Darius."

Agent Grigg's voice became urgent. "Darius has contacted you? How? When?"

I explained, falteringly, how I was sure that Darius was trying to send me a message in his video. As I told her about Rostam and Count Dooku, I realized how ridiculous it all sounded. A US embassy had been attacked. People had *died*, and here I was talking about Persian mythology and Star Wars.

"I know it sounds stupid, but Darius *had* to be talking to me in that video. He had to."

Agent Griggs was quiet for a half a heartbeat longer than she should have been. I could tell she wasn't buying it. "Has Darius been in *actual* contact with you?" she asked, the urgency gone from her voice.

"That's what I'm trying to tell you," I said. "I think he's trying to talk to me in the video. I think he's trying to tell us he's innocent. That he's a prisoner. Somebody's making him do all this."

"But he hasn't contacted you *directly.*"

"No," I said, frustrated. She wasn't taking this seriously. "But—"

"Thank you for the information, Kamran," Agent Griggs said. "Be sure to call us if Darius tries to contact you directly."

I felt the chance to help Darius slipping away. *Be loyal*, I thought, remembering the Code of Honor. *Never give up.*

"Darius isn't a traitor," I said quickly, but Agent Griggs had already hung up.

CHAPTER FOURTEEN

I WAS WATCHING THE EMBASSY BOMBING VIDEO again for the thousandth time when Dad knocked on my door.

"Kamran, dinner."

I had skipped school for the past week, glued to my computer in my room. Mom and Dad had let me stay home, and both of them had taken off from work. None of us wanted to brave the reporters camped out in our street. We didn't want to go to work or school and feel the eyes on us, hear the whispers. Adam had texted me a couple of times asking how I was, but I never wrote back. Sometimes I wondered who Adam was going to take to the Super Bowl, or who Julia Gary might be dating now, or who was starting in my place on the football team, but mostly I didn't care.

I didn't have time for that stuff. I didn't have time to care about anything except proving Darius wasn't a traitor.

I dragged the video slider back to the six-minute-thirty-nine-second mark and hit play. "I'm busy," I said.

"We have family business to discuss," Dad said.

Family business? We'd never had "family business" to discuss before. But now we did: dealing with Darius was our family business now.

I dragged myself out of my room, my back and legs stiff. I'd been sitting in that chair day after day, staying up late into the night watching the videos over and over again. Darius made at least one reference to our old Rostam and Siyavash games in each one, and I was sure they were supposed to mean something. Something only I could understand. But I didn't know what.

Mom and Dad waited at the table, looking as dismal as I felt. Mom had made lubia polo—an Iranian dish with rice pilaf, meat, and green beans. It was one of my favorites, but I had no appetite. Apparently my parents weren't very hungry either. No one ate.

"Your mother and I have discussed moving," Dad said without prelude. "Maybe changing our name."

"*What?*" I said. "You're kidding, right?" I was stunned. We were the *Smiths*. We lived in Phoenix. That's the way it had always been. "Change our *name*? Move where?"

"Mexico, maybe," Mom said quietly. "Or Canada."

I gaped at her. "*Canada or Mexico?* I thought you were talking about California or something. You want to leave *America*? That's just great. How's that going to look?"

"Kamran—" Dad started.

"We can't just move to another country! We're *Americans*, no matter what Darius has done."

The phone rang again. Dad got up from the table to answer it while I fumed.

"No comment," he said after a minute. "No. Please don't call here again."

He'd no sooner hung up than the phone rang again. He frowned as he answered it. "Hello? No, I— No. No comment. Please don't call again."

While he was talking, Mom's cell phone started to ring.

We were still getting calls every day, but not this frequently. This was like the night of the homecoming game, when Darius's first video had appeared. Which meant only one thing:

Darius had done something bad again. Really bad.

CHAPTER FIFTEEN

THE HOUSE PHONE RANG FOR THE FOURTH TIME AS I turned on CNN.

An American journalist had been beheaded. On TV.

Darius hadn't held the sword, but he'd stood by in the background.

Stood by, and not done anything to stop it.

I sat down on the couch and stared. There was no message this time. No code. Just Darius standing there while an American citizen was brutally murdered on television. My stomach churned. I think the only reason I didn't throw up is that I hadn't eaten in two days. Tears rolled down my face, spilling onto my T-shirt. I cried for the journalist, for the journalist's family, for Darius, for the whole awful world. How could something like this happen? How could Darius *let* something like this happen? What had happened to our Code? What happened to being the bravest of the brave and helping the helpless? What happened to killing all the monsters?

What had happened to Darius?

Mom ran to her bedroom and shut the door. Dad kept fielding phone calls. I sat and watched the TV like a statue, unblinking. Like it was my duty to watch. Like I owed it to the journalist and all those soldiers and civilians who'd died in raids Darius had been a part of. I couldn't even hear what was being said over the ringing phone. But it didn't matter. I just had to watch.

Suddenly, the screen changed. CNN showed the now-familiar photo of Darius, clean-cut in his army uniform. Then they showed a live picture of the front of a house. I blinked, dully realizing I was looking at the front of *my* house, the house I was sitting inside right that second.

The camera zoomed in on a man in our front yard wearing jeans, a T-shirt, and a backward Diamondbacks baseball cap. He had a handkerchief tied around his nose and mouth like an Old West outlaw, and he was shaking something up in his right hand. I frowned and leaned in close, trying to understand what I was seeing.

The man reached up and spray-painted a giant letter T just below our front window.

"Dad—Dad! Somebody's spray-painting our house!"

Dad looked up from the phone and frowned, trying to process what he was seeing on the television. The man had followed the T with a large letter E.

"He's spray-painting our house!" I said again. "Right now! He's out there right now!"

Dad ran for the front door, and I followed him. Camera lights found us as soon as he opened the door, and reporters swarmed across the lawn like locusts.

"You!" Dad called to the vandal. "Get out of here!"

"Come make me, Osama!" the man called back. He kept spraying. He wasn't scared of us at all.

The reporters reached us, lights blazing, questions flying, and Dad backed us both into the house.

"Dad, he's still out there," I protested.

"Just leave it alone, Kamran," he said, closing the door.

I went to the TV. The vandal was almost finished. In big, crooked red letters he'd painted the word TERRORISTS across the front of our house. Right there for our all our neighbors and CNN and the rest of the world to see. Someone pounded on our front door and rang the doorbell. A reporter climbed over the fence in our backyard. Dad ran around locking all the doors and pulling all the shades down. It felt like we were under attack. Like all of America was going to break down our door and come for us.

And then, later that night, they did.

CHAPTER SIXTEEN

WAS I IN AN ELEVATOR? IT WAS HARD TO TELL with the sack on my head. I could feel a slight vibration under my feet. And something about the closeness, the hum in the small space, told me it *was* an elevator. I was with two other people. I knew because they'd led me along, one at each elbow, steering me through whatever building they'd brought me to.

"Where are you taking me?" I asked for the thousandth time. "Where are my parents?"

For the thousandth time, nobody answered me.

I hate to admit it, but I was so scared I cried.

I'd been dragged from my house, wrists bound and a sack over my head, and thrown in a car. We'd driven for a while, the black bag hiding everything from me, and then I was taken out of the car and put on a plane. I recognized the sound of jet engines warming up. Knew what the short climb up metal stairs meant. My hands were recuffed in front of me so I could fit in a seat, and I was buckled in and told not to remove my seat belt. I asked again where I was being taken, where my parents were, but got no answer. Someone put a cold plastic bottle in my hands and told me it was water. "Drink," they told me. They pulled the sack up just enough to free my lips, and I drank, if only to prolong the wonderful sensation of fresh air on my chin, my mouth.

After that I got sleepy. Passed out. I don't even remember the airplane actually taking off or landing. I woke up again in another car, on the way to wherever I was now. As the grogginess wore off, the realization slowly dawned on me: *I had been drugged.* They'd put something in that water to knock me out. Make me easier to deal with.

I had been taken from my home, handcuffed, hooded, and drugged.

My skin crawled with goose bumps. If I had been scared before, I was terrified now. This was deadly serious.

I heard the elevator doors slide open. Hands grabbed me by the elbows, and we were walking again.

Where had they taken me? If we got on a plane, we probably weren't in Arizona anymore. Some government facility in New Mexico, maybe? Colorado? Nevada? The air force had all kinds of bases out west. It could be any of them.

I was walked down an echoey corridor and led inside a room. A chair squawked as it was pulled out for me, and the hands pushed me down into it, my arms landing on an empty metal table. There was a clink of chain, and someone attached my handcuffs to the table with a click.

Then, right before the last person left the room, they pulled the black sack off my head.

I sucked in cool, fresh air with relief as the door clicked shut behind me. I was alone. Alone in a small white room with a mirrored window along one side and a camera with a glowing red light up in the corner. I'd seen enough cop shows to know what the big window was for. That's where people sat and watched you while you were being interrogated. This was an interrogation room. There was nothing else there besides me, the table I was handcuffed to, and two more chairs.

"Hello?" I called. I turned to the mirrored window. "Is anybody there? Where am I? What's going on?"

Nobody came. Nobody answered. Somebody might've been watching me behind that glass, and on that camera, but I was all alone.

I put my head down on my arms and tried not to cry.

CHAPTER SEVENTEEN

THE DOOR OPENED BEHIND ME, AND I JERKED MY head up. Had I been sleeping again? How long had I been in this room? I didn't know. I didn't have my phone to tell the time.

A white man and woman came in and sat down. The man was older than my father, but younger than my grandfather. In his fifties maybe? I always had a hard time guessing people's ages. He was wearing suit pants and a rumpled white shirt with no tie. He had dark brown hair that looked like it hadn't been combed since last week, and stubble that was closer to the beginning of a beard. His mouth was small and thin over a short, sharp chin. His forehead was creased in a frown or a look of concern, or maybe both. He sat back in his chair and studied me with his gray-blue eyes.

"Do we really need the handcuffs?" he asked.

The woman ignored him. She set a thick file folder on the table and sat down, clasping her hands over it. She was thin and pretty and wore a business suit with a skirt. Her face was round and soft, but the way she wore her blond hair pulled back made her look hard. Tough. Everywhere the guy was laid-back and sloppy, she was neat and professional. She sat so straight her back didn't even touch the chair.

"Kamran Smith? I'm Special Agent Tomaszewski." She didn't introduce the man, and he didn't offer his name.

"Where am I?" I asked. "Why did you bring me here? I don't know anything."

"You're a guest of the United States government," the woman said.

I tried to lift my hands away from the table where they were chained. "A 'guest'?"

"We'd like to talk to you about your family," Special Agent Tomaszewski said.

"Where are my parents? Can I see them?"

"Not right now," Special Agent Tomaszewski said. She flipped open the file folder.

"I want a lawyer," I told her. I didn't know why I needed a lawyer. I just wanted someone here with me besides these government people, and I'd seen people say that on TV.

"I'm afraid it doesn't work that way," she told me. "You're not officially under arrest."

"Then can I go?"

"No. As I said, you're a guest of the United States government."

"Until when?"

"Until we get the answers we need," Special Agent Tomaszewski said. "Now. Let's talk about your mother."

"My mom?"

"She was born in Iran, is that right?"

Here we go, I thought. *We're all terrorists because my mom was born in Iran.*

"Yeah. So what?"

"She came to America in 1978 to escape the Iranian Revolution and the rise of the Islamic Republic," Special Agent Tomaszewski read from her file.

"If you already know, then why are you asking?" I said.

"Kamran, this will be a lot easier for you if you cooperate."

"What's that supposed to mean?" I asked.

"Your mother eventually settled in the Phoenix area and attended Arizona State, which is where she met your father. Is that right?"

I shrugged. "Far as I know. I wasn't around then."

"Your father is a Christian, is that right?"

"Kind of," I said. "He doesn't go to church or anything. But he was raised that way."

"And your mother is a Muslim?"

I glowered at her. "It's a free country," I said, even though I wasn't feeling so free right now.

"Please answer the question."

"Yes, my mom was raised Muslim," I said wearily. "But she isn't anything anymore. None of my family are. We don't go to church or mosque or anything. My mom was born in Iran, but she became a US citizen after she moved here. My dad's American. I was born in America. Darius was born in America. We're *Americans*. The only other country I've ever been to is Mexico, on vacation. We're not terrorists, or members of al-Qaeda. *Darius* isn't a terrorist. Look—my mom is Shi'a. Al-Qaeda is Sunni. If Darius suddenly got religious—which he didn't—he'd be a Shi'ite. Not a Sunni. Al-Qaeda wouldn't even *want* him."

"Unless they just needed an American Muslim to be the poster boy for their jihad."

I let out a long, frustrated breath and tried again. "We have a code of honor we live by. Darius and me. He's a United States soldier taken prisoner and being forced to do things against his will. He's told me. There's a secret code in his videos. I've been trying to tell you guys that."

"A code of honor. Secret codes. Lots of codes," Special Agent Tomaszewski said, flipping pages in her folder. "All right. Let's talk about this secret code, then."

CHAPTER EIGHTEEN

FINALLY. I TOLD HER EVERYTHING I'D TOLD THE other agent on the phone: about Rostam, and how Darius and I used to make up adventures, and the Sith Lord reference, and what I thought it meant.

"There are others, too, in the newer videos. References to the games we used to play together. I just don't know what they mean yet."

The man behind Special Agent Tomaszewski stirred, his eyes going to her. He looked like he was going to say something, but she went on.

"Do these games you played as children have anything to do with this?" she asked. She pulled a glossy photograph from the folder and pushed it toward me on the table. I gaped at it. It was a picture of the Code of Honor Darius and I had written up as kids. The same Code of Honor I'd dug out of the stuff from Darius's desk a few days ago. The DHS had taken a picture of it. Given it an evidence number.

Evidence of what?

"Yeah," I said at last. "This is—Darius and I made this up. It's the Code of Honor our hero Rostam lived by in our stories."

"A Code of Honor you and your brother also lived by, is that correct? That's what you just told me."

"Kind of. Yeah. I mean, they're good rules for living your life."

Special Agent Tomaszewski nodded. "Be strong. Be brave.

Tell the truth," she said, skimming the list. "Be loyal." She paused. "Loyal to whom?"

"What?"

"Loyal to whom?" she asked again. "It says 'Be loyal,' but it doesn't say whom you should be loyal *to*."

I shrugged. "Your friends, I guess. Your family."

"Your country? Your faith?"

"Sure," I said. "I guess." Where was she going with this?

"Be loyal. Never give up. Kill all monsters." She paused. "What monsters?"

What did this have to do with anything? "Dragons, demons, vampires, ninjas. Sauron, the Joker, Voldemort, Darth Vader. Stupid stuff. We were kids. We made that when I was like five."

Special Agent Tomaszewski clasped her hands in front of her again. "So it wasn't about killing real monsters, then," she said.

I laughed. "Maybe you haven't noticed, but there *aren't* real monsters."

"Aren't there?" she asked, dead serious. "Some people call the United States government monsters."

"Yeah," I said, slumping back in my chair as far as my handcuffs would let me. "I'm thinking maybe they're right."

The man beside Special Agent Tomaszewski sat up straighter. When he spoke, his soft voice was laced with an Irish lilt. "Whoa, now. Listen, son, I don't think you should—"

"Are you familiar with the Persian legend of the Seven Labors of Rostam, Kamran?" Special Agent Tomaszewski asked me, cutting her partner off. He slouched back in his chair.

"Sure," I said. "My mom used to tell us those stories."

"So Darius would have been familiar with them, too?"

"Sure."

Special Agent Tomaszewski read from her file. "Rostam fights beasts, dragons, demons . . . those the kinds of monsters you and your brother swore to kill?"

"Yeah. I guess. I don't see what—"

"What's the last of Rostam's Seven Labors, Kamran? Do you remember?"

"He kills the White Demon and saves the king."

Special Agent Tomaszewski nodded. "There are some scholars who believe that last story is a metaphor. That it's really about the struggle between the Persians and invaders from the north. *White* invaders. That Rostam is a hero in Iran because he fought the white invaders who meant to conquer his kingdom, and won."

I saw where she was going with this, but it was crazy. "But—I—we never thought of it that way. The White Demon was just a giant wizard. He was Voldemort and Grawp rolled into one. He didn't represent any white invaders or anything to us. We were just kids!"

"But now you're not," Special Agent Tomaszewski said.

"So you're saying . . . what, that Darius thinks Americans are monsters he has to kill because he signed some made up Code of Honor in middle school? That doesn't make any sense! Why would he hate America? He joined the US Army! He's a Ranger!"

"Let's talk about Darius," Special Agent Tomaszewski said. She flipped to another part of her folder, and I sank lower in my chair. I was starting to really hate that folder.

"Straight As in high school. Varsity football. Strong SAT scores. West Point. Volunteered for the Army Rangers. Made captain before the age of twenty-five. All very impressive. Just as impressive as your record so far, Kamran. Almost identical. Trying to follow in his footsteps?"

That was a loaded question, and we both knew it. Yes, I was following in Darius's footsteps. But I thought he was an American hero, and she thought he was a terrorist. I didn't answer, and she went on.

"During his senior year, Darius spent a week in Washington, DC. Strange place for a seventeen-year-old boy to go on spring break. What did he do while he was there?"

"I—I don't know." I vaguely remembered that Darius had taken a road trip there with some friends. From the photos on Facebook, it had looked like they'd had a lot of fun. "Visited the White House? Took pictures. Did touristy stuff."

"Not conduct reconnaissance for al-Qaeda?"

"Conduct—*no!*"

Special Agent Tomaszewski turned a page. "Tell me about the incident when you were younger. When the two boys who lived down the street called you names."

I couldn't believe it. How in the world had the Department of Homeland Security heard about *that*? Somebody who lived on our street must have told them. Maybe Ben and Steve themselves. Which meant they'd interviewed all my neighbors, trying to dig up dirt on us. What was she going to ask me about next, the Halloween I rolled a neighbor's house with toilet paper?

"Kamran?"

I shook my head. "It was nothing. These two kids called me names. They didn't even know what they were saying."

"And how did your brother react? He was angry, wasn't he?"

Aha. Now I understood what she was getting at. Big bad Darius, neighborhood terrorist. "Yeah. He beat them up," I told her. There was no point lying about it. She obviously already knew the whole story.

"And 9/11. How did he react to that?"

"I don't know. I was three."

"But Darius would have been . . . eleven. That's a difficult time to suddenly have everybody look at you like you might be a terrorist."

"It's tough to have people look at you like a terrorist *any* time," I told her. "Like right now, for example."

The guy beside her tried to swallow a grin. Point for me.

Special Agent Tomaszewski wasn't put off in the slightest. "It must have been an impressionable time for him."

I shrugged. "Maybe it was. Maybe that's what made him want to be a hero."

"A hero to whom?"

"To the United States of America. In case you missed it in your folder there, he's been fighting for freedom in Afghanistan for three years. Darius is an American hero."

"Darius Smith has been seen on film training al-Qaeda militants and is responsible for the deaths of fifty-three people at the US embassy in Turkey, including twenty-two civilians. He also stood by and watched while an American journalist was beheaded yesterday."

My face got hot. I lurched forward, the handcuffs clinking where they were attached to the table. "He didn't do any of that! Not on purpose! He's a prisoner! They're just making it look like—"

"Why would Darius throw everything away?" Special Agent Tomaszewski cut in. "What would make him want to abandon his friends, his family, his country?"

I sat back and glared at her. I had already told her the truth. She just didn't want to hear it.

"Did you know that Darius is a devout Muslim, Kamran?"

"I told you already, he isn't—"

She slid another photo around from that folder of hers. "Do you know what this is?" she asked. It was a picture of a string of black wooden beads with a tassel on the end of it.

"It's a string of beads," I told her.

"It's a misbaha," she said. "A string of prayer beads. Muslims use these to keep count of their prayers. We found this in your brother's apartment."

I frowned. Why would Darius have prayer beads? "He's not religious," I told her.

Special Agent Tomaszewski slid more papers in front of me. Printouts from websites. "Our search of your brother's computer says otherwise. Somebody from his computer's IP address has been asking for rulings on questions of Islamic law in an online forum under the name Rostam90. 'Is it still forbidden to shave my beard if my job requires it?' 'Can I go to parties where alcohol is being served even if I don't drink?' 'Is it permissible to pray in my army boots?'"

I stared at the printouts. Rostam90 had to be Darius. He was born in 1990. Had Darius really become a Muslim? And if he had, did that even mean anything?

"I'll ask you again, Kamran," Special Agent Tomaszewski said. "Loyal to *whom*?"

CHAPTER NINETEEN

I SAT ON THE BED IN THE LITTLE HOLDING CELL THAT had become my new home, thinking about Darius. He was all I thought about now. All I *talked* about.

I'd been here—wherever "here" was—for over a week now. Every day was the same: wake up in this cell, have some stale cereal brought to me for breakfast, and then get taken to the interrogation room down the hall. Special Agent Tomaszewski and the silent, nameless guy would meet me there with her folder full of papers, and we would go over everything again. Or she would bring up some new part of Darius's life and spin it, making it sound like just another reason for him to become a terrorist, another explanation for why he'd turned traitor and joined al-Qaeda.

Then I'd be brought back to my cell for lunch, and sometimes I'd be taken back to the interrogation room in the afternoon to go over it all again with two different people. I still hadn't seen my parents. I had no idea if they were even in the same building. And I still had no idea when I was ever going to get out of here, or what was happening with Darius.

Day after day I argued with Special Agent Tomaszewski and the others, telling them that Darius wasn't a terrorist, but after a week of hearing why he might be one, I was beginning to wonder. To doubt. And I hated myself for doubting. I felt like I was betraying Darius for even thinking it.

But what if Darius had betrayed *me*? What if Darius had betrayed everyone and everything he loved? What if Darius had never really loved any of us to begin with? What if he had been pretending all that time, playing the part of the All-American son, getting straight As and playing football and joining the army, always with the plan to get to Afghanistan and run to al-Qaeda, where he could at last be himself? Finally let the real Darius come through?

I stood and kicked my flimsy wooden bed. I hated doubting Darius, I hated that Darius had ever given me reason to doubt, and I hated Darius for getting into trouble like this in the first place.

We would all have been better off if he died in Afghanistan.

No. No, I couldn't think that. I could never think that. I didn't want Darius dead. I wanted him alive, and back home, and proven innocent.

But what if he wasn't innocent? Special Agent Tomaszewski certainly didn't think he was. She had him pegged for a terrorist from age eleven, maybe even earlier. Was Darius still mad at the Ben and Steve Hollises of the world? Did he hate all the haters? Had they called him "monster" with their looks and their whispers and their prejudice so often that he had finally decided to become what they said he was?

And the codes. The secret codes I kept trying to tell them about. Was I just imagining things? Maybe my brother had really gone insane. Maybe he was just mixing up the real legends of Rostam with the stuff we'd made up as kids.

I sat down on my bed again. I felt like I didn't know anything anymore, least of all my brother.

Someone knocked on the door like they did when they were bringing me food or taking me to the interrogation room. But it was late. My dinner tray had already been taken away, and they never came for me after dinner.

I took a deep breath. What did they want from me now?

CHAPTER TWENTY

THE DOOR OPENED, AND THE MAN WHO'D SAT IN ON all my interviews with Special Agent Tomaszewski stepped inside, carrying a chair. The guy with the Irish accent. He still looked rumpled and unshaven. It was good that he'd brought his own chair, especially if he was planning to stay. I had no other furniture besides my bed and the toilet and sink in the corner.

My guard came in with the handcuffs they put on me to take me from place to place, but the Irish guy stopped him. "We won't be needing those for this, Sergeant. Will we?" he asked me.

I shook my head. Whatever was going on, we could do it without the cuffs. I hated those things. They hurt my wrists. Worse, they made me feel like I'd done something wrong.

"That's what I thought." The Irish guy set his chair down, and nodded the guard toward the door. "I'll be fine. I'll call if there's trouble."

My guard looked at me doubtfully and left. He probably had no idea who I was or what I'd done to get myself locked up here. For all he knew, I was a violent criminal.

The Irish guy sat in his chair, facing me straight on. He crossed his legs and leaned back. "Hello, Kamran. I know all about you, but you don't know me so well," he said. "My name's Mickey Hagan. I'm an analyst with the CIA."

An analyst with the CIA. I swallowed hard. I was in way over my head here.

"I—I came to—well—" Mickey Hagan paused. "Ah, for the love of God. I don't know *what* I came here to do."

I hadn't expected that. He was quiet for a long time—longer than was comfortable—but I didn't say anything. They'd made me talk all day in the interrogation room, and I wasn't in the mood to say anything more. I sat back on my bed and crossed my arms.

"That's not entirely true," Hagan said at last. "I do know why I came here. I came to tell you a story."

Great. A story from a CIA analyst who'd been sitting in on my interrogations for a week. He must have seen my lack of enthusiasm written all over my face.

"I know, I know," he said. "Just—just hear me out. It has a lot to do with you. All to do with you.

"I wasn't born here," he went on. "I'm an American citizen now, like your mother, but I was born in Northern Ireland, so long ago now I don't care to mention. Do you know anything about Northern Ireland?"

I shook my head.

"It's just as well, I suppose. If you'd grown up when I did, you'd have heard all about it on the news. It's the wee top part of Ireland. Ireland's hat, if you will," he said, his eyes flashing with something like humor. "Northern Ireland, you see, doesn't like to think of itself as part of the rest of Ireland. They're Protestants there, mostly. Church of England types. And they'd rather Mother England still ruled the whole island."

I didn't see how any of this had anything to do with me. Hagan waved a hand like he understood he needed to get on with it.

"There's still plenty of Catholics there, though, the rest of Ireland being full up with them and all. They sort of spill over, you see? That was me when I was a lad—a Catholic Irishman in a country that didn't want one. My older brother, Conor, he was always getting into trouble with the law when we were boys, but that was the way of things. If you were Catholic in Northern Ireland, you had the deck stacked against you, you see. They sent us to separate schools. We had to eat in separate cafés. If you were Catholic, no Protestant would hire you for any job of work, and the Protestants in Northern Ireland, they own all the companies. Eventually they built a *wall* between the Protestants and the Catholics, in case we didn't get the memo that we were to have nothing to do with each other.

"But the wall did very little to keep the peace. For decades, Northern Ireland was torn apart by what they benignly called 'The Troubles.' The Republicans, the ones who wanted Northern Ireland back in Ireland proper, they fought the Loyalists, the ones who wanted Northern Ireland to stay part of England. They set fire to each other's homes, put bombs in their places of business, shot each other in the streets. And it didn't matter if you didn't have an opinion one way or another. If you were a Catholic, the Protestants always looked at you like you had a bomb under your coat. But maybe you know what that feels like already."

I did know what it felt like, and he knew it.

"If you lived on either side of that wall in Northern Ireland, you were a part of it, sure as I'm sitting here. Whether you wanted to be or not," Hagan said. "You were just as likely to die by accident in Northern Ireland as you were on purpose."

Something about saying that made Hagan get quiet for a few seconds. Then he rallied and went on.

"So the Hagan family, we did what any good down-on-its-heels Irish family does when the going gets tough: we up and moved. Away from Northern Ireland and its troubles, down to Galway, in the good old Republic of Ireland. Without the

Protestant government there to tell us what we could and couldn't do, we settled in nicely, thank you very much, and we thought that was the end of it. I went to school, got good enough grades that my parents didn't cuff me on the ear, and spent my every last minute mooning over girls and playing football. The real kind, not what you Americans call football."

I couldn't help but smile at that. It'd been so long since I'd last smiled I'd almost forgotten how to do it.

"But Conor was still getting in trouble with the law," Hagan said, "even after it weren't Protestant policemen doing the hassling. He'd learned in Belfast not to trust the law, you see, and it was a hard thing to unlearn. He'd become a fair hooligan in Belfast, too, and that's a tough path to leave once you've started down it.

"Me? I went the other way. After graduation I joined the army—the Irish Army—and soon I was angling for a career in military intelligence, if that isn't an oxymoron for the ages. So while Conor found himself in and out of jail, I found myself on the other side of things, defending him, pulling strings to get him square again in the ever-watchful eyes of the law. He'd never done anything really bad, I kept telling myself. Just a little rabble-rousing now and again. Yes, he was political. Yes, he wanted reunification with Northern Ireland. Fifteen years in Belfast had made him a zealot. But in a free society, you're allowed to have opinions, am I right? Or so the brochures say. Conor would get arrested at a Sinn Féin meeting, and I'd stick up for him with my superiors. Because Conor wasn't truly guilty. He couldn't be. I'd grown up with the lad. Knew him better than anyone else. And *Conor Hagan wasn't a terrorist.*"

So there it was at last. The connection to me. How many times had I said the same thing about Darius in that interrogation room? *Darius Smith isn't a terrorist.* He couldn't be. And what was my best argument? Because I'd grown up with him. Because I knew him better than anybody else, and I couldn't believe it. Because if Darius Smith was a terrorist, I would have known about it.

Wouldn't I?

CHAPTER TWENTY-ONE

"SO HERE'S ANOTHER STORY FOR YOU," HAGAN SAID. "The other story about me and my brother growing up in Northern Ireland, that one isn't finished yet. We're just taking a little break from it. Call it poetic license.

"In 1982, a long time before you were born, God help us all, a young man working for the Irish Republican Army went into a fish shop in Belfast, Northern Ireland, carrying a bomb. Now, the Irish Republican Army isn't the Republic of Ireland Army, mind you. They're two different things. I worked for the Republic of Ireland's army, the ones with the tanks and the planes and the fancy uniforms; this lad worked for the Irish Republican Army, the IRA as they were known, a terrorist organization hell-bent on bringing Northern Ireland back into the fold by any means necessary—which usually meant a petrol bomb or a machine gun.

"The Ulster Defense Association, an equally bloody-minded terrorist group fighting to keep Northern Ireland independent, was supposed to be having a meeting upstairs of the fish shop this lad entered with the bomb, you see. The plan was for this young man to enter the shop disguised as a deliveryman, scare the customers downstairs away with a gun, and then set his time bomb on a short fuse that would give him just enough time to get away before blowing the UDA leadership to heaven or hell, I don't know which. But something went wrong. The bomb went off before it was supposed to. Before any of the innocent people downstairs could be chased from the shop. Blew the whole building up, it did, raining down wood and brick and mortar, killing the eight Protestants inside and wounding fifty more on the street outside. Killed one UDA man, too—the fishmonger—but no others. They'd canceled the meeting, you see, and the bomber, he didn't know. He died, too, of course. Wasn't supposed to, but when the bomb went off early, he went with it. Killed him right off."

Mickey Hagan stared at his shoe, visibly building up the courage to continue.

"The bomber was my brother Conor, of course," he said at last. "You'll have figured that out already, bright lad that you are. It weren't two stories but one. The beginning and the end of the tragedy. The bomber was my brother, the one I'd sworn wasn't a terrorist till I was blue in the face. Stupid me, I'd believed him when he'd told me he was off to see Galway United play football. I'd believed everything he'd ever told me, every last lie, and now he was dead for it. We both were, in a way. But maybe you know a little bit about how that feels, too."

Darius wasn't dead—not that I knew, at least—but I knew what Hagan meant. All my life I'd thought one thing about Darius, and now he was maybe something else, and it was like his whole life was a lie. And mine, too, for believing him.

So that's why Mickey Hagan was here. To tell me a story about his brother. The brother he trusted, believed, defended, only to watch his faith and loyalty go up in flames. He was here to help me accept the fact that Darius was a terrorist.

"I just . . ." I said, "I was just so sure."

Hagan nodded, understanding.

"Even after everything," I said. "After everything he's said and done, I still can't believe Darius is a terrorist."

"And neither can I," Hagan said.

CHAPTER TWENTY-TWO

WAIT—THIS CIA GUY WAS TELLING ME HE THOUGHT Darius *wasn't* a terrorist?

"But you just got done telling me that story about your brother. About how you thought he was innocent, but it turned out he was guilty all along," I said.

"Because I wanted you to understand what happened to me," Hagan said. "And I knew you, of all people, would understand. All week I've watched you slowly lose your confidence in your brother, the same way I did. The truth is hard enough to accept. You fight it. Deny it. But when you do come 'round, you start to question everything. You start looking for signs your brother was a terrorist in every little thing he said and did, and then you beat yourself up for being so blind."

I nodded. I'd been doing that very thing when he walked in.

"After Conor died, I was a wreck," Hagan said. "Not just because I'd lost my older brother, the boy I'd looked up to and idolized all my young life, but because I doubted myself. If *I* hadn't seen that Conor, who I knew better than anyone else, was a terrorist, how was I supposed to ever be right about *anybody*? I couldn't trust my hunches anymore. My intuition—my gut." He thumped a fist on his chest. "From that moment on, I was forever second-guessing myself."

"My coach always says, 'No distractions, no doubts, no second guesses,'" I said.

"Wisdom of the ages, that is," Hagan said. "After Conor died, I was haunted like a banshee by all three. I was distracted. I doubted myself. I second-guessed myself at every turn. And when you do that in the spy business . . . well, it's over. You're done. The Irish Army didn't want the brother of a known terrorist in their ranks anyhow, so I did what any good down-on-his-heels Irishman does—"

"You up and moved," I finished for him.

Hagan smiled wryly. He liked that. "Indeed. Came to America, as so many of my blessed people have, where it turns out they didn't mind so much that my brother was an IRA terrorist, as the IRA had no beef with the USA. Got a job with the CIA as a counterterrorism analyst, and here I am: a well-traveled, very experienced counterterrorism expert with a very high pay grade, but no confidence to make the tough calls and too much seniority to be let go. And what does that get you? You're the rumpled old man in the interrogation room who isn't allowed to ask questions. You're nobody. Nothing. A joke."

Hagan ran his hands over his face and up through his unkempt hair, then slapped his knees, surprising me.

"I want to *believe* again, Kamran. I want to be the man I once was, the man who believed my brother was innocent. No—who *knew* my brother was innocent. I want to stop second-guessing every last thing. I want to have a gut feeling about something and be *right* about it for once. And I've got a gut feeling about your brother, Kamran. I think he's what you've been saying he is all along: a loyal American soldier who got captured, and who's now doing his damnedest to tell us everything he can about what his captors are up to so we can stop them."

I couldn't believe it. Just when I'd started to think everybody else was right about Darius, somebody finally came along who believed what I'd been saying from the start. I was all mixed up inside. I wanted to believe, like Hagan. Wanted to go back to that innocent, naive Kamran who wouldn't hear anybody say a bad word about his older brother. But *could* I go back? Could I forget everything I'd learned about Darius this week? Could I ever see the events of his life as anything but the path to terrorism?

"Everybody else in this building thinks your brother is a traitor to his country," Hagan said. "And they may be right. I don't know. That's my curse. I can't trust my gut anymore. But I want to *try*. So I'm choosing to believe in you, Kamran. In you and your brother and your Code of Honor. The only question now is, do *you* still believe?"

That was a good question. And one I wasn't sure I had a good answer to.

"I—I don't know if I do anymore," I told him. "But I want to."

"Good enough," Hagan said. He stuck out his hand and I shook it.

"Now," he said, "if you've got a bit of free time on your hands, I'd very much like to go over those tapes of Darius again with you."

CHAPTER TWENTY-THREE

"THERE," I SAID, POINTING TO THE VIDEO OF THE embassy attack. "See how he's wagging his finger? It's like the pattern to the knocks. We used to send messages to each other through the wall, letting each other know when we could sneak into each other's rooms and talk at night."

Hagan and I sat in a dark room full of TV monitors and computers. It was the first time I'd been somewhere other than my holding cell or the interrogation room. Hagan had even brought me a can of Coke and a bag of chips. This was living large.

Ha. A couple of weeks ago my definition of "living large" was dancing with Julia Gary and going to the Super Bowl with Adam. It's funny how little things can become big things when you've got nothing anymore.

"So what's the message?" Hagan asked me, his face lit up by the glow of the TV screen.

"I—I don't know. I never could figure it out," I said, feeling lame.

"That's because you're seeing it, not hearing it. Let's get it audible."

"But there's no sound."

"A little creativity wouldn't go amiss, I'm thinking," Hagan scolded. He rewound the video and we watched it again. This time, Hagan knocked on the table as Darius wagged his finger. "Anything?" he asked.

I shook my head. It wasn't sounding like any of our codes. Maybe I'd been wrong.

No. Stop second-guessing yourself.

"Not yet," I said.

"You say you used these codes at night, through the wall, yes? Close your eyes. Go back to being little and listening for your brother to knock to you through the wall."

I did what he said. Pictured myself smaller, younger, waiting in bed to hear the signal from Darius that the coast was clear. Looking forward to sneaking into his room and watching him act out a new story he'd made up about Rostam with his G.I. Joes.

Hagan knocked. Knocked again. Knocked again. I was ready to sneak out, to go see Darius, but—I suddenly knew I couldn't.

"Mom and Dad are coming!" I said aloud. "That's what that knock means. Mom and Dad are coming!"

"Brilliant," Hagan said. At first I thought he was being sarcastic, but he was scribbling notes in a black notebook.

"But—what's that supposed to mean? Mom and Dad don't have anything to do with this."

"No," Hagan said. "But put yourself in Darius's army boots for a moment. You're taken prisoner in Afghanistan. Forced to train al-Qaeda soldiers—or at the very least, pretend to look like you are on film. Yes? This is good. It's an opportunity for you to get a message to America. Maybe you've heard the militants talking about a strike on a US military installation. Or an American embassy. You want to tell us. Warn us. You know you can't just say it out loud on camera—they'd never post that to the Internet. You have to be sneaky. You have to say it in some way that your captors won't understand. You need a *code*. And luckily, you already have one. One that you and only one other person in the *world* understand. That no one else in the world could ever crack. That's the best kind of code. Unbreakable."

"But the knocks, they're not like letters or words you can rearrange. It's just, this one means 'Mom and Dad are coming,' this one means 'The coast is clear,' this one means 'I'm coming to you.'"

"Right. Okay. So your vocabulary in this code is limited. But it's all you've got for now. So don't take the message literally. Think about what 'Mom and Dad are coming' *means*. At its very core."

"I don't know. Uh, look out? Danger?"

"Precisely. That's it in a nutshell: *danger*. Right from the start, Darius was warning us. *Trouble is coming.* And I have to say, he was right."

It made sense. Even if he wasn't able to say what the trouble was, it meant something to just say "look out!"

"So you send your message as best you can," Hagan said, queuing up another video. "And you wait. And you listen. And then, lo and behold, there comes another miracle: they tell you to read a speech directly to the camera. They ask you to *talk*."

It was the second video, the one where Darius took responsibility for the attack on the US embassy. Hagan knew right where the Sith Lord reference was, and he moved the slider to the exact minute and second. He'd been listening to me all those times I told them Darius was trying to communicate with me. He'd taken notes. Watched the video over and over again, trying to understand. Trying to believe me. I was so grateful to him in that moment I could have hugged him. You know, if that wouldn't have been really weird.

"So now you can slip something in, maybe, but you still have to be tricky," Hagan said, his eyes still on the video. "Here you don't have a code, not like the one you used on the wall. But you do have a language you and only one other person share. Again, a language that no one but you and your brother can ever understand, can ever translate. The language of a shared childhood. 'Rostam in the cave of the Sith Lord.' It's brilliant. It's so utterly confusing, so random, so *cryptic* that it makes no sense. It sounds like the delusional ramblings of a prisoner. Or perhaps someone pretending to be a convert."

CHAPTER TWENTY-FOUR

"YOU THINK HE'S DOING THAT?" I ASKED. "PRETEND-ing to be on their side?"

"It's an effective way to survive when there is no other option open to you," Hagan said. "If you can make them believe you. And he may think it will make him privy to more insider information he can pass along."

Hagan loaded the next video. The third one. It was another rant from Darius, read from a piece of paper. This one didn't claim responsibility for anything or come on the heels of an attack.

"Here," Hagan said, clicking ahead. "At the four minute, thirty-seven second mark. Another Rostam reference."

"Rostam and the Death Eaters," I said. I knew what it was. I'd watched it again and again, trying to understand what Darius was trying to tell me.

"A Harry Potter reference," Hagan said smugly. "Don't look so surprised. Just because I was born a hundred years before you and work for the CIA doesn't mean I live under a rock. I've read each and every one of them," he said, "*Goblet of Fire* being my favorite, of course. But I want to hear *your* version."

I thought back to the story we had invented. "Okay, so, Rostam and Siyavash are tracking down this Death Eater, Bellatrix Lestrange."

"A devious and dangerous witch, to be sure," Hagan said, taking notes in his black book.

"Right. We find out that Lord Voldemort has sent her to capture an old Auror named Reginald Lumpbucket."

Hagan looked up from his notebook. "Is that a name I should know?"

"No. We made it up."

"Well, it's a good one," Hagan said. "Very English."

"Do you think that's the clue? Darius heard them planning something about somebody named Lumpbucket?"

"No," Hagan said. He motioned again for me to keep going.

"So, we track down Lumpbucket to this old house, where he's supposed to live. Bellatrix Lestrange is there, too, looking for him, and we fight."

"Naturally," said Hagan.

"But while we're fighting, we find out from his old house elf that he's not there. Turns out Lumpbucket died a long time ago."

"Voldemort is foiled, then," Hagan said.

"No," I said. "There's still his portrait."

Hagan sat up. "His portrait?"

"Yeah. You know how in the Harry Potter books, all the paintings are alive? Lumpbucket's portrait is in a museum, and Bellatrix Lestrange flies off to steal it."

"She robs a museum?" Hagan asked. He put down his notebook and swung around to one of the computers.

"She tries to. We stop her, of course. But I still don't understand it. What Darius means with the story, I mean."

"I think I do," Hagan said. He turned the computer screen toward me. On it was an article from *Time* magazine, with a picture of an American soldier standing next to the charred metal door of a small building. "The National Museum of Iraq has been undergoing extensive renovations since it was damaged during the 2003 Iraq War," Hagan explained. "While those renovations have been taking place, the museum's remaining antiquities were moved off-site to a hidden location, guarded by American forces. Only the United States military knew where those objects were being hidden, yet two weeks ago armed militants raided the location, stealing a truckload of Mesopotamian artifacts, some of which were more than five thousand years old."

"Darius!" I said. "Darius might have known the location."

"Maybe he was the one to tell them, maybe not. But I think we can definitely say that he was warning us that a museum was about to be robbed. Look at the date on the article, and the date on the video."

They were days apart—and Darius's warning had come first.

"Why would terrorists want to steal a bunch of old artifacts?" I asked.

"*Money*," Hagan said simply. "Guns and bombs and trucks cost money, and those artifacts are worth a great deal of it on the international art market. That they liberated cultural artifacts from the control of American soldiers probably didn't hurt, either." Hagan grabbed my shoulder and squeezed it. "This is a terrific breakthrough!"

"But we're too late. They already stole the stuff. It's probably long gone."

"Yes, yes. There's a marine colonel still in charge of recovery efforts from thefts during the Iraq War. I'll pass along who we think perpetrated the crime to him, see what he and his team can do. But don't you see what this means? We have proof, Kamran. Proof! It's a dead cert that your brother is sending us coded messages. He dropped the name of a story about a museum robbery, and three days later museum artifacts were stolen in Iraq. That's proof that we were right. Both of us."

We were right. *I* was right. Darius really was trying to talk to me in those videos. I felt awful for ever doubting him. It was me and Darius against the world.

No, I realized. Not anymore. It was me and Darius and *Mickey Hagan* against the world. I finally had an ally.

"Let's keep going," he said.

"So. *Goblet of Fire*'s your favorite?" I said while he called up the next video.

"Of course," Hagan said. "Ireland wins the Quidditch World Cup in that one. Closest we'll ever get to winning the World Cup of anything."

CHAPTER TWENTY-FIVE

HAGAN MET ME AT THE DOOR TO THE VIDEO ROOM, where my guard now dropped me off every day.

"Got a new one," Hagan told me.

"A new video?"

He steered me toward a chair and hit play. It was Darius again, looking dirtier, more haggard. His beard was fuller now, and he wore a turban on his head. I barely recognized him. It had only been what—about a month and a half since the very first video? But for Darius, it had been a lifetime.

For me, too.

We'd been going over the videos for days, piecing together the clues and the events Darius had been referring to. I told Hagan the made-up Rostam stories Darius mentioned, and Hagan used his experience and knowledge of foreign affairs to link them to recent incidents in the Middle East. What Darius meant with some of his references was still a mystery to us, but a new video trumped everything. This was what we'd been waiting for. If Darius dropped a clue in this one and we were able to decipher it, we might be able to stop whatever it was before it happened.

Maybe even find a way to rescue Darius.

I focused on what Darius was saying. Most of it was the usual ranting about America and the infidels.

Then he made another Rostam reference.

I almost stood and cheered. Hagan was excited, too, I could tell. He hurriedly rewound the video so we could hear it again.

"Like Rostam taking on the Joker's smiling goons, we will score a victory for justice!" Darius said.

Hagan was scribbling in his notebook. "Like Rostam taking on the Joker's smiling goons, we will score a victory for justice," he repeated.

"That one? Seriously?" I said. My elation of a moment before was gone, replaced by a feeling of hopelessness.

"Why? What is it?" Hagan asked. "What's the story?"

"That's just it," I said. "It isn't much of one."

Hagan waited, pen hovering over a page in his notebook.

I sighed. "One day we were playing football in the backyard, one on one, just throwing the ball back and forth. And Darius had the idea that the football had a bomb in it."

Hagan looked up. "A bomb?"

"We pretended that the Joker from Batman had put a nuclear bomb in the football, and that Rostam and Siyavash had to score a touchdown with it to defuse it."

Hagan looked up at me skeptically.

"We were kids!" I said for maybe the hundredth time since we'd started this. All our games and stories were stupid. Everybody's games and stories were stupid when they were little, because you didn't know any better. "I'm just telling you what it was."

"Right, right," Hagan said. "What else, then?"

"The smiling goons were Joker henchmen he'd used his laughing gas on. Like . . . scary clowns with football helmets on. Darius and I—Rostam and Siyavash—had to get past them to score."

"What else?"

"That's it. That's what I'm saying. There's nothing to it. We just mashed up playing football with our Rostam adventures. I don't know what good it does us."

We watched the rest of the video to see if Darius gave us any more clues. Right toward the end he dropped another reference to Rostam. Hagan and I both sat up straight again.

"And then when our work is done and the last heretic is swept from the face of the earth, like Rostam at the World's End we will go to our final rewards," Darius said solemnly.

"Okay. Okay! There's lots more to this story!" I said, happy to once again be useful. "Rostam and Siyavash have to help Optimus Prime steal back the AllSpark from Syndrome, the bad guy from *The Incredibles*."

"You've lost me on this one, I'm afraid," Hagan said. "We've moved beyond Harry Potter, yes?"

"Optimus Prime is a Transformer."

"Carry on," said Hagan.

"So we're fighting one of Syndrome's giant robots, and we're winning, when Syndrome implants nanobots in Optimus Prime and turns him against us. So now we have to fight one of our allies."

"As you do," Hagan said.

"We manage to lock Optimus Prime in truck mode, but the nanobots, they activate Optimus Prime's self-destruct device. If we can't get rid of him, he's going to blow up and take out half of Phoenix. So Rostam jumps on board him and—"

Oh. Oh no. No no no no no, I thought.

"And what?"

"And he drives him over a cliff at the World's End. Optimus Prime hits the bottom and explodes. Rostam dies to save the city."

Hagan gave me a dubious look. "But he lives, right? He's your hero. Heroes never die in the storybooks."

"No," I said. "No, Rostam really dies. The whole next story is about Siyavash tracking down Syndrome to avenge his death.

It turns out Syndrome's nanobots can rebuild Optimus Prime and Rostam, and they're brought back to life."

"So there you go," Hagan said.

"But—but, Mr. Hagan, there aren't really nanobots that can bring you back to life."

Hagan knew that, of course. What he hadn't considered was what the story might actually mean. Not until that moment. He hadn't thought what I had: that Darius was telling us he was going to sacrifice himself.

That Darius was going to die.

CHAPTER TWENTY-SIX

THE ONLY SOUND IN THE ROOM FOR A FEW MINUTES was the low hum of the computers and televisions.

Hagan leaned back in his chair. "All right. Let's take them one at a time. As for the first story, I have to say, it's not much to go on. But let's see what we can do. All the other clues we've figured out have been about events in the Middle East—Afghanistan, Iraq, Turkey, Saudi Arabia. Clearly that region is their base of operations. It's still a big area, but it gives us a place to start."

"Not a lot of people playing football over there," I said.

"I don't think we should be focusing on the football angle," Hagan said. "There's another part of that story that as a CIA counterterrorism analyst I find highly interesting."

"The nuclear bomb," I said.

"The nuclear bomb," Hagan agreed. "There are only nine countries in the nuclear club right now: the US, the UK, China, France, Russia, India, Pakistan, North Korea, and Israel. Israel won't say if they have nukes or not, but we know they do, so they count. Just don't tell anybody. State secret."

"I—I wouldn't—" I stammered.

"Israel's for sure not going to give them one of theirs," Hagan went on, "so the most likely place for our terrorists to get one is Pakistan, which shares a fifteen-hundred-mile border with Afghanistan, most of which is barren, unpatrolled desert and mountains. Easy to sneak across, is what I'm trying to say there. And Pakistan is where al-Qaeda's leaders go to ground when the drones start buzzing too close to home. It's their bunker away from bunker, if you will."

"So, what, you think Darius might be telling us somebody's moving a bomb?"

"It's possible. American football is all about moving the ball forward. Gaining . . . territory."

Something had clicked for Hagan. I could hear it in his voice. See it in his face. He swung around to a computer to look something up.

"But what about the other story? The one about Optimus Prime and the nanobots? Does it mean what I think it means?"

Hagan found whatever it was he was looking for and leaned back again.

"I think it might mean everything we think it means. Even a game of football."

I didn't understand.

"It came to me when I said 'American football,'" Hagan told me. "Your brother, he mentions a story about football, and a bomb. You think it's one thing, I think it's another. But what if it's both? There happens to be a slightly massive football tournament about to happen next summer in Canada. *The Women's World Cup.*"

"What? You mean soccer?"

"Yes. Well, the rest of the world calls it 'football.' And your brother would know that, being the international traveler he is now. Have you any stories about soccer?"

"No," I told him. "None that I can think of."

Hagan nodded. "So he would have had to use your version of football to send his warning. In this World Cup, you have a target truly worthy of a jihad. Infidel women running about outdoors without veils, showing indecent amounts of skin—to a radical Islamist, at least. And what better place to attack? Close enough to the United States to make a point, but not so close as to necessitate actually sneaking a bomb across America's borders." He turned the screen toward me, showing me Women's World Cup schedules and tables. "And your United States team is all set to play Australia in the first round."

"You think—you think they're going to set off a bomb at the Women's World Cup in Canada?"

"I do," said Hagan. "And I'm sorry, Kamran, but I think the other story means Darius is going to be the one to wear it."

CHAPTER TWENTY-SEVEN

MICKEY HAGAN SWEPT A HAND OVER A PIZZA BOX and a two-liter of soda. "I come bearing gifts," he said.

Pizza! I'd existed on nothing but cafeteria food and cartons of milk delivered to me on metal trays for as long as I'd been here. Just the sight of a pizza delivery box and I was practically drooling already. My guard left me in the video room with Hagan and went to stand outside.

"What's the occasion?" I asked.

Hagan looked a little embarrassed. "Well, it's Christmas," he said.

I sat down in one of the chairs. *Christmas.* It had been November when all this started. And now it was *Christmas.* If this had been any other year, I'd be home with my parents right now, opening presents. Watching basketball.

Trying to get through to Darius on Skype.

I suddenly pictured our house. Cold. Dark. Empty. No Christmas tree. No food cooking in the kitchen. No music playing. No friends and family. Where were my parents? How long would it be until we finally got out of here?

"I didn't know if you celebrated Christmas or not," Hagan said.

"Yeah. We do," I told him. I sighed. "I miss my parents."

"I know, son. I'm sorry. It's not my call."

I nodded. I felt like Mickey Hagan was the only person in this whole building who cared anything about me.

"At the very least, your efforts in helping us decipher those messages in Darius's communications deserve some reward," Hagan added.

He flipped open the box, revealing a large thin-crust cheese pizza. Right then, it was the most delicious-looking pizza I'd ever seen. He gestured at the pie, and I dug in.

"Not good enough to get me out of here?" I asked between a mouthful of pizza and a swig from the two-liter.

"I'm afraid not," Hagan said. "If anything, it's proven they were right to bring you here."

I stopped chewing. "Seriously? I thought cooperating would help get me *out* of here."

"It will," Hagan said. "Eventually. And more importantly, it will save lives. Possibly even your brother's."

"So they're doing something about it? The Women's World Cup?"

"The proper authorities have been notified. Security will be doubled. A special team is being sent to look for the bomb. I can't go into too many details, of course, but rest assured, measures are being taken."

"And Darius?" I said, sipping again from the two-liter. "What will happen to him?"

Hagan took a slice of pizza for himself. "It's hard to say, isn't it? A lot of that will depend on what Darius does, if and when they catch up to him. Oh, wait," Hagan said. "I've got some kitchen paper here somewhere."

While his back was turned, I quickly closed the lid on the pizza to look at the restaurant flyer taped there. Underneath a picture of George Washington in sunglasses, it said WE THE PIZZA. The address was 1776 51st Street NW. No city. Weird name for a pizza place. I'd never heard of it. Definitely not an

Arizona chain. Colorado maybe? California? The area code was 202. I didn't know that one, either.

Hagan turned back with paper towels, and I flipped the box open again.

"There we are," Hagan said, handing me a napkin. "Now your mother can't complain when you see her again."

Ha-ha. We both knew Mom and Dad and I had plenty to complain about, and not using napkins was about 1,976,242nd on the list.

"So now what?" I asked. I'd been brought to the video room, but we'd already figured out everything we could from Darius's messages.

"DHS wants us to go back over the tapes," Hagan said. "Look for anything else Darius might be trying to tell us."

I sagged. "But we've been over those videos dozens of times," I told him. "What else is there to learn? We've listened to them over and over and over again."

Hagan sat up. "You're right." He wheeled his chair over to the computer monitors and called up the al-Qaeda training video again. I groaned.

"No, wait," he said. He put the video on one of the big screens, dimmed the lights in the room, and hit play. But this time, he muted the monitor.

"What are you doing?"

"You're right. We *have* listened to these videos ad nauseam. Now let's *watch* them."

CHAPTER TWENTY-EIGHT

I WHEELED MY CHAIR OVER, BRINGING THE PIZZA and soda with me. It was strange, sitting in the dark with my feet up on the desk, eating pizza and drinking soda and watching Darius put al-Qaeda militants through their paces like I was at home on a Saturday night watching a DVD with Adam.

Adam. He'd be at home with his family today, opening presents. We always called each other later in the day, told each other what we'd gotten. I might even have walked over to his house that night to play our new video games.

Forget Adam, I told myself. *He's certainly forgotten you.*

I watched as Darius silently called out commands to the troops, tapping his leg. We'd already figured out that code. More "Danger coming." I slid my focus from Darius to the men he was training, to the guns they carried, to the obstacles they jumped and ducked and rolled behind. The camera was jerky, like it was being held in somebody's hand. It moved around the small patch of desert, capturing Darius's training session from all angles.

"Wait. Stop," I said.

Hagan practically fell over himself getting to the mouse to stop the video, his wheeled chair carrying him backward as he lunged forward.

"What? Did you see something?" he asked.

"Rewind it. There," I said. "That mountain silhouetted in the background. I know it."

Hagan looked at me skeptically. "You can't. This is Afghanistan. *Maybe* Pakistan."

"No. No, I'm sure I've seen that mountain before." I'd seen it a few times, I was sure. Not recently . . . but I'd thought about it recently. When . . . ? Then I had it. When I'd been remembering playing Rostam and Siyavash with Darius in the desert! Me and Darius, looking down through scraggly bushes at a dry riverbed, the orange sun setting over that same mountain in the background. "Superstition Mountain!" I said. "That's Superstition Mountain, outside Phoenix!"

"Kamran . . ." Hagan said.

"No, I *know* it is. And look. There. That plant. That's desert sand verbena. Rakhsh likes to eat it."

"Are we talking now about the stories you and Darius used to make up, or the real world, Kamran?"

"I mean the real Rakhsh. One of the horses at the ranch where my mom works. She named him Rakhsh after Rostam's horse. I used to go riding those trails in the Tonto National Forest all the time, all around Superstition Mountain. Rakhsh and the other horses love to eat that stuff. And I'm pretty sure the Sonoran Desert is the only place it grows. At least I think that's one of the plants native to Arizona. We had to learn all that stuff in fourth grade."

Hagan squinted at the screen. "It's hard to tell *what* it is," he said. "As for that mountain—that could be any mountain, anywhere. You can barely see it."

"Mr. Hagan, you gotta believe me. *Darius is right here, in Arizona!*"

Hagan put up his hands. "Hold your horses, cowboy. First let me run this by the CIA's geologists and botanists, see what they have to say about it."

"You've got geologists and botanists?"

"Naturally," Hagan said. I couldn't tell if he meant that as a pun. I think he did. "We'll see what the rock and plant folks have to say about it, at the very least. We shall leave no stone unturned, as it were. But, Kamran, I'm telling you right now: Darius isn't in Arizona. No matter how much you'd like him to be. He's in Afghanistan. That's where he was captured. That's where the broadcast came from."

"But if the attack is going to be in Canada—"

"Then they would have smuggled him into Canada, by way of a seaplane from Greenland. They would never risk bringing him to America just to smuggle him across the border into Canada. Kamran, believe me. When you watch one of these things again and again and again looking for the tiniest of little clues, it's been my experience that you tend to find them. Whether they're really there or not."

I sagged again. But—

"I tried to tell them," Hagan said. "Told them we'd got all the blood we could from this stone, but do they listen to Mickey Hagan? No. Not anymore."

I sighed. I was so *sure* it was Superstition Mountain in that video. But now that he'd said all that, pointed out how far-fetched it was, I realized it was probably wishful thinking. The silhouette of the mountain in the video was small. Cut off. Blurry. And the scrub grass was just as hard to see. It could be anything, really.

I was trying to put Darius somewhere else. Somewhere away from all the real trouble. Somewhere closer to home. Darius and I hadn't gone riding out there in a long time, but he'd have to have recognized he was in Arizona, if that's where he really was. Wouldn't he?

No. I was sure. I'd seen the mountain in the background. It was Superstition Mountain.

"It doesn't make sense, I know," I told Hagan. "Why would terrorists kidnap Darius in Afghanistan, then bring him all the way back here, through all that security, only to take him north into Canada for a suicide attack on the Women's World Cup?"

Hagan's eyes slid to the TV monitor. "They wouldn't, of course," Hagan said, his thoughts elsewhere.

"But they did," I said. "I don't know why, Mr. Hagan, but they did. *Darius is in Arizona.*"

CHAPTER TWENTY-NINE

NEW YEAR'S CAME AND WENT—I MARKED IT IN THE calendar I'd begun keeping in my head—but for me there were no parties, of course. No bowl games to watch.

I didn't worry too much about it. All I could think about was Darius in Arizona. When I wasn't in the video room trying to convince Mickey Hagan, I was pacing my cell, comparing my memories to that video. I was sure now. *Darius was in Arizona.* It didn't make any sense, but I *knew* it was true. But if I knew it, why didn't Darius? And if he knew it, too, why didn't he *say* anything? Was he counting on me noticing, just like I noticed his hand signals and the Rostam clues? I almost didn't catch those. Wouldn't have if I hadn't gone over every second of those videos. If Darius knew he was in Arizona, he would have said something, dropped some clue. Which meant he didn't know.

Or he did, and he was deliberately hiding the fact from us.

That thought hit me like a sixteen-ton weight. I'd been so sure Darius was an innocent victim in all this. Then the CIA and Homeland Security had convinced me he might be what everybody else thought he was. Then Mickey Hagan talked me down from the ledge. But what if Darius really was messing with us? What if the clues he was feeding us were deliberate fakes? What if he knew he was in Arizona all along, and was dropping these clues to throw me off the scent, knowing I would be the one person in the world who would do anything I could to find him?

I sat down on my bed and put my head in my hands. I didn't know what to think anymore. The only thing I was sure about was that the mountain in the background was Superstition Mountain, and that Darius was in Arizona. The rest of it—the rest of it made me sick. All this second-guessing would have made Coach Reynolds's head spin.

There was a knock at the door, and Mickey Hagan came in. He didn't bring a chair, and he didn't look happy.

"The geologists have been over the videos, Kamran. They say that mountain in the background could be any of a dozen in Afghanistan's Chagai Hills—let alone the rest of the world."

"But—"

Hagan held up a hand. "I know. You're sure. But these people, they're experts. They've been over every inch of that terrain on their computers."

"I've been over it on horseback!" I told him. "What about the verbena?"

"Too blurry to tell, Kamran. But most likely another variety of verbena that does grow in Afghanistan. I'm sorry."

I stood and paced again. "They're wrong. He's here, Mr. Hagan. I know it!"

"Well, I asked for a reconnaissance plane to take pictures of the area around your mountain, just to be sure."

"And?"

"And they didn't see anything unusual, Kamran. Just hikers and riders and Forest Rangers. And desert. Lots and lots of desert."

"But there are caves up in those mountains," I argued. "They could be hiding out anywhere up in there, and no one would ever know! One flyover might not catch them."

"Kamran—"

I kicked the bed against the wall. It made enough racket that the guard outside came in, his hand on the pistol at his side.

"We're all right, we're all right," Hagan told him. "Just letting off a bit of steam."

The guard wasn't so sure everything was all right, but Hagan outranked him. The guard scowled, backed outside, and closed the door again.

"Now, there's no reason to go giving out, son," Hagan said. "That won't do anybody any good, most of all you."

"Makes me feel better," I grumbled.

"Well, that it might. But I'm only after what's best for you. I hope you know that. And what's best for you right now is to keep a lid on that temper of yours. All right?"

"It just—it just sucks so much to know I'm right and have no one listen to me!"

"I'm listening," Hagan said. "But the DHS, they have their answer. And the answer is Afghanistan. And they know it for a fact."

This was new. "How?" I asked.

"The plot we uncovered, the one Darius told us about with your delightful ticking time bomb football story—it's been foiled."

CHAPTER THIRTY

"AT 21:52 LOCAL TIME, A NAVY SEAL TEAM RAIDED a building in a village outside Zarghun Shahr, near the Afghanistan-Pakistan border," Hagan said. "They intercepted a small team of highly trained terrorists with the blueprints for Investors Group Field in Winnipeg, Manitoba, Canada—the location of the United States Women's team's first World Cup match—and enough explosives to flatten it."

"Nuclear?" I asked.

"No, mercifully," Hagan said. "But the rest of the intel was good, Kamran. Very good. You saved a lot of lives today."

"Did anybody die in the raid?"

"Seven militants. Two Navy SEALs," Hagan said quietly.

"And—and Darius?" I asked. I almost didn't want to know. "Was he caught?"

"He wasn't there," Hagan said. "Neither was the man we think is behind all this business, an Iraqi terrorist named Haydar Ansari."

"So there you go," I said. "This Ansari guy and Darius, they weren't there because they're *here*. In America."

"Kamran, even if they were able to smuggle Darius back into the country, there's no way Ansari is here with him. He's on every international watch list from here to Australia. He's infamous. He would never leave the Middle East. It would be too dangerous for him. And he's too much a coward."

"Then just Darius is here," I said. "Please, Mr. Hagan. I'm begging you. Something else is going on."

Hagan shook his head, but I could tell he had doubts. That he was second-guessing himself as much as I had been.

"What does your gut tell you?" I asked him.

"My gut tells me I missed dinner."

I wanted to kick my bed again, but I didn't. Instead I turned my back on Hagan and walked as far away from him as I could in the little room.

"*Kamran,*" he said apologetically. "Kamran, let's say I do believe you."

"Then—" I started, but Hagan cut me off.

"*Let's say I do believe you, Kamran.* It's not about my gut this time, or yours. My gut told me you were right about the code—and you were. That was the clue we needed. We averted a terrible thing, and that's a fact. But this business about Arizona, I've done all I can."

"Have you?" I challenged him. "Have you really?"

"Yes," Hagan said coolly.

"Have you gone to the media?"

"Kamran, that's not how we do things here."

"Have you contacted the Forest Rangers, then?"

"No, Kamran—"

"Sent in a SEAL team?"

"*Send an elite spec ops force into a national forest outside Phoenix?*" Hagan said. "Kamran, be serious."

"How far up the chain have you taken this? To your boss? What about your boss's boss? Or his boss? The National Security director, or whatever?"

"Kamran—"

"You're not trying!" I yelled at him.

"I've tried all I can!" Hagan shot back. "I'm not the one you want for an ally here, Kamran! You've got the wrong man. This

Code of yours, this intelligence, the raid. This was a win. A big win. Just getting them to listen to me was a victory in and of itself. A victory that won me points at this agency, and that's a fact. Points I could *maybe* spend pushing this Arizona angle. But no matter how many shillings I have in the bank, no matter how hard I push, there's always going to be a wall I can't knock over. No win is ever going to wipe my slate entirely clean. I'm always going to be the ignoramus who second-guesses himself so much he can't write an intelligence brief without contradicting himself. Who isn't good for anything more than sitting in on the interview of a high school student. *I'm always going to be the damned fool who didn't know his own bloody brother was a terrorist thirty years ago.* That's who I am," he said, finally calming down. "That's all anyone will ever remember."

"It's all anyone will ever remember if you let it be," I told him.

"I'm sorry, Kamran. I—I've done all I can," Hagan said, and he left me alone.

CHAPTER THIRTY-ONE

MICKEY HAGAN DIDN'T COME FOR ME THE NEXT DAY.
Or the next. Neither did Special Agent Tomaszewski or any of
the other interrogators. The only person I saw for the next week
was my guard when he brought my meals. I paced my cell like
a caged lion. I banged on the door and asked for Hagan. I left
my food untouched on its metal trays.

How could Hagan just roll over like that? How could he
not do everything he could to convince them of the truth? He
knew there was something wrong. I could see it in his eyes.
Hear it in his voice. That day I'd realized the video was filmed
in Arizona, I'd said it didn't make any sense, and he'd agreed
with me. They wouldn't have brought Darius all the way to
America, snuck him across the border, and hidden him away in
the Tonto National Forest just so they could turn around a few
months later and make him carry a suicide bomb into the
Women's World Cup in Canada. Hagan and I both knew that
was stupid.

But Darius *was* in America. I was sure of it. Which meant
only one thing: the terrorists were planning on using Darius in
a strike *here*. In America. And soon. Hagan knew it, too. If one
was true—Darius was in America—the other was true—Darius
would soon be used against an American target.

So why hadn't Hagan done everything he could to convince
them of the truth? I kicked my bed. My guard was so used to it
by now that he didn't bother to put in an appearance, and I
kicked it again just for him.

Frickin' Mickey Hagan. After all we'd been through, I thought he was on my side, do or die. But I saw now it was all just a trick. I thought he'd been my friend, just like I'd thought Adam and Julia and all the rest were my friends. But they weren't. Not deep down. They were friendly enough when it didn't matter, but when push came to shove, they abandoned ship. Every last one of them.

Even Mickey Hagan.

It had all been a trick. That story about his brother, all that camaraderie, the pizza and sodas, it was all to get me to open up. To pump me for information. The story about his brother was probably just made up, I realized—a way in, and a way out. It was all spy tricks. All those people who'd interrogated me, that hard-looking lady who convinced me Darius was a terrorist, they were the "bad cops," like on TV. Hagan was the "good cop." He came in afterward and told me I was right, told me he believed in me, just to get my help. Just to get the "good intel." And then when he got what he wanted, he dumped me faster than Julia Gary.

I kicked the bed again, and my food tray skittered across the floor. I didn't care. I knew the truth now. I was all alone in this. In everything. All alone except for Darius, trapped in some cave somewhere in Arizona.

Maybe, I thought.

No. No doubts, no second guesses. I remembered our Code of Honor, the one that lady had thrown in my face like it was the reason Darius had turned traitor. *Be loyal.* I knew who I was loyal to: Darius. Darius was innocent. He was being held in Arizona by terrorists and didn't know where he was. *Never give up.* If Mickey Hagan couldn't believe that—wouldn't believe it—I would. I wouldn't give up. I wouldn't let go of the truth.

But what was I going to *do* with the truth?

Mickey Hagan had been my ally—my voice at the CIA. When I'd stuck to my guns about the code in the videos, he'd been the one to convince his superiors I was right. I was sure that Darius was being held prisoner in Arizona, that he was going to die in a very real, soon-to-happen suicide attack right here in America. Darius was going to die, and who knew how many more people with him. He was going to die and everybody was going to think he really was a terrorist.

But here I was, helpless. Trapped in this cell. A prisoner of the United States government—the very country I wanted to help defend. I had to do something.

But what, Kamran? I asked myself.

The answer came to me with perfect clarity.

I had to escape.

CHAPTER THIRTY-TWO

IT WAS CRAZY. STUPID. IMPOSSIBLE. ESCAPE FROM A US government facility? Me?

But I had to try. Darius was my brother. I had to do everything I could to help him, or . . .

Or die trying.

I nodded, like I'd been talking to myself. Like I'd been having an argument, and had finally been convinced.

I had to break out of here and get to Arizona. Find Darius in the mountains outside Phoenix.

And then what, genius?

And then tell the authorities. Take them there. They'd arrest me. Put me back in a cell. But it wouldn't matter. I'd tell them right where Darius was, exactly how to find him and this Ansari guy or whichever terrorists were with him. Even if the authorities didn't believe me, they'd come for me, wherever I told them I was, and then they'd see—they'd see there really were terrorists right here in America. Right in the mountains outside Phoenix.

I was starting to sound a little crazy, even to myself. But I had no other choice. Mickey Hagan had abandoned me. Given up. Crawled back into his hole of regret and self-doubt. But not me. I wasn't going in there with him.

I was ready to get out of my hole.

I heard murmuring outside my door.

I quickly put my ear to it and listened. My guard was talking to somebody with a big, deep voice. Not Hagan. Somebody new. I had no idea what it was about, but I heard the jangle of keys. The guard was going to open my door.

My eyes roamed the room half crazily, searching for something to use as a weapon. I looked up at the camera in the corner. I can't imagine how I looked in that moment, my back to the door, eyes bulging out of their sockets, unshaven, unbathed. Like some cartoon madman. They'd see me. Whatever I did, they'd know. But I had to get out of here. Get back to Arizona. Find Darius. Stop the terrorist plot.

The metal food tray. My eyes locked on to it, and I snatched it up like it was a fumbled football. I hefted it in my hands, taking the weight of it. Not too heavy. But when swung at a face . . .

The guard's keys jangled in the lock, and I flattened myself against the wall, ready to strike.

CHAPTER THIRTY-THREE

THIS WAS IT. MY ONLY CHANCE TO ESCAPE. MY ONLY chance to find my brother. To save Darius. I had to. I was the only one who could do it. My breath came short and quick, and a bead of sweat rolled down the hollow of my back.

No. Relax, I told myself. *Breathe. Do like you do when you're standing behind the quarterback, waiting for the snap. Waiting for a hole to open up to run through.*

I closed my eyes. Took a deep breath. I embraced the anticipation. The adrenaline. Let them fill my head like white noise, let them push out everything else but my goal. No distractions, no doubts, no second guesses. On the football field, there was nothing but me and the defense, and here, now, there was nothing but me and that guard.

Me, the guard, and the metal tray I was going to brain him with.

The door opened. The lights flickered on. A burly, broad-shouldered African American soldier stepped inside.

"Kamran Smith?" the soldier said. "I'm here to transfer you to another—"

I swung the metal tray like a club, aiming right for his face. They met with a jarring clang and the soldier went straight down like he'd been clipped in the back of the legs.

"What was that?" the guard in the hall said. He was drawing his gun as he came into my cell. I put my shoulder into the door like I was hitting a tackle dummy, slamming the soldier between the door and the frame. He dropped his gun and staggered, but he didn't go down. I hit him with the door again. And again. He finally fell on top of the first guard, unconscious.

I was panting. I glanced up at the camera again, sure my attack had been witnessed. I waited for the yells, the alarms, but all I could hear was my own heartbeat thundering in my ears. I took a step toward the door, and my legs almost gave out, like I'd just run a hundred wind sprints. But I didn't have time to collapse. I didn't have time to calm down. If I wanted to save Darius, I had to get out of here. Now.

I peeked out into the hall. Empty.

The second guard was still lying half in, half out of the door, and I dragged him inside by the arms. I stood over the two men, looking down at their unconscious faces. *Oh my God. What was I doing? What had I become?* A couple months ago my life had been high school, football practice, Julia, Adam, West Point applications. It all seemed so insignificant now. So far away. But as insignificant as it was, if I walked out that door now, if I ran, it was all gone for good. Football and college and girls and all the rest of it. If I ran out that door, there was no going back. Not ever.

I pushed the fear down deep. *No distractions. No doubts. No second guesses.*

I took the first guard's gun from his holster, locked the soldiers in my cell, and ran.

CHAPTER THIRTY-FOUR

I WAS TWO CORRIDORS AWAY FROM MY CELL WHEN the alarm went off. It wasn't loud—not like a house alarm meant to scare away crooks. It was more like a persistent, low beep. *Beep. Beep. Beep. Beep. Beep. Beep.* In a way, it was more ominous than a blaring alarm. It was like the little flashing red light up near the ceiling every few feet was saying, "I just wanted to let you know: Kamran Smith escaped from his cell. But we're not too worried about it. We know we're going to catch him. Carry on." *Beep. Beep. Beep. Beep. Beep. Beep.*

There were doors all down the hall. Closed doors, without windows in them and each marked only by white numbers on little black plastic squares. Were these more cells? Were my parents behind one of these doors? Some other prisoners? That's what we were. Me and my parents, and anyone else being held here. We weren't "guests." We were prisoners of the United States government.

Whatever was behind those doors, I was in perpetual fear that one of them would open and someone would step out and grab me. Or worse, make me use the gun.

The gun. I looked down at the gun I'd taken from the guard. It was cold and black, with more buttons and switches on it than I thought guns had. Could I really shoot someone with it if I had to? Would I?

There was a turn up ahead. Another corridor. An emergency exit sign pointed left. The way out. That's what I wanted. I had to get outside the building and run. Run all the way back to Arizona from wherever it was they had taken me—New

Mexico, or Colorado, or California, or wherever—and find Darius before it was too late. For him, and for whoever it was he was supposed to kill.

I slinked down the hallway. I was almost to the end when a radio squawked around the corner. I was just about to run into a guard!

I grabbed the handle of the first door I found and tried it. Locked! I lunged for the door across the hall. It opened. The lights flickered on automatically as I threw myself inside. I was in a little office break room. Refrigerator, cabinets, coffee-maker, microwave, table, two chairs, trash can, soda machine. The smell of burned coffee and liquid cleaner.

A door opened and closed nearby. They were searching the rooms! In a panic, I looked for any place I could hide. The cabinets were all filled with shelves and packed with random mugs and paper plates and half-empty boxes of coffee filters. The trash can was too small to fit inside, the table too tiny to hide under. Idiotically, I threw open the door to the refrigerator, thinking I could hide in there. I couldn't, of course. I'd have to dump all the soda cans and plastic tubs full of moldy old lasagna and half-eaten cans of soup in the trash and find some place to hide the glass shelves. And then, you know, probably suffocate.

I spun around, trying to think what to do. Where to go. I still had the gun. I could hide behind the trash can, wait for whoever it was to come inside, and shoot them. Run past their dead body, and out the exit, and disappear.

I stared at the gun in my hand. It was heavy. Heavier than I thought a gun would weigh. A lot heavier than all the water pistols I'd played with as a kid.

Too heavy.

I couldn't do it. I couldn't shoot an American soldier in cold blood. Even if they were coming to take me back to my cell. Even if I was never going to see daylight again.

Not even for Darius.

Another door closed. Footsteps close by. The squawk of a radio. I was busted.

And then an idea came to me. A memory, really, of another time there had been alarms, and chaos, and panic. A crazy, stupid idea that would have been funny if I hadn't been freaking out. I opened the refrigerator and grabbed the half-empty soup can. At my sixteenth birthday party, Adam had put a can of soup in the microwave without knowing any better and almost burned my house down.

I hurried over to the microwave and tried to shove the can inside, but there was a spoon sticking out the top and it wouldn't fit. I took the spoon out and almost tossed it in the sink before I realized it was better in the microwave. More metal, more sparks. I tossed it in with the can and yanked open drawers, stuffing more silverware into the microwave. When it was full I slammed the door closed and punched the button for popcorn.

Vmmmmmmm. The microwave lit up and started humming, the can and all the silverware rotating inside. I could already hear the metal popping and crackling as I ducked behind the trash can.

The door opened. A soldier in fatigues stepped inside, his gun held out in front of him in both hands. His eyes went straight to the sound of the microwave the moment it burst into flames. The soldier recoiled. The sprinklers in the room came on, suddenly dowsing everything with rain. The fire burned on, the microwaves still bouncing crazily off all that metal. Another alarm—shrill, and far louder this time—pierced the air. The soldier lunged for the fire extinguisher on the other side of the room.

I burst from where I was crouching behind the trash can and ran. Out into the hall. Around the corner. A glowing green exit sign above a door beckoned, promising escape. I didn't look back to see if the soldier was following me. I banged through the door, expecting to see a starlit field, a parking lot, a road.

But I wasn't outside at all. I was still *inside*. I was in a stairwell, with simple concrete stairs going up and down.

The door clicked shut behind me, muffling the sound of the alarms, and I saw the words painted on it:

SUBLEVEL 22.

I had twenty-two flights of stairs to climb just to reach the ground floor.

CHAPTER THIRTY-FIVE

THE DOOR HAD BARELY CLICKED SHUT BEHIND ME before I was running up the stairs, taking them two at a time. *Twenty-two flights.* All this time I'd been twenty-two levels underground! I'd had no idea.

I was huffing by sublevel 17. But I had to run. They had to know I'd made the stairwell. I'd set a microwave on fire just outside the exit door. Any second now, somebody would—

I heard a door burst open in the stairwell. Heard boots on stairs. Coming fast. But from which direction? The sound echoed up and down the stairwell. If they were coming up, I might be able to beat them to the ground floor. *Might.* If they were coming down, they'd catch me for sure. And there was nowhere to hide in here. It was just level after level of stairs and doors. There was only one thing to do: I had to get out of the stairwell.

I tried the door at sublevel 15. Locked! A digital keypad beside the door was the only way in. I ran up the next set of stairs to sublevel 14. It was locked, too, with another keypad beside it. I stopped, breathing hard, and made myself think. Had all the doors been like this? Yeah. I could see them: little keypads just like this one outside every door. If every one of those doors had one, sublevel 13 would, too. And 12 and 11 and 10 and 9 . . .

If I wanted out of this stairwell, I had to get through one of these locked doors.

Boots thundered. Another door opened and closed. More soldiers. I had to move. But I didn't know the code! I punched in four random numbers on the keypad. A little red light came on. I tried another four. Another red light. The footsteps were getting closer. *Come on come on come on*, I told myself. *Think. What's the code?* This was sublevel 14. I tried 1414. Red light. 4141. Red light. 1234. Red light. 4321. Red light. In frustration I mashed all the buttons with my fist.

The keypad hesitated for a second, and I held my breath—

The red light came on.

I cursed. The soldiers were almost on top of me! Wait—I still had the gun. I still wasn't going to shoot any soldiers. I wasn't even going to pretend to. But I could shoot the keypad! The soldiers would hear it, and they'd see what floor I was on from the bullet hole, but if it worked, if the door opened, I'd at least be out of the stairwell.

I aimed the gun at the keypad. Turned my head away. Slowly squeezed the trigger, waiting for the bang.

The door made a chunking sound, and a green light blinked on the keypad. The door had unlocked. But I hadn't even fired the gun! What'd I do, *scare* the keypad into opening?

I didn't have time to figure it out. I twisted the handle, pulled the door open, and slipped inside, gun at the ready.

CHAPTER THIRTY-SIX

BROWN-AND-RED-PATTERNED CARPET. GRAY CUBI-cles. Fluorescent lights. A water cooler. A mail cart. The soft click of fingers typing on computer keyboards. Suddenly I wasn't in a secret US government detention facility. I was in an office building. A US government office building, I was sure, but not another floor full of locked doors and interrogation rooms.

I heard footsteps behind me. Boots running in the stair-well, and I backed away from the door. The nearest cubicle was empty, and I slipped inside and hid under the desk. I waited for the door to fly open, for dozens of soldiers and security officers to come pouring through and catch me, but nothing happened. The door didn't open. No soldiers came charging through. Of course! They wouldn't have expected me to be able to get past the keypad security. They didn't know I'd come through onto this floor. They had run on by, still expecting to find me some-where in the stairwell.

I had time to catch my breath, but not too much time. Pretty soon now they'd figure out that I had to have made it through one of those doors, and they'd trip the alarm. Start searching all the other floors.

The alarm! I listened: there wasn't an alarm going off on this floor, and you couldn't hear the alarm from downstairs all the way up here. Maybe the people on this floor didn't know there was a prisoner loose. Maybe the people on this floor didn't even know there were prisoners in the building at all. That was a chilling thought.

I peeked up over the edge of my cubicle. There was a woman in the next cubicle with her back to me, typing away at her computer with headphones on. One whole wall of her cubicle was filled with pictures of a black-and-brown dog. A German shepherd maybe. On hikes. At the lake. On the couch. This lady loved her dog.

The cubicles stretched out across the room, interrupted every now and then by big white pillars. I saw somebody stand up in one of the cubicles, a man, and I ducked instinctively. He went the other direction, though, and I watched him walk to a copier on the far side of the room, near the elevators.

The elevators. I couldn't go back in the stairwell. They'd be looking for me there. But the elevators—they were my ticket out of here.

But they were all the way across the room. And I didn't exactly look like I worked here. The man and the woman were both wearing business suits. I was wearing jeans, sneakers, and one of my T-shirts that they'd brought to me from home when my stay as a "guest" became more like "semipermanent resident." I didn't look like a government agent. I looked more like the pizza delivery boy.

Delivery boy. I peeked around the cubicle door at the mail cart parked by the stairs. I might not look like I belonged in a cubicle, but maybe I would pass for a mail room delivery guy. Unless the mail room delivery guys in secret US government facilities wore suits, too. Or were soldiers or something. But it was worth a shot. I certainly couldn't go back the way I came.

The mail cart was like a two-decker shopping cart, with a handle on one end and wire baskets on top and bottom. The top was filled with file folders with names on the labels. People who worked on this floor, I guessed. The folders were all empty—

somebody had already delivered all the mail. That was good. I wasn't going to be doing any real delivering.

The bottom part of the cart had a bunch of brown 9" x 12" envelopes in it, each one with three columns of spaces on each side where you could write in the name of the person inside the building you wanted the envelope to go to. Interoffice mail. These were empty, too.

An ID badge hanging off the top basket had a picture of a guy named Chad Dill, Position: Mail Clerk, on it. He didn't look a thing like me.

What the heck. I buried my gun in the pile of envelopes, took a deep breath, picked out the elevators across the room, and started pushing.

CHAPTER THIRTY-SEVEN

I WANTED TO SPRINT, WANTED TO RUN WITH THE cart like I used to do in the parking lot of the grocery store, hop on, and zoom past all these cubicles. But I had to be cool. I had to walk slow enough so that when people saw me pass their cubicles they would barely even look at me. If any of these people were working on Darius's case, if any of them recognized me, it was all over.

The mail cart wheels squeaked so loud I jumped. I tried it again, going easier this time, but it still squeaked loudly in the quiet office. It was like a bullhorn announcing my presence. "Here I am! Kamran Smith! Escaped fugitive! Come and get me!" But there was nothing else to do. The mail cart was my costume. My disguise. I needed people to see *it*, not me.

Well, one thing was for sure: they were going to *hear* it.

I squeaked past the dog-obsessed lady, but she didn't even look up. I didn't know if she couldn't hear me with her headphones on, or if she was so used to the squeaky mail cart by now that she just ignored it. I pushed on, squeaking the whole way. The elevators looked impossibly far away.

Another woman came out of the cubicle right beside me, scaring me to death. I froze, and she squeezed on by without a second look. I breathed again. Okay. Test number one complete: I looked like the mail guy. Maybe not Chad Dill, but *some* mail guy. That's all that mattered.

It was time to get moving again. That alarm might sound any second now, and then I wouldn't be overlooked. I pushed on, a little faster this time, threading my way through the cubicles. At first I kept my head down, but when it looked like nobody even cared that I was there, I started peeking into the cubicles, watching people as I passed. It was night (at least I thought it was night), but there were still a lot of people at work. Maybe they worked in shifts, like at a factory. The Intelligence Factory. At the Intelligence Factory, your secrets are our business!

I couldn't tell what people were doing exactly, besides typing on computers, watching videos, and reading newspapers in foreign languages. It all looked pretty boring. Nothing like Q's secret gadget lab in James Bond. Where were the exploding pens and electromagnet watches?

"Hey there. Hold on," a man called.

I put my head down and kept pushing, hoping he wasn't talking to me.

"Hey, I said hold up," the man said, closer now.

A hand grabbed my shoulder and spun me around.

I was busted.

CHAPTER THIRTY-EIGHT

I FROZE. I WAS MORE THAN HALFWAY TO THE ELEVA-tors, but too far away to run for it. My eyes went immediately to the pile of envelopes in the bottom basket where my gun was hidden.

"Sorry," the man said, letting me go. He came around in front of me, blocking my way. He was average height, young-ish, white, with brown hair and a receding jaw. He wore gray pants, a white long-sleeved shirt with the sleeves rolled up, and a red tie. He smiled. "You must not have heard me. Got your earbuds in?"

He still thought I was the mail clerk! "What? Ah, no. Sorry," I said, trying to cover my unease. "I was just—my mind was somewhere else."

"Yeah," he said. "Totally get that. These late-night shifts, man. I didn't think they ran mail overnight."

I didn't know what to say to that, so I shrugged. Luck-ily, the guy didn't seem to really care. He was just making small talk.

"You got any of those interoffice envelopes?" he asked. He scanned my cart, spying the stack of them in the bottom basket.

The stack hiding my pistol.

"Here we go," he said. He bent down to grab an envelope.

I dropped down with him. "I'll get one for you!"

"I got it," he said. He put his hand in and fished around. I glanced up at the top of the elevator across the room, calculat-ing how fast I could get there.

"Huh. What's this?" he said.

Run, I told myself. *Just run.*

The guy held up an envelope. "Here's one with every line used up," he said. "Never thought I'd see one! But I guess it has to happen sometime, right? Like Bigfoot sightings."

"Yeah," I said. Sure. Just *please please please* let me go.

"Here," he said, giving me the envelope like there was some special ceremony for envelopes that had all the address lines used up. Then he put his hand back in the basket, looking for another envelope. Not again! I watched his hand, wishing it away from the gun I'd hidden in there. He grabbed an envelope, and I sighed with relief.

Until I saw the barrel of the gun sticking out from among the envelopes.

The guy stayed where he was, stuffing a piece of paper he'd brought with him into the envelope. I stared at the barrel of the gun the entire time, waiting for him to see it while he was writing the recipient's name on the envelope. I had just decided to reach out and tug at one of the envelopes to cover the barrel when he finished and looked up at me.

"There we go," he said, handing me the envelope. "You're good to go."

"Thanks," I said.

"Let me know if you run into Bigfoot, too," he said, and he disappeared back into his cubicle.

I chucked the envelope he'd given me in the basket, covering the gun, and hustled for the elevators. I didn't care if anybody saw me moving fast. I wanted out of there.

I got to the elevators without anybody else stopping to talk to me about Bigfoot and I slapped the up button. The elevator dinged as it arrived on sublevel 14. Luckily, there was no one else inside. The other elevator arrived beside it with a ding, and I hurried into mine before whoever was getting out of the other one could see me. I mashed the ground-floor button and punched the close-door button over and over again. The door slid closed just as another woman in a business suit walked past. I thought I saw her look inside, thought her eyes caught mine for a split second, but then the door was closed and the elevator was lifting me up to safety.

For now.

CHAPTER THIRTY-NINE

I WATCHED THE RED DIGITAL NUMBERS ON THE ELEvator tick by slowly. Excruciatingly slowly. Sublevel 13. Sublevel 12. *Come on come on come on.* This had to be the elevator I'd taken into the Department of Homeland Security building that first night, the one I could barely tell was moving. It was slower than watching a soccer game.

The World Cup. Hagan had been so sure the target was the Women's World Cup. But it couldn't be. Not the real target. I was sure of it. Darius was still in danger. The *United States* was still in danger.

And if they weren't going to do anything about it, I was.

Sublevel 11. Sublevel 10.

The elevator dinged and stopped. *No no no no no.*

The doors opened, and an Asian man in dark business slacks, a white dress shirt, and a dark tie got on, his ID badge glinting where it hung on his belt. I stared down at the mail cart, trying to be invisible as he punched the button for the floor he wanted. Did he know who I was? Did he know there was a prisoner on the loose in the building? If he recognized me, would he call security? Try to grab me and drag me back to my cell?

My eyes went to the basket on the bottom of the cart. The gun was buried there. I wasn't going to shoot anyone. I already knew that. But you didn't have to shoot a gun to use it. Couldn't I just threaten him with it? Hold him off until we got to the top floor, and then make a run for it when the doors opened? I could be out the front door before he even called security.

"How's it going?" the man asked.

I jumped. He'd settled in beside me in the elevator, both of us facing the door, and we were already moving to sublevel 9.

He looked at me. I was taking too long to answer. I had to do something. *Say* something.

"Good," I said at last, my voice croaking.

Smooth, Kamran. Real smooth. Stare at the floor like a five-year-old, wait so long to respond to somebody saying hey that you draw attention to yourself, then sound as awkward and guilty as possible. James Bond you're not.

"Sorry," I said. "Long day."

The guy nodded sympathetically. "Yeah. Tell me about it."

And that was it. Enough, at least, to get him to stare at the elevator door again and forget all about me. *Just be cool, Kamran,* I told myself. *You're the mail guy. You look the part. Now act it.*

I'd never understood Julia's love of drama club and acting. It wasn't my thing. I mean, I went to all her plays and pretended to be interested, but before we'd dated, you couldn't have paid me to go see a play. Whenever they'd brought the whole school into the auditorium to watch whatever play the drama club was putting on that semester, I'd hunkered down in my seat and closed my eyes, grateful for the afternoon away from classes but otherwise totally bored out of my mind. But now, suddenly, I had a real appreciation for what it took to get up onstage in front of other people and pretend to be someone you weren't. I was scared speechless. I wouldn't be surprised if my stinking, soaked armpits didn't give me away.

Then on sublevel 8, the elevator dinged and the doors opened again.

CHAPTER FORTY

A WHITE WOMAN IN A GRAY PANTSUIT GOT ON, NOD-ding to the other guy and me. She pushed a button. The elevator moved. I stared at my cart.

The elevator dinged and stopped *again*. Seriously? It was nighttime! How many people were working late?

Too many. A white guy in a suit got into the elevator, and I worked my way farther into the corner. At least now there were so many of us no one felt forced to talk. You know how it is: If there's just two of you, it's awkward not to say something. If the elevator's full of people, you can just pretend you're all alone, even if you're squeezed in like a package of Peeps. Safety in numbers, isn't that what they say? I was surrounded by people who might recognize me, might bust me any second, but in a weird way having more people in the elevator made me more invisible.

The first guy to get on the elevator with me got out at sub-level 3. Only three more floors to go! I took a deep breath and thought about what was going to come next. I'd wait for everybody else to get off the elevator on the ground floor, and then I'd follow them out. Ditch the mail cart around a corner somewhere. Slip outside. Make a run for it. I wouldn't be in Arizona, I was sure of that. But hopefully I could find a way back. Catch a ride with someone. Beg money for a bus. I'd walk if I was close enough. But I couldn't worry about that now. Right now I had to focus on just getting out the front door.

The elevator dinged, and the little red numbers said we were on the ground floor at last. I played the part of the courteous mail room guy, holding the door open as the more important people left.

That's when I saw the main floor beyond the elevator.

Between me and the dark glass doors at the front of the building were perhaps a dozen people, most of them guards. Soldiers in black fatigues and helmets patrolled the lobby, automatic weapons in their hands. Video cameras hung in the corners. The only way *into* the building was past the guards working metal detectors and scanners, and the only way *out* was past another guard at a turnstile that only worked when you checked out with your ID card. This was no generic office building with an empty lobby and a single security guard watching basketball on his monitor. It was a heavily secured government facility. One I wasn't walking out of.

CHAPTER FORTY-ONE

I PULLED BACK INTO THE ELEVATOR AND SLUMPED into the corner. What was I thinking? Where did I think I was? *Who* did I think I was? *I was a prisoner in a US government building.* I was an idiot to think I could just run down the hall from my cell, bang open a door, and run off into the night. I was trapped. I had no way out. Maybe I should turn myself back in and beg for understanding.

The doors began to close like the stage curtain closing at the end of a play, and I watched in despair as my only way out disappeared.

"Hold the door!" a woman called. I shrank back, but she stuck her hand in, catching the doors before they closed. She was one of the most beautiful women I'd ever seen. She was young, and fluid, and alive, even here in this cold, gray government building. *Especially* here. She could have been on television. She had light brown Middle Eastern skin, dark hair and dark eyes, and full lips. She was wearing a dark blue skirt and jacket over a form-fitting white shirt. If she'd passed me at the mall I would have stared.

But I wasn't at the mall. I was on the run, in the elevator of a secure government facility. I dropped my eyes to the mail cart, still panicking. Still trying desperately to think what to do.

"Hello," she said, turning her thousand-watt smile on me. I was so flustered I didn't even say hello back.

"You missed the mail room," she added.

I was usually cool around pretty girls at school, but this woman was so beautiful I could barely put two words together.

"I—huh?"

"It's on sublevel four, isn't it? Where the trucks come in?" she said.

"What?" I said dumbly.

"Sublevel four," she said again. "The mail room. That's where the big trucks come in from outside."

"Uh, yeah," I said. *Yeah! The mail room!* Trucks! Outside access—probably without all the scanners and cameras and metal detectors! "Yeah!" I said.

She smiled at me again. I felt like my own personal guardian angel was pointing me the right way. My own gorgeous guardian angel.

"Oh, silly me—I forgot to push my button," she said. She leaned over and pushed the button for sublevel 12. "Want me to push four for you?" she asked me.

"Um, yeah," I said. "Thanks."

We stood next to each other, me trying to ignore how pretty she was and failing miserably, her probably already having long forgotten I existed. She hummed a song while we waited, and distantly I recognized it as that old NSYNC song, "Bye Bye Bye."

The elevator dinged and I started to move my cart toward the door, but this was just sublevel 3. One more floor to go. The doors opened and a white guy in a suit started to step inside.

"Rick!" the woman said. "Just the man I was coming to see." She intercepted him, putting her arm in his and walking him back off the elevator. The doors closed on them, and I let out the breath I didn't know I'd been holding.

I silently thanked my guardian angel and punched the sublevel 4 button again, even though it was already lit. I had a second chance. Maybe there was some way I could say "Bye Bye Bye" to this place after all.

CHAPTER FORTY-TWO

I STEPPED OFF THE ELEVATOR, PUSHED THE MAIL cart through thick pieces of hanging plastic, and entered the building's mail room. It was a huge facility with conveyor belts, wheeled canvas carts big enough to crawl inside, stacks of smaller plastic mail tubs, and huge sorting areas. At the back of the room were long concrete loading bays and garage doors where semis could back in. Miraculously, one of the bays was open. An unmarked trailer was parked backward in the stall, and the garage door at its head was wide open. I could see darkness outside. And freedom. I was giddy just thinking about how close I was. Just a little farther, and I would be outside and on my way to Darius.

But first I had to get past the dogs.

There were two of them. German shepherds, led around on leashes by two US soldiers in black fatigues with automatic rifles over their shoulders. The rest of the mail room was almost empty except for the two men in jumpsuits wheeling boxes off the truck on dollies. The soldiers walked in and out of the truck and around the boxes, their dogs sniffing everything.

The truck I had to sneak past to get outside.

One of the dogs raised its head and looked straight at me, and I hurriedly pushed my mail cart behind a sorting machine.

I peeked out again, but the soldiers and mail room guys hadn't seen me. The dogs knew I was there, but they were trained to sniff for explosives and toxins, I guessed, not to be watchdogs. But they'd be onto me the second I got anywhere close to that truck. And just when I was so close!

I debated just leaving the gun where it was, but eventually I pulled it out from its hiding place under the envelopes. What was I carrying the thing around for if I wasn't going to shoot at anybody with it? I sighed, knowing I still couldn't do it. But I had to find *some* way around that truck.

I watched the workers and the soldiers with the dogs, trying to look for some pattern to their movements, some opportunity for me to slip through. But this was no video game with NPCs who marched around on set routines so you could sneak up behind them and knock them out. These were real people. Real Americans, with jobs and families and lives. I had to get away, but I couldn't hurt anybody doing it.

There—on the wall. A fire extinguisher! Right beside where the workers were stacking the boxes, and the dogs were sniffing them. Adam and I had once watched a video on YouTube of some idiots shooting fire extinguishers. The red canisters erupted like geysers when they were shot, spraying a thick white cloud of carbon dioxide everywhere. Harmless, but really hard to see through the cloud. And they'd make a terrific distraction until these guys figured out what hit them.

My hand trembled a little as I propped the gun on a conveyor belt that wasn't running. I took aim very carefully. The fire extinguisher seemed a lot farther across the room than when I'd first come up with the idea, but I was sure I could do it. I shot stuff at this distance all the time in video games. I just had to wait until the four men were close enough to the fire extinguisher to be swallowed up by the cloud, but not so close that I would hit one of them if I missed. I waited, watching them move back and forth, my heart pounding in my chest, and then I saw my chance. I squared up my aim and pulled the trigger—

CHAPTER FORTY-THREE

NOTHING HAPPENED. THE TRIGGER DIDN'T BUDGE.

I pulled the gun back and stared at it. Why didn't it shoot? Wait—guns had safeties on them, didn't they? So you couldn't shoot yourself in the foot by accident when you were pulling your gun out of your holster. I searched the sides of the pistol, trying to figure out which of the switches and buttons was the safety. I felt way in over my head.

I flicked a switch near my thumb to what I figured was "shoot" (or "un-safe" maybe?) and took aim again. I had to wait forever for everyone to be going the same direction again, but then at last I had another chance. I squinted down the short barrel of the gun, held my breath, and squeezed the trigger.

The gun kicked like a line drive taking a bad hop, and I ducked reflexively, my ears ringing like crazy. The bang was so loud! Then the air was filled with yelling and barking. I peeked out from behind the machine. The fire extinguisher was still there—I'd missed it! And now the soldiers and workers thought somebody was shooting at them. They had all ducked behind boxes, the soldiers scanning the room with guns in hand.

No! I'd ruined everything. I was going to be caught. Thrown back in my cell. Handcuffed. I had shot at United States soldiers! They would never believe me when I told them I was shooting for the fire extinguisher.

The soldiers were yelling into walkie-talkies. In minutes, seconds, security would pour in through the hanging plastic, and I was done for. I had to make a run for it. But I couldn't, not without being seen.

I aimed at the fire extinguisher again. They were all still huddled around it, but at least this time they were hiding out of the way. I pulled the trigger, and the gun exploded again. Another miss. The soldiers ducked. I tried again. And again. And again. Nothing! Dang it! How hard was it to hit a fire extinguisher from across the room?

The soldiers had figured out where I was from the gunshots. One of them was taking aim at me as I tried one last shot.

THOOM!

The fire extinguisher exploded, swallowing everything on that side of the room in a white cloud. Yes! I scrambled up from where I knelt, my arms sore and my whole body shaking. I sprinted along the side of the tractor trailer away from the yelling soldiers and barking dogs and into the cold night air. I was free! I'd made it outside!

I couldn't stop running, though. Not until I was far enough away from the building to hide someplace. I ran up a long, wide concrete ramp to a big dark parking lot, slipping in the snow as I stopped to get my bearings.

Snow? I shuddered in the freezing cold air. I'd forgotten it was mid-January. But this was definitely not Arizona. Or Nevada. Or New Mexico. Colorado maybe? Up in the mountains?

I couldn't stand around figuring it out. I ran in among the scattered cars in the parking lot and crouched down, trying to hide. I had to figure out which way to run before I really put my legs into it. I peeked up through the snow-covered car windows and my eyes fell on a giant white obelisk in the distance with two blinking red lights on the top. Dully, I realized what I was looking at.

It was the Washington Monument.

The gun slipped from my hand and clattered to the ground as I stood and stared.

I wasn't in Arizona, or Nevada, or California, or Colorado.

I was in Washington, DC.

CHAPTER FORTY-FOUR

WASHINGTON, DC.

I knew things were serious. That this business with Darius was big-time. But not *this* big-time. Not fly-Kamran-Smith-to-Washington-and-detain-him-in-the-Department-of-Homeland-Security-*Headquarters* kind of serious.

I realized I was standing in plain sight and dropped back down between the cars. I couldn't see the Washington Monument anymore. Almost like it had been a dream.

But it hadn't been a dream. I was in Washington, DC. Something like two thousand miles away from home.

I heard shouts from the ramp down to the mail room. I had to run. I would have to figure out how to get back home later.

Two thousand miles?

There were trees in the distance, beyond the parking lot. I grabbed the gun out of the slush and hurried toward the trees, still crouching low. I came to the end of a Volvo, looked both ways for guards, and sprinted across the open road to the next line of cars. Safe. I was almost to the end of a big white SUV when I heard a shout behind me and turned to look. I couldn't see anything but cars, but that was a good thing—it meant they couldn't see me, either. Just a few more rows, and then I would be to the woods.

I turned to run again, and the burly African American soldier who'd come to my cell to transfer me stood in my way. I knew it was the same guy because there was dried blood caked around his nose where I'd hit him. And he looked seriously unhappy about it.

In a daze, I remembered I still had the gun and raised it, my arm moving like I was underwater. Then the gun wasn't in my hand anymore. It was in the soldier's hand. He'd taken it from me in the blink of an eye. Somebody hit the fast-forward button and he punched me in the chest. Knocked the wind out of me. Spun me around. Caught me before I sank to my knees. Put me in a headlock, one arm around my neck, the other covering my gasping mouth.

And just like that, it was all over. I was caught.

CHAPTER FORTY-FIVE

MY SNEAKERS CUT PATHS THROUGH THE SLUSH IN the parking lot as the big soldier dragged me backward, away from the Homeland Security building. A white van screeched up behind us, and its side door flung open. Hands grabbed me, dragged me inside, and the door slid shut with a bang.

"*Go,*" the soldier said, his voice deep and urgent.

The van accelerated. It was dark inside, windowless, and it took me as long to catch my breath as it did for my eyes to adjust. I was on the floor of an empty cargo van. There were two seats at the front, only one of them occupied. The driver was a young white guy with sandy brown hair, wearing all black, but that's all I could make out from my angle. The big soldier sat on a low metal bench welded to the van wall behind me, his huge black army boots by my head. Another man, tall but thin, sat in shadow on a bench on the other side of the van, facing me.

"Well," the shadowy man said, his voice instantly familiar. "I have to say you certainly made that a lot harder than it had to be."

"Mr. Hagan?" I said.

It was. A passing streetlight lit up the inside of the van, illuminating his thin, stubbly face.

I sat up. "*Mr. Hagan?* But what—how—why—?"

"All very good questions," Hagan said. "Have a seat and I'll try to answer them all. We don't have much time."

A phone rang, and Hagan pulled his out of his pocket and looked at the screen. He held up a finger. "I need to take this," he said. He answered it and held it to his ear. "Hagan." He waited. "Escaped, you say?" He feigned surprise and looked right at me. "Now, how did he do that?"

I climbed up onto the bench beside the soldier as Hagan listened, and I purposefully slid a few inches away. My chest still throbbed from the big guy's punch. I had been hit a lot in football games, but I'd never taken a shot as hard and painful as that man's fist.

"Did he, now," Hagan said. "Did he, now? Incredible. And you think he had help? I see. Do you have a description of the vehicle? Yes, I see. Yes, of course. I was already headed in. I'm in the car as we speak. If I see the van, I'll do what I can to detain it. Yes. All right."

Hagan hung up and put the phone back in his pocket. "It seems you've managed a daring escape, Kamran Smith. Far more daring than the more prosaic one I had already arranged for you."

"But you said—"

Hagan put up a hand. "I always meant to break you out. The moment the higher-ups told me we were finished, that they had their one and only terrorist plot all taken care of, thank you very much, now get back to your cubicle, Mickey Hagan, I knew I had to do something. *We* had to do something. And that meant getting you away from there."

"So you believe me," I said. "About Darius being in Arizona." I felt a huge weight lift off my shoulders. I'd been so convinced I was alone. I'd been ready for it. Ready to go it solo, to sacrifice everything to help my brother if I had to. But to know I had at least one ally—and a smart, connected one at that—was a huge relief. "You believe me again," I said.

"No," Hagan said. "I never *stopped* believing. But I couldn't very well come into your cell and say, 'Kamran, I'm sending in a friend of mine with all the right papers to transfer you to another facility, but he's really breaking you out.' You noted, of course, the camera in the corner."

I turned to look at the big soldier. Hagan had sent *him* to get me out? And I'd smacked him in the face with a metal tray. The soldier didn't look at me. He was busy disassembling the gun I'd taken from him, and that he had taken back so easily.

"They'd have heard me, seen me for sure if I'd tried to tell you," Hagan went on. "I had to play it the other way, in fact. Convince you we were finished, so as to allay suspicion when you did escape. I'd be suspect number one in helping you escape, you see, close as we were. So I came to you and played the part of the insecure intelligence agent, the role I was born to play. I don't mind playing the fool, but I hated to hurt you like that. I'm sorry, Kamran."

I shook my head. It didn't matter. All was forgiven. I was in a van, speeding away from the building where I'd been held. Speeding *toward* Darius and Arizona.

"So I went home to watch telly and sent Dane Redmond here in for you," Hagan said, nodding at the big guy. "Dane's an old friend of mine. His speciality is getting people in and out of dangerous places. He's ex–Special Forces."

I knew what that meant. Special Forces soldiers were Green Berets—highly trained elite soldiers who specialized in un-conventional warfare. You could drop a team of Green Berets behind enemy lines, and in a week the twelve of them would walk out again with the warlord they'd been sent in after, with-out anybody else ever knowing they were there. They were the best of the best.

"I was only after a routine snatch and grab," Hagan said, "but you made it anything but routine."

The young, sandy-haired driver laughed, a real, delighted laugh, like he enjoyed any kind of chaos. "First time I ever seen somebody get the drop on Dane!" he said, cackling. "Took his gun, too!"

"Kamran, meet Jimmy Doran. Jimmy's our tech guy," Hagan said. The driver waved. "He's the one who looped the video on your room when Dane went in. He's also the person who unlocked that key-coded door for you in the stairwell."

"He—you—?" I stammered.

Jimmy laughed again. "Wouldn't have had a clue where you were until the system registered all those wrong tries. Mashing all the buttons was a particularly nice touch," he said. "I killed the alarm you should have triggered and unlocked the door for you."

Dane ejected the bullet clip from the butt of his gun and frowned at it. "There's six bullets missing," he said. He turned his hard eyes on me. "You shoot somebody?"

"Uh, no," I said.

"The only thing Kamran killed was one very stubborn fire extinguisher," Hagan said with a grin.

"Saw that on the security camera feed," Jimmy said from the front seat. "Nice trick! I was about to kill the lights for you, but you did all right on your own."

"It took you six shots to hit one fire extinguisher?" Dane said.

"I've never shot a gun before, all right?" I said.

"Ooh—hang on, guys," Jimmy said. "I *gotta* pick up this hitchhiker. She's a real looker."

What? I looked at Hagan, trying to understand. We couldn't stop for hitchhikers!

Hagan's eyes told me to wait. The van slid to a stop, and the gorgeous woman from the elevator climbed into the passenger seat.

CHAPTER FORTY-SIX

JIMMY FLOORED IT AGAIN, AND THE BEAUTIFUL woman turned and waved at me. Even here in the van, just the flash of her smile made me blush.

"Aaliyah Sayid, counterterrorism expert and CIA consultant," Hagan said. "I had her in the building, just in case. Good thing, too. When you went rogue we had to steer you to the mail room, and Aaliyah was gracious enough to drop the hint."

The late-night transfer, the key code in the stairwell, the hint in the elevator—my entire escape had been watched over, orchestrated even, by these *three* guardian angels. For all I knew, Dane had sent security on a wild goose chase after they found him, buying me more time. I never would have gotten out without their help. And here I thought I'd been so clever. So smart. I was an idiot. Without their help, I would have been caught a dozen times over.

Hagan seemed to read my mind. He laughed. "Kamran, did you ever happen to hear the story about the man who asked God to help him escape from a flood?"

"You mean, like, Noah?"

"No, not that flood. A wee bit smaller one. It goes something like this: there's a flood, see, and the waters, they chase the man in our story up onto his roof. The rain keeps falling and the waters keep rising, but our man's not worried. That's because he's sure his God is going to save him. Well, in short order a rowboat comes along, and the man rowing it tells our man on the roof to jump in. 'No, thanks,' says he, 'I'm waiting on God to save me,' and the man in the rowboat goes along his way. Well, the waters rise, getting ever closer, and along comes a motorboat. But our man's response is the same: 'Go save someone else,' he says. 'God will save me.' So off goes the motorboat, and the waters, they come up to our man's feet. Last of all comes a helicopter, and they drop our man a ladder. But what does he tell them?"

"God will save me," I said.

Hagan nodded. "He sends the helicopter packing and settles in, waiting for God to save him. Well, the rain keeps falling and the water keeps rising, and our man, he's swept away and drowns. Being a pious lad, he goes straight to heaven, but when he gets there, he's got a bone to pick with his maker. 'I had faith in you,' he tells God, 'I prayed to you. Believed in you. You said you would save me, but you never did. What's up with that?' God shrugs. 'I sent you a rowboat, a motorboat, and a helicopter,' says he. 'What more do you want?'"

Dane snorted a laugh.

"You," Hagan said to me, "you're like our man on the roof—only you jumped in and tried to swim before I could even send you the rowboat."

"So if Dane's the rowboat, and I'm the motorboat, and Aaliyah's the helicopter," Jimmy said, "what's that make you in this story, Mickey? God?"

Hagan grinned. "How close are we?" he asked Jimmy.

"Five minutes."

"You got all these people together just to break me out?" I asked. I was feeling a little unworthy.

"Not just to get you out," Hagan said. "To go with you to Arizona. To find your brother and stop a terrorist attack."

CHAPTER FORTY-SEVEN

MY PULSE QUICKENED. SO I REALLY WAS GOING TO do it. *We* were going to do it. My escape had been worth it after all.

"Don't think it will be easy," Hagan warned me. "These three are good—the best—but you'll still have work to do to find your brother, and the authorities will be after you at every turn. And then there's Haydar Ansari."

Ansari. The Iraqi terrorist Hagan had told me they thought was behind everything. He hadn't been captured with the al-Qaeda cell planning to blow up the Women's World Cup. Did that mean he was here, in America?

"Aaliyah will brief you on Ansari," Hagan said. "Jimmy will keep me in the loop via a secure connection. Dane's in charge of the mission." Hagan leaned forward, his gaze serious. "This is dangerous, Kamran. Make no mistake. I'm only sending you along with these three because you know everything there is to know about your brother and where they might be keeping him. But you're to do everything they tell you and anything *I* tell you, Kamran. No arguments. Do you understand?"

I nodded, glad to have people who actually knew what they were doing to tell me what to do.

I glanced at the gun in Dane's hand. "And what about Darius?" I asked.

"I've told Dane: Darius isn't to be harmed, if at all possible. We're operating under the assumption that he's innocent, and has been working to help us stop Ansari."

"And if he hasn't?" I asked. "What then?" I was ashamed to doubt my brother, but it had to be said.

"Then I'll deal with it," Dane said.

I shuddered. It didn't take much imagination to think what that might mean.

"Trust each other," Hagan told us. "Work as a team. Time is of the essence. We don't know how long we have before they strike. I'll do everything I can on my end to keep the authorities off your trail."

The van slowed. "We're here," Jimmy said.

Dane slid the van door open and hopped outside. After a quick look around, he nodded to Hagan. Hagan motioned for me to follow him. He led me around to the back of the van, where a midsize sedan with government plates was parked in a hidden spot off the road. It was cold out, way colder than anything I was used to in Arizona, and I buried my hands in my pockets and shivered.

Hagan pulled a card from his jacket pocket and gave it to me. The only thing written on it was a phone number.

"Memorize that, then throw it away," Hagan told me.

"What is it?" I asked.

"A phone number of last resort," he told me. "One last fail-safe. You call that number from any pay phone, any landline, any cell phone in the country, and the cavalry will come riding over the ridge to save you. And, may I remind you, to arrest you. Consider it a 'get thrown back into jail free' card. Which would presumably be safer than the alternative. You call that number, and it's all over. Understand? Last chance saloon."

I nodded.

"I'm putting you in harm's way, Kamran, which is a wicked thing for me to do to a lad of seventeen."

I started to protest, but Hagan held up a hand.

"Spare me the 'I'm a man grown' speech," he said. "You're a senior in high school, and you've no business playing at cloak and dagger. But the simple fact is I need you. Your country needs you, as the cliché goes."

"My brother needs me," I said.

"Aye. That he does," Hagan said. "You're a good kid, Kamran, and an even better brother." He held out his hand, and I shook it.

"Thanks, Mr. Hagan. For everything."

"Call me Mickey," he said.

Dane came around the back of the van. "We need to do this," he said.

Hagan nodded and sent me back inside the van. He got in the sedan and pulled it out into the dark, lonely road, across both lanes. Jimmy backed the van out and pulled it up to a stop in front of the car, as though Hagan had blocked our path.

"What are you doing?" I asked Jimmy, but Aaliyah shook her head at me.

Ahead of us, Mickey Hagan got out of his car with a gun.

"What's he doing? What's going on?" I asked, but nobody answered me.

Mickey came around the side of the van. Dane opened the sliding door, raised his gun, and shot Mickey Hagan in the leg.

"No!" I cried, lunging for the door. "Mickey!"

Dane held me back. "Go," he told Jimmy. Jimmy floored it, and the van swerved off the road, around Mickey's car, and down the road.

"What the—? What'd you do that for?" I cried.

"Get down," Dane said, and he pushed me to the floor.

Bullets ripped into the van, punching holes in the metal doors on the back. The front windshield shattered, but stayed in place.

"Geez, Mickey!" Jimmy cried. The van swerved. Screeched. Straightened. I heard more gunshots, but no more of them hit the van. "We're good," Jimmy said at last.

Dane helped me up off the floor. "It was Mickey's idea. To make it more convincing he had nothing to do with your escape."

Mickey's idea? To let Dane shoot him in the leg? This was way more serious than I'd thought.

"Get us to the backup van," Dane told Jimmy, and he settled down on one of the benches to take his gun apart again.

I crawled up on the bench across from him, staring at the bullet holes in the back of the van. Mickey had missed anything important on purpose, but the next time we ran into the authorities—the real authorities—we might not be so lucky. I was officially a wanted fugitive now, and this was officially real.

CHAPTER FORTY-EIGHT

THE MOTEL ROOM WAS EMPTY WHEN I CAME BACK in with a bucket full of ice. Jimmy was still in the bathroom, and Dane and Aaliyah hadn't come back from the van yet. We were in some little town in West Virginia, well off the main route anybody would take to Arizona. The CIA, the DHS, the FBI, they all knew by now that I thought Darius was in Arizona, so it only stood to reason that's where I'd be headed. Unless my "abductors" were taking me somewhere else.

I still couldn't believe I'd sat there and watched Dane shoot Mickey Hagan. I'd seen people get shot before in movies and TV shows, but being there for the real thing was shocking. Guns were loud. Made you jump. And to see the bullet rip into Mickey's leg, to know that it was real, and not some special effect . . .

I popped open one of the cans of soda Jimmy had brought with him and poured it over a plastic cup full of ice, trying not to think about Mickey. It felt like such a treat now, such an indulgence, to have a soda on ice, after weeks of milk and juice from cartons.

I sipped my drink and turned on the TV to distract myself. I shouldn't have. A photograph of me—my junior yearbook photo, of all things—was on the first channel I went to. I winced. It had been weird to see Darius's picture all over the news, to hear famous announcers talking about him. It was even weirder to see *my* picture and hear people talking about *me*.

Apparently the secret of Kamran Smith was out. Nobody had known I was being held prisoner, but now they all knew

I had escaped. The manhunt was on, Anderson Cooper said. Homegrown terrorist on the run, said Sean Hannity. Rachel Maddow called it a sad new chapter in an increasingly sad story. But the story was the same all over: Kamran Smith and his brother, Darius Smith, were American terrorists. One of the "experts" Hannity had on his show, some think-tank guy I'd never heard of, said Darius and I had both wanted to join the army so we could "take down America from within." They talked about my application to West Point, my time at East Phoenix High School, my run-ins with other kids.

Was this really happening?

They showed the front of my high school. Then Omar Maldonado, my old teammate, was on camera. "He always acted all high-and-mighty," Omar said. "Like he was better than everybody else."

"I knew he was a terrorist. It was just—the way he looked at you, you know? Like he hated all of us," said Rachel Dubois, a junior girl I had literally never seen before in my entire life.

Nobody interviewed Adam or Julia or anybody else I'd thought had been my friends. But maybe they were saving that for the morning shows.

Jimmy came out of the motel bathroom waving a Zippo lighter around. "Dude. Sorry about that. That's going to linger."

I clicked the TV off. I'd seen more than enough.

Jimmy flipped his lighter closed and went straight for the ice, pouring a Red Bull for himself.

Jimmy must have been only a few years older than me. He looked like somebody from a college garage band, with long, sandy blond hair, multiple ear piercings, and expensive sneakers. The arms that stuck out from his black Arctic Monkeys tour T-shirt were toned and tattooed. Black numbers ran up and down his left arm.

"You like my ink?" he said, catching me staring. He pulled the sleeve of his T-shirt up to show me his whole arm. The numbers were big and small, stacked horizontally and vertically in all different kinds of fonts. "IP addresses," he told me. "Every super-secure site I've cracked is on here." He pointed to different numbers as he said their names. "Pacific Bell. Microsoft. London *Times*. Bank of America. NASA."

"You're a hacker," I said.

"No. A *cracker*. Hackers just find the exploits. Crackers take advantage of them." Jimmy grinned. "I'm what they call in the business a 'black hat.' At least I used to be. Now I guess I'm a white hat. One of the good guys."

"What happened? Why'd you change hats?"

Jimmy pointed to one of the largest numbers on his arm. "This one right here. United States Department of Defense. That's right: the Pentagon. I was just going in to punk them. Honest. I was going to replace the DoD website with one that looked like the game choices Matthew Broderick gets when he dials in in *WarGames*. You know, Chess, Poker, Tic-Tac-Toe, Global Thermonuclear War?"

I shrugged and shook my head. I had no idea what he was talking about.

Jimmy threw up his arms. "Nobody watches the classics anymore! Anyway, they caught me. Stupid, really. I should have bounced the signal through a few more onion layers of symmetric encryption. Got cocky, got caught. So I cut a deal: I'd tell them how I got in—and how to fix it—and they wouldn't throw me in jail for the rest of my life. Opened up a whole new career for me. Now all kinds of companies pay me to test out their Internet security." He pretended to take off a hat and put another on. "Black hat off, white hat on. I never made so much money. I've even done work for the CIA. That's how I met Mickey. 'Course, the DoD still makes me wear a GPS ankle monitor."

Jimmy hiked up his pants leg to show me a black gizmo strapped to his ankle.

"*You're wearing a GPS monitor?*" I said. "But that means they can track you! Track us!"

"Chill, dude," Jimmy said. "I cracked this thing the day they put it on me. As far as the good old US of A knows, I'm at a video game convention in Orlando."

Dane and Aaliyah came back with armloads of bags and equipment, and I hurried to take one of them from Aaliyah. She smiled at my zealous chivalry like she was onto me, but still appreciative. She had changed clothes from before, trading in her business suit for jeans and a T-shirt that read BACKSTREET BOYS and showed a printed photo of the band.

"What happened?" I asked, nodding at her T-shirt. "Did you have to go shopping at the Goodwill?"

Aaliyah's bright smile suddenly switched off, and she gave me an icy stare. I knew immediately that I'd made a mistake, and my heart sank.

Jimmy hooted. "Ooh-hoo! You've done it now, kid! Nobody makes fun of the Boys around the princess and lives!"

"I—I'm sorry," I said, my face hot with embarrassment. "I didn't mean—"

"You only get one warning," Aaliyah said, perfectly serious. "And I'm not a princess," she told Jimmy.

"You check the room for bugs?" Dane asked.

"Yeah, yeah," Jimmy said. "Gave the place the sweep. We're clean."

Aaliyah latched the door and flipped the security lock.

"Are we—are we all sleeping in the same room?" I asked. "I mean, is Aaliyah—"

"Yes," Dane said. "It's more secure."

Jimmy grinned. "You were thinking maybe you two could share a room, cowboy?"

My face must have been as red as Jimmy's soda can. "No, I didn't mean—"

"Just ignore him," Aaliyah said. She set up a laptop on the little table by the window and pulled out a chair. "Now have a seat, Kamran. It's time you learned all about Haydar Ansari."

CHAPTER FORTY-NINE

"HAYDAR ANSARI," AALIYAH SAID. "AKA 'THE LION.'"

Aaliyah called up a picture of a boy playing soccer. There were other players in the foreground, and the picture was kind of blurry, but the shot was clear enough to see that Ansari was a good-looking guy with olive skin and dark, curly hair.

"He's just a teenager," I said.

"Was. He's in his forties now. But this is the only confirmed picture we have of him," Aaliyah said.

I stared at the picture. It could have been me, playing soccer instead of football. We didn't resemble each other all that much, but for at least one brief, innocent moment, both our lives had been about nothing more than scoring a goal or a touchdown, not politics.

"Haydar Ansari was born into a well-to-do family from Tikrit, Iraq, the same city where Saddam Hussein was raised," Aaliyah explained. "Ansari's distantly related to Hussein, in fact—third cousin, three times removed."

"Father's brother's nephew's cousin's former roommate?" Jimmy joked. He hopped on one of the beds with his laptop and groaned. "Ow. Who picked this motel? These mattresses are like stone."

Dane thumped a heavy canvas duffel bag on the other bed. "I've slept on stone before," he said. "This is better."

Aaliyah ignored them. "Ansari's family was rewarded with power and wealth when Hussein took power. Wealth and power they lost when Baghdad fell and Saddam was defeated during Operation Desert Storm."

"You were in that one, weren't you, Dane?" Jimmy asked.

Dane didn't look up from the bag he was rooting through. "I was in that one," he said.

"As a part of the ruling Baath Party, Ansari's family lost everything in the war. To escape persecution from the new Shi'a government, they fled to Syria, where Ansari spent the rest of his youth angry at the United States for ruining his life. It wasn't long, of course, before he fell in with al-Qaeda."

"As you do," Jimmy said.

"As you do," Aaliyah said. "Ansari went on to make a new name for himself, going to university and becoming a successful businessman in his own right. We now know he was funneling much of that money back into al-Qaeda. When Osama Bin Laden was killed in 2011, al-Qaeda effectively splintered into dozens of smaller, autonomous cells around the world, which was how it was designed to operate in the first place. Soon after, Haydar Ansari went from merely funding militant activities to leading them, becoming the leader of a particularly dangerous cell in Afghanistan."

My eyes went from the picture of the young Haydar Ansari to the file on him on Aaliyah's screen. The beginning read like the bio of any regular guy. Born. Went to school. Married a Syrian woman named Bashira. Had kids. A home. A career. But in 2011 he'd given it all up. Left it all behind to become a black-masked face in an al-Qaeda video, leading terrorist attacks from a hidden bunker somewhere inside Afghanistan.

"Ansari's cell has been responsible for some of the worst attacks on US servicemen and civilians in years," Aaliyah said. "We know it's him, but we still haven't been able to catch him." She called up a picture of a bombed-out building in a dusty desert town. "We thought we'd killed him with a drone strike three years ago, but six months later he claimed responsibility for a bombing in Egypt that killed six Americans. He's like a cockroach. We step on him, but he just comes back."

"Just like Lindsay Lohan," Jimmy said.

"We don't know where he is, but we do know that he's alive," Aaliyah said. "If you and Mickey are right, and he *is* in America . . ." Aaliyah shook her head.

"If he is here, why? What's his target?" Dane asked.

"Ansari's trademarks are intricate plots and false clues. It's all about misdirection," Aaliyah said. "Which is why I agree with Mickey—he meant for us to uncover the Women's World Cup plot. He wants us to think we're safe. That's when he'll strike. And it'll be big, whatever it is. He wants an audience. He wants to scare as many people as possible."

"And if he is in America, he'll want to do it soon, before he's discovered," Dane said.

"Here's something that might help," Jimmy said. He turned his computer around. "Mickey just sent us your brother's latest music video."

CHAPTER FIFTY

ANOTHER VIDEO FROM DARIUS?

We all gathered around Jimmy's computer. Darius read another prepared statement off a piece of paper. He looked older. More tired. His beard was long now. I almost didn't recognize him. There was almost nothing of the old Darius I knew and loved there on the screen.

Is this how Haydar Ansari's wife and children felt as they watched him transform into a terrorist? Watched him become someone they didn't know anymore?

I tried to focus on what Darius was saying. It was the usual death to America stuff. And then Darius dropped two Rostam clues.

The first was Rostam versus Godzilla, a story we'd made up after watching a bunch of Japanese monster movies on cable one afternoon.

The other was the bit about the Joker's goons again.

I sat back on the rock-hard bed, deflated.

"What?" Jimmy asked. "What is it?"

"It's the same code he used before," I said. "The one about football."

"But the other clue is new, isn't it?" Aaliyah said. "About Godzilla?"

"Yeah. Rostam and Siyavash have to fight Godzilla. We couldn't beat him, so we lured him into a rocket ship full of hot dogs and blasted him into space."

Jimmy snickered.

"*We were little kids,*" I argued for what felt like the millionth time. "What I want to know is why Darius is still talking about the Women's World Cup."

"To make sure you got it," Dane said.

"But we took care of it already," I said. "The CIA. The army. Whoever. They stopped it."

"Maybe they haven't heard," Jimmy said. "Maybe they've got their heads buried too far in the sand."

"No," Aaliyah said. "I refuse to believe Ansari doesn't know. Even if their contacts didn't tell him, it was all over the news, in every newspaper in the world. It was even on ESPN. *Haydar Ansari knows*—his World Cup bomb plot was foiled. But I think he wanted it to be."

"Plans within plans?" Dane asked.

"Precisely," Aaliyah said. "Give the CIA a bomb plot in Canada to throw us off the scent of what he's really up to here in America. Something he's kept so secret not even Darius knows about it. Unless there's a clue to it in your Godzilla story."

"Ansari's going to fire a rocket full of hot dogs at us!" Jimmy joked.

"Yes, it doesn't *sound* very helpful," Aaliyah said.

"But why give the Joker's-goons clue again?" I asked.

Aaliyah shrugged. "I suspect your brother's access to information from the outside world is more limited, and he doesn't know that the Women's World Cup plot was foiled. As Jimmy says, he's just making sure we get the message. And as long as Darius doesn't know anything, we don't know anything." She bit her lip. "We really needed a new clue right about now, but this video is worthless."

"No," I said. "No, it has to mean something. The Godzilla clue is new."

I had Jimmy play the video again for me. I stared at Darius as he read. *What are you trying to tell me, Darius? What are you trying to say? I know you're trying to tell me something!*

He came to the part again about the Joker's goons, and I remembered playing football with him that day in the backyard.

And then, suddenly, I had it. What Darius meant the first time, and what he meant now. What Haydar Ansari was doing in America. What he was going to attack.

"Oh my God," I said. I hopped up and started pacing the room. "Oh my God! We were so stupid!"

"What?" Aaliyah asked. "What is it?"

"Okay. So. Okay," I said, still pacing. Thoughts were coming at me like a quarterback blitz. I couldn't find the words. Where to begin. "Okay. Yes. Sorry. So, what if Darius *does* know there's another plot? What if the thing about the Joker's goons *did* mean the Women's World Cup the first time, but means something different this time?"

"Something different?" Aaliyah said. "But it's the same story. The same reference."

"The clue was all about a bomb in a *football*," I said. "Mickey thought that meant football like soccer."

"It was," Dane said. "They found the cell with stadium plans and everything."

"But you said Ansari was all about misdirection. Tricks. He's clever, and he likes to show it. So what if this attack's the same, but different?"

Everybody was frowning at me. I wasn't explaining it right.

"Look. Okay. We know Ansari's in America, right?"

"We think so, or we wouldn't be here right now," Aaliyah said.

"So he's here in America. In *Arizona*. And he wants a big target, you said. Something with an audience," I said.

I waited for them to get it, but they just stared at me. In frustration I grabbed the remote control and turned the TV on. Instead of one of the news channels, I clicked over to ESPN.

"And welcome back to SportsCenter," an announcer said. "With Super Bowl Forty-Nine just a week away, all eyes are on host city Phoenix, Arizona, where the teams met the media today. For more on the press conference, we go to Emily Reed live at the University of Phoenix Stadium. Emily?"

"Oh, frak," Jimmy said.

Emily Reed, microphone in hand, started talking about the upcoming Super Bowl. I turned to face the others in the room.

"You want a big audience?" I said. "You want to scare the most people you possibly can? What about setting off a bomb in front of a *hundred million viewers* on TV?"

Aaliyah got up and started pacing. Dane stared at the floor.

"No," Jimmy said. "No. Way. The security on that building the day of the game will be like the Pentagon. And trust me, I know what that's like. We're talking barricades, metal detectors, dogs, a thirty-mile no-fly zone patrolled by F-16s. That place is a *fortress*. Nobody's crazy enough to hit the Super Bowl."

"It makes sense, though, doesn't it?" I asked. "Why bring Darius to America if the target is in some other country? Because it's not. It's right here. And it's always been about football. Mickey thought that meant soccer. Darius, too, at first. That's the distraction. The misdirection. But it's always been about *American* football. Darius must have figured it out!"

"A plan within a plan," Aaliyah said.

"You can't possibly be serious!" Jimmy said. "I'm telling you, it's impossible."

"Impossible or not, we need to get DHS on this," Dane said. "FBI. CIA. Tell Mickey."

Jimmy tossed his laptop on the bed. "I need another Red Bull." As he dipped his plastic cup into the ice bucket, Dane grabbed his wrist.

"Who got ice?" Dane said. His voice was low and scared, like having ice in the room was the worst thing that had ever happened in the history of the world.

"Me," I said, confused.

Dane's dark eyes turned on Jimmy like he'd just betrayed us all. *"You let him out of your sight?"*

Jimmy yanked his wrist free and rubbed it. "I had to go to the can!"

Dane turned on me, his eyes still smoldering, and I shrank back. "Did anybody see you?"

"I—I don't know. Maybe," I said. "There was this guy going into a room, but—"

Dane hurried to the front window and peeked out behind the curtain. Red lights glinted on the glass.

"Everybody down!" Dane cried, and a tear gas cartridge trailing white smoke came crashing through the window.

CHAPTER FIFTY-ONE

A WHITE CLOUD WAS ALREADY STARTING TO FORM in the room as I dropped to the floor. I could feel my eyes tearing up, my nose and throat beginning to burn.

Dane dove between the beds for the smoking cartridge. He came up with it in one hand, the other arm wrapped around his face. It looked like a Roman candle, one end of it burning bright and pouring white smoke. I couldn't believe it—who grabbed tear gas cartridges? What was he doing? The smoke was making me hack up a lung and I was halfway across the room.

Dane stuffed the smoking cartridge into the ice bucket flame-first, and it fizzled out. "We don't have much time," he said, his voice ragged. "Bathroom vent."

Jimmy disappeared into the bathroom, and seconds later I heard the fan running, drawing out the tear gas still in the air.

Bullets shattered what was left of the window, and I hit the deck. Dane grabbed one of the mattresses and flipped it up against the broken window. I threw my hands over my head and tried to become one with the sticky motel carpet.

Dane tossed Aaliyah a smaller duffel bag. "Back wall," he told her, and she hurried to the bathroom vanity at the back of the room as Jimmy came out. Dane flipped the other mattress up against the far wall, like a pillow fort. "Get him underneath!" he yelled.

Jimmy grabbed his laptop, then me, and together we scrambled for the space between the mattress and the wall. I didn't see how it was going to help. The bullets were shredding the mattress up against the window.

They were shooting at us. I couldn't believe it. "They're shooting at us!" I said.

"Yeah," Jimmy said. "They tend to do that when you shoot your way out of a Department of Homeland Security facility."

"I only shot a fire extinguisher!" I said.

A bullet hit the TV, and Emily Reed disappeared with a spark and an electric sizzle. Dane yanked the busted TV off its base and chucked it against the door, piling the table and chairs on top of it. He didn't want the soldiers getting in, and clearly that wasn't the way he was planning on getting out.

Jimmy hastily stuffed his computer into his backpack. "They'll be through that door any second now," he said.

Dane pulled his pistol, flipped the safety off, and pointed it at the door.

"He's not going to shoot them, is he?" I asked. "The point here is to prove I'm *not* a terrorist, right?"

Dane heard me above the gunfire and pulled his gun back. "Aaliyah?" he called.

"Explosives set!" Aaliyah cried.

"Explosives?" I said.

Dane pushed me and Jimmy under the mattress propped against the wall and Aaliyah crammed in with us.

THOOM. The room shook as the explosives went off, taking out the whole back wall where the bathroom had been. Water from the broken pipes sprayed little fountains among the shredded wooden studs and broken drywall. Out the back, through the hole, was the rear parking lot—and in it, our van.

CHAPTER FIFTY-TWO

THE VAN'S TIRES HUMMED ON THE BLACKTOP, ITS headlights cutting a dozen yards of road and trees and hills out of the darkness. Dane was at the wheel, driving so fast it felt like we were flying. None of us spoke for a long time, each of us, I think, listening for the sound of more gunshots. But eventually, there was nothing but the rattle of the van. We wouldn't stop again that night, I knew. Not after the debacle at the motel. If it were up to me, we wouldn't stop again until we got to Arizona.

"Call Mick," Dane said at last, his voice waking us all like an alarm clock.

Jimmy flipped open his laptop and went through an elaborate series of windows and screens until one of them finally showed a sleepy-eyed but still fully dressed and awake Mickey Hagan. He was somewhere with a lot of bookshelves behind him. Maybe his house.

"Kamran, Aaliyah, Jimmy," he said. "Is Dane with you? Are you all right?"

"Yes," Aaliyah told him. "But just barely. We were made at the motel."

"I know," Mickey said.

"You knew?" I said. "And you didn't warn us? They were shooting at us! Tear gas! Real bullets! We could have been killed!"

"I'm sorry," Mickey said. "I knew they were coming for you, but I couldn't warn you. They let me find out about it in advance—'accidentally on purpose,' I think—to see if I was a leak. To see if I was really in communication with you."

I still couldn't believe it. There had to be some way Mickey could have gotten us word. Tipped us off.

Jimmy saw the anger and confusion on my face and laughed. "Welcome to the spy business, kid. It's all part of the game."

"What bothers me is that they were so obvious about it," Mickey said. "Nobody includes you in briefings for twenty years, and then all of a sudden you're pulled out of the hospital and driven to Langley. What a load of bollocks."

The hospital? *Mickey's leg.* Of course. Dane had shot him! The image of that bullet punching a bloody hole in Mickey's leg would be forever stuck in my head. "Is your leg okay?" I asked.

Mickey smiled. "It's kind of you to ask. Yes. Hurts like the devil, but I've had worse. Dane knows his business. It was a clean shot, straight through. No broken bones, nothing that won't heal. It is what it is. All part of the game, as Jimmy says." He held up a cane. "On the plus side, now I have something to shake at the neighborhood children when I tell them to get off my lawn." He smiled weakly. "I'm just knackered, is all. It's been a long day. Did you have a chance to watch the new video from your brother?"

Aaliyah and I told Mickey all about our guess that the football clue was really about the Super Bowl, and the story of Rostam and Siyavash versus Godzilla. When we were finished, he looked as horrified at the thought of an attack on the Super Bowl as we were.

"It does make sense," Mickey said. "Though Jimmy's not wrong—the security around that stadium on game day will be better than what the president got when he visited Afghanistan. But that shouldn't stop us from investigating it. I'll pass it along as though I'm putting my own interpretation on it. If they don't buy it, we'll have to trust Super Bowl security to stop whatever it is. And the Godzilla story?"

"Hot dogs," Aaliyah said. "Maybe something to do with food services at the Super Bowl?"

"Aye. That's good. Gives me a place to start, anyway. I'll look into it. In the meantime, try to get to Arizona as quickly as possible without getting yourselves killed."

CHAPTER FIFTY-THREE

THE ADRENALINE RUSH FROM THE ATTACK ON OUR motel room kept me awake for a little while longer, and I spent the time memorizing the phone number Mickey had given me. After about an hour, though, I crashed. Hard. When I woke on the roll-out foam mattress on the floor of the van, I was stiff and sore, and the sun had already come up. Jimmy was now at the wheel, Aaliyah had her eyes closed listening to music on headphones in the passenger seat, and Dane sat on one of the benches in the back, eating an apple.

"Hungry?" he asked, holding a banana out to me.

I realized I was famished, and took it from him greedily. It took a little while for the grogginess and stiffness to wear off, but the banana helped. So did the silence.

"Where are we?" I asked at last.

"Just past Louisville, Kentucky," Dane said. "Making good time. You drink coffee?"

I didn't. Dane passed me a bottle of grapefruit juice instead. Dane and I had been together now for almost a full day, and I hadn't really looked at him. In fact, I was always doing anything I could to look *away* from him. He was big, strong. His biceps seemed as big as my thighs. His hair was cut short on top, almost close enough to make him bald, and he had a black mustache. The main thing about him was his stillness. He never seemed to move unless he had to.

His nose was bandaged with taped white gauze.

"Sorry about your nose," I told him.

His head turned. It was as unsettling as watching a statue's head swivel slowly to look at you. "Don't be," he said. "Initiative is good. Sometimes it's the only thing between life and death. You didn't know I was there to help you, so you helped yourself. But you're not always going to have a metal tray around. You'll learn more when you're a cadet at West Point, but I can teach you a few quick and dirty defensive moves now, if you want."

"I—Yeah. Yeah, that'd be great," I said. "But I'm not going to West Point."

"Mick said you were."

"Well, I *was*. But I'm pretty sure I'm not going now."

"You'll get back in after we clear your brother's name," Dane said.

I was touched. "You really believe Darius is innocent?"

"Of course," Dane said. "He's a Ranger. Rangers don't quit, and they don't turn. 'Surrender' is not a Ranger word."

And that was that. Dane believed down in the core of his being that my brother was innocent for no other reason than because he was a United States Ranger. It was unthinkable to him that a Ranger could ever turn on his own country. I wished everybody thought that way.

Dane ejected the cartridge of bullets from his pistol and cleared the firing chamber, clicking the trigger a few times with the gun pointed down and away at the floor just to be sure.

"Let's say somebody's got a gun on you," Dane said. "You don't want to die. What's the first thing you do?"

"Try to take it away."

"No," Dane said. "You do nothing. You don't want to die, you do what they tell you. You're being robbed, you give them whatever you've got. Your life is always worth more, and trying to disarm somebody else is the number-one way to get yourself shot. Second, if you can, you run. Get as much distance and obstacles between you and the gun as possible. You engage, your odds of getting shot go way up. Got it?"

I nodded.

"Now," he said, "if you *know* your assailant is going to shoot you, you want to try to disarm him." He aimed the empty gun at me. "Take the gun away."

"Here?"

"You think your attacker is going to move someplace more convenient if you ask him?"

I stared at the gun in Dane's big hands, then tried to grab it as fast as I could.

Click. The bullet he would have fired would have gone straight in my brain.

"Don't grab up," he told me. "Grab down. Again."

Click. I grabbed down, but I was gut-shot before I could pull the gun free.

"Get yourself out of the direct line of fire. Go toward the side with the gun. It's easier for me to come around across my body than it is for me to swing out wide, see? Again."

I moved. Grabbed his wrist. Pushed down.

Click. Still dead. Or at least shot in the leg like Mickey.

"Better," Dane said. "Grab the weapon, not the wrist. Your goal here is to control the weapon." He put my hand on the gun. "Bend my wrist back with the weapon in your hand. All the way back, that's a joint lock. Hardest position for me to do anything with my hand. Then, while you've got my weapon locked away from you, that's when you counterattack."

"Counterattack?"

"Something fast. Something painful. Kick him in the groin. Hit him in the throat. Claw at his face."

"That's not very honorable," I said.

"Honor's got nothing to do with it. This is about survival. It's you or him." Dane released the tension in his arm, and I let go. "You use leverage and pain to get the weapon. Then, when you got it, you unload it. Discharge it. Kick it or toss it away."

"Shouldn't I aim it at my attacker?"

"You got it from him, who's to say he won't get it back? No. Not until you're a trained soldier. Even then, the best way to survive a gunfight is to not be in one. Worst he can do without a gun is beat the snot out of you. Worst he can do *with* one is shoot you dead. You get rid of the weapon, and you run away. Call for help. Let's do it again. Just the leverage part."

I tried to do everything he told me. Twisted. Grabbed the gun. Tried to push his wrist back into a joint lock. It was like trying to snap a telephone pole. I was strong for a high school senior, but I was still just seventeen. Dane kept the gun pointed right at me. He let me struggle helplessly for a few seconds before pulling the trigger.

Click.

"And the last part of the lesson is the most important part of the lesson," he said. "Don't ever try this stuff on somebody a lot stronger than you."

"Great," I said. "So I just need my attacker to be either my grandmother or a freshman in high school."

Dane laughed. "You'll get bigger, and the army will make you stronger, cadet."

"If I get in," I said.

"I told you. You'll get in," Dane said. "Let's do it again. I'll go easier on you this time."

We practiced the move again and again, Dane pushing back, but not so much that I couldn't push him back. By the end, I at least knew what I was *supposed* to do, even if I wasn't doing it all that well.

"Mickey just sent the signal," Jimmy said from the driver's seat. He had his cell phone in his hand, reading the screen. "He wants to chat."

CHAPTER FIFTY-FOUR

JIMMY PULLED INTO A GAS STATION. WE REFILLED, bought snacks, and made bathroom runs, then huddled around Jimmy's laptop to talk to Mickey together. I ate a Slim Jim and sipped a Dr Pepper as Jimmy finished the complicated process of establishing the secret, secure connection.

This time Mickey was sitting in his car. He looked better, though. More rested. He hadn't slept on the floor of a van like me.

"I ran the Super Bowl idea by the big brains," he said. "They're as incredulous as you are, Jimmy. Still, I think they at least said something to Super Bowl security, so they'll know to be on higher alert, such as it can get any higher. But it's all the more reason for us to have gotten you out of there, Kamran."

"I don't understand," I said.

"If the CIA isn't going to do something about this, *we* have to," Mickey explained. "I ran down your food services angle, Aaliyah. The food concessions for the Super Bowl are being supplied by Kendall Food Services, which distributes out of Nashville, Tennessee."

Dane glanced at Jimmy, who immediately pulled out a tablet to look them up.

"So far it's the best interpretation of Darius's clue we've got—assuming he really is talking about the Super Bowl. The food delivery isn't supposed to leave Nashville until later tonight. Dane, I want you and the team to check it out."

"But—what about Darius?" I asked. "The Super Bowl's in four days. We have to find him."

"Our priority is preventing an attack on the United States," Mickey said. "Darius knows that."

"He's a Ranger," Dane said. "He's ready to die for that."

Mickey quickly held up his hands. "Not that we aren't going to do everything we can to prevent that from happening, Kamran," he assured me. "But Dane's right. Your brother is a soldier. A very good one until just a few months ago, by all accounts, and perhaps even better since. He's doing what he can to stop this terrorist attack, and now we have to as well. If the target is the Super Bowl, we have time. Not much time, but time. And if we *do* foil whatever it is Ansari has planned, it'll all be over well before then."

It'll all be over, and then they won't need Darius anymore, I thought. *We'll kill Haydar Ansari's terrorist plot, and Haydar Ansari will kill Darius.*

CHAPTER FIFTY-FIVE

"CAN YOU CHECK AGAIN?" AALIYAH SAID TO THE security guard behind the desk at the Kendall Food Services warehouse facility. "My name is Hana Nazari. N-A-Z-A-R-I. Channel Five News?" She held up the microphone she was carrying like she was talking into it. "You haven't seen me on TV?"

Aaliyah certainly looked the part. She was prettier even than ESPN's Emily Reed, who also had dark hair and olive skin. Aaliyah had changed back into the sharp gray business suit and black high heels she'd worn at the DHS building. I couldn't help staring at her, then chided myself for it.

"I'm sorry," the security guard said. A badge pinned to his shirt said "Voss." I didn't know if that was his name or the security company's name. "I don't have any record of anybody agreeing to let a film crew in here tonight," he told us.

"It's just a puff piece," Aaliyah said. "'Supersize Food Trucks Off to the Super Bowl.' 'Nashville Feeds the Super Bowl's Hungry Fans'? Great publicity for Kendall Food Services."

The outside door opened, and Jimmy came into the lobby wearing a blue jumpsuit and white hard hat, and carrying two bags of tools. "BellSouth," he said. "Somebody called about phone line repair?"

"Yeah," the security guard said. "Down the hall and—"

"Chris, what was the name of the person we talked to?" Aaliyah interrupted. She was talking to me. Chris was my alias for this little performance. I was supposed to be her cameraman. Though how anybody could take me seriously with the video camera Jimmy had given me, I didn't know. It wasn't a little home handheld version, but it wasn't one of those big things you had to lug around on your shoulder, either.

Aaliyah was waiting. I picked a name from the directory on the wall over where I stood, like I was supposed to.

"Murray?" I said. "Murphy? Something like that?"

"William Murphy?" the security guard said. "In public relations?"

"*Yes*. That's the one," Aaliyah said. "Could you call him?"

"Ma'am, it's ten forty-five at night."

"Which means the eleven o'clock news starts in fifteen minutes," Aaliyah told him.

"Hey, bub," Jimmy said. "Router room?"

"Sorry," the guard said, flustered. "Down the hall and to the right. Sign's on the door."

Jimmy nodded and strolled off down the hall.

Aaliyah stalled, babbling on to the security guard about recent features she'd done, to give Jimmy time to get where he was going.

"Okay, go," Jimmy said. I almost jumped as his voice came through loud and clear in the earbuds Aaliyah and I wore.

"Please? Could you call him?" Aaliyah begged the security guard. "I don't know why Mr. Murphy didn't leave word, but we did talk about it, and I'm supposed to go live in twenty."

The security guard relented. "I'll call."

I looked around nervously while the security guard picked up the phone and dialed. I didn't understand how this next part could work, but Jimmy had assured us he could do it.

"Mr. Murphy?" the security guard said. He put a finger to his other ear like he was trying to hear the phone better. "Mr. Murphy? This is Clifford Voss, night security at the distribution center. Yes. I'm sorry to interrupt your party, but there's a Miss—"

"Nazari," Aaliyah told him. "Channel Five."

"—Miss Nazari here from Channel Five, and she says she— Yes, sir. That's right. No, sir."

Somewhere down the hall, not very far from here, Jimmy had patched himself into the warehouse's outgoing phone lines. The name I'd read out while he was in the lobby had told him who the security guard was going to call, and all he'd had to do was intercept the call and pretend to be Mr. William Murphy. I hadn't believed him when he'd said it would be a piece of cake, and I still worried that the person Clifford Voss was talking to on the other end of that line was the *real* William Murphy.

"I see. All right, sir. Thank you. Sorry to bother you. Yes, sir. You too." Mr. Voss hung up and looked at us suspiciously. My eyes flicked to the door, ready to run.

CHAPTER FIFTY-SIX

"MR. MURPHY SENDS HIS APOLOGIES," THE SECURITY guard said. "He says he talked to you, but he just forgot to leave word with security."

"Well, of course he did," Aaliyah said. She was already walking for the door to the warehouse. "Thank you, Mr. Voss. We know where to go."

"I'll call the floor manager on duty tonight and let him know you're on the way," Voss said.

"Terrific," Aaliyah called over her shoulder as I hurried along behind her. "Thank you!"

The swinging doors thumped closed behind us, and I let out a breath. Aaliyah didn't seem a bit nervous, though, clicking briskly along the concrete corridor in her high heels.

She put a hand to the four-way communicator she wore in her ear. " 'Hey, bub'?" she said quietly, imitating Jimmy from before. "Who are you, Wolverine?"

"She knows the Wolverine!" Jimmy's voice came through on her earbud and mine. "Be still, my fanboy heart! Kamran, you've got competition, kid."

I blushed. I'd hoped my mini-crush on Aaliyah wasn't quite so obvious.

"Cut the chatter," Dane said through the earbuds. He was linked in, too. He could hear everything we said to each other. "We've got a job to do. Jimmy, we need shipping manifests, authorization papers—"

"Yadda yadda yadda," Jimmy said. "I know the routine.

Give me ten minutes and I can tell you what the CEO had for breakfast this morning."

Jimmy's job was to hack into the warehouse's computers and look for evidence that anything was amiss.

I brushed against a water cooler, almost overturning it in a clumsy attempt to keep up with Aaliyah's brisk pace. She slowed down for me.

"You're nervous, aren't you?" she said.

"Yeah," I admitted. I was supposed to be studying for midterms right now, not going undercover with an elite ops group. I didn't want to mess up, but I had another worry, too.

"You're doing great," Aaliyah told me. "Just keep following my lead."

"If we—if we do find something," I said, giving voice to my greatest fear, "if we do uncover some kind of plot and stop Haydar Ansari, and Ansari's been using Darius to feed us false information, doesn't that mean he won't need Darius anymore? That he could . . . could kill him?"

Aaliyah nodded, her eyes sympathetic. "It's possible. But I'm not going to give up on him, Kamran. When this is over, we'll find him and clear his name, no matter what."

"Why are you doing this?" I asked.

"What?"

"This. Helping me. Helping Darius. Working for Mickey."

Aaliyah took a deep breath, and for a few moments the only sound was her heels clicking along on the floor. We came to a door and pushed through it. Between us and the loading docks at the far end of the compound was a long warehouse full of boxes marked KENDALL FOOD SERVICES. There wasn't a soul around—it was, after all, almost eleven o'clock at night.

"How old were you when September eleventh happened?" she asked at last.

"Um, three." I felt very young all of a sudden.

"I was fourteen," she said. "A freshman in high school. Exeter. You know it?"

I shook my head.

"Big fancy boarding school in New Hampshire. Hadn't even been there a month. Didn't have any friends, wasn't in any clubs yet. And after September eleventh, nobody *wanted* me to be their friend, or be in any of their clubs."

It was exactly the same thing that had happened to me when Darius hit the news. I knew exactly how she must have felt—the looks, the whispers, the snubs—and I told her so.

"Right. So take what you went through for two weeks and multiply that by *four years*. My father wanted to pull me out of Exeter, send me to school in Switzerland. But I begged him to let me stay. Maybe a little bit of it was out of stubbornness. But mostly it was because I loved America. I'd dreamed of coming here since I was a little girl. I loved American TV, American movies, American food—"

"American boy bands?" I said.

She smiled. "No. I *worshipped* American boy bands."

"She tell you who played her sweet sixteen birthday party?" Jimmy cut in on our earpieces, making me jump all over again. I'd forgotten he and Dane were still listening in. "*NSYNC.* Her rich daddy paid them to play just for her."

"Justin kissed me," Aaliyah said dreamily. "Right here." She pointed to a place on her cheek and I laughed, but she was totally serious. "Everybody from school was there, of course. So excited. But they just came for the concert. They were never really my friends, none of them. They never got close enough to me for that. You asked me why I do this, and that's why. September eleventh . . . crystallized me. Changed me. Made me want to prove to all the haters that not all Muslims are radical terrorists. So after I graduated, I went to Georgetown to study international relations, specifically Arab relations with the West. That's where Mickey found me. He hired me right out of college as a CIA consultant, and I've never looked back. When he told me about your and Darius's situation, I was in. No-brainer."

I nodded. Living in my little bubble in Phoenix, it had never occurred to me that there could be somebody else out there who got what I'd been going through so completely. Somebody who had experienced the same prejudice I did, and was doing everything she could to undo it.

At last we reached a warehouse where a skeleton crew was filling refrigerated tractor trailer trucks with pallets of plastic-wrapped Kendall Food Services boxes, and I did a double take.

I knew one of the people loading the trucks.

CHAPTER FIFTY-SEVEN

IT WAS DANE! HE WORE THE BROWN PANTS AND work shirt of Kendall Food Services, and he was checking off loaded pallets with an electronic scanner. I knew it was his job in this little performance to infiltrate the warehouse "unofficially" through the back door, but I was still surprised at how thoroughly he'd done it. The Green Berets really were amazing at getting into a place and blending in without causing a ripple.

A red-faced white guy in a white shirt and brown tie hustled over to us. Fresh sweat stains ringed his armpits, and he dabbed at his balding, sweaty head with a handkerchief.

"I—I'm Fred Sorenson," he said, stopping us in our tracks. "I—nobody told me you were coming." He looked at my camera like it was a bazooka. "You want to film the food being loaded onto the trucks?" He looked around. "Why?"

"Puff piece," Aaliyah said again, slipping easily back into character. "'Nashville Food Company Feeds Hungry Super Bowl Fans.' It's Super Bowl all the time on TV right now."

Fred Sorenson swallowed and patted his head again with his handkerchief. The man looked like he was about to have a heart attack. Aaliyah had to notice it, too.

"Well, maybe just some shots of the food trucks leaving, then?" he said.

Jimmy's voice was suddenly in our ears again. We could hear him, but Fred Sorenson couldn't. "*This* is interesting," Jimmy said. "All the other food—French fries, nachos, popcorn, candy—came from their usual vendors. But their usual hot dog vendor couldn't deliver. Last-minute refrigeration failure at the hot dog supplier's facility in Chicago. Kendall Food Services had to go to a secondary supplier in Houston. Hot dogs just came in this afternoon."

Hot dogs! That's what Darius and I had pretended to lure Godzilla into the rocket with.

"Actually," Aaliyah said to Sorenson, super smooth, "we thought we might open a box or two. Show the actual food that's being shipped out. Something *American.* Something that says 'football.' A box of hot dogs, for example."

Fred Sorenson practically spluttered. "H-hot dogs?" Behind him, Dane left one tractor trailer and hopped up into another to look for the boxes of hot dogs. "I—I don't think that's—I don't think that's a good idea," Sorenson said. "You really ought to go. *Please.*"

Dane's voice came low and steady in our ears. "Got 'em. Only the top boxes are filled with hot dogs," he said. "The rest are filled with plastic explosives. C-4. Enough to level an entire stadium."

CHAPTER FIFTY-EIGHT

AALIYAH DROPPED THE MIC, GRABBED THE FLOOR manager by the shirt, and slammed him up against a stack of boxes. "Why are those hot dog boxes filled with C-4?"

Fred Sorenson collapsed into a sobbing, spluttering heap. He was afraid. Really afraid. And his fear was contagious. I had never seen a grown man cry like that, and it scared me. "I'm sorry. I'm so sorry!" he blubbered. "I knew it was wrong, but I couldn't—They told me if I went to the police, they'd kill her."

"Kill who?" Aaliyah asked.

"My daughter," he said, sobbing. "They have my daughter."

"Who?" I asked.

A shot rang out, startling me. A red stain spread across Sorensen's shirt, and with horror I realized he'd been shot. His eyes went wide and his mouth opened like he was trying to say something, but he was dead before he hit the floor.

Before I had time to gasp, Aaliyah grabbed me and yanked me down to the ground. Bullets ripped through the boxes above us. My heart thudded as we scrambled to safety behind the boxes while Dane returned fire from the protection of a tractor trailer. The other employees, the skeleton crew who'd been loading the trucks, leaped off their forklifts and ran for the exits.

I ducked as guns fired, not sure where the bullets were even hitting. "Who's shooting at us?" I cried.

"Whoever kidnapped Sorenson's daughter," Aaliyah said. "Whoever arranged for those explosives to end up on those trucks."

She pulled a small gun from the inside of her suit jacket. Bullets tore into the metal wall behind us, pinging like hail on the roof of a car. I wanted to disappear. But Aaliyah popped up from behind the boxes and squeezed off a couple of shots. She dropped back down and put a finger to her ear. "Jimmy, we're under attack!"

"I know!" came his response. "I was watching the parking lot security cameras. These guys didn't drive up. They were already here."

Bullets pinged off the tractor trailer where Dane was hiding, and I flinched.

"They're going to set off the explosives!" I said.

Aaliyah stood, fired, and ducked again. "Plastic explosives don't work that way. It takes a blasting cap." She put her finger to her ear again. "Dane, I make six hostiles with body armor and automatic rifles along the south wall. Maybe more."

"Roger that," Dane's voice said in my ear. "Four more are making their way around the stacks on the west wall."

Bullets chewed up the boxes all around us. Aaliyah returned fire with her pistol, but it was nothing compared to the firepower our attackers had.

"We can't beat ten guys!" I cried.

"Jimmy," Aaliyah asked, "can you do anything for us?"

The fire alarm suddenly went off, red lights flashing and sirens shrieking.

"Great," I said. "Anything else?"

"It's all I can do," Jimmy's voice said. "Nothing else here is automated. Wait—I hear somebody. They've found me!"

"Get out of there!" Dane said. "You too, Aaliyah. It's our only option."

"Where?" she said. The attackers blocked the way we'd come in, and were along the wall with the emergency exit, too.

"Where the trucks come in and out," I said, thinking fast and pulling Aaliyah in that direction. "That's how I got out of the DHS building—"

The boxes right by my head exploded, spraying us with frozen French fries. Aaliyah yanked me back down.

"Or not," I squeaked.

"Back exit's covered," Aaliyah told Dane.

"Then we go up," Dane told us.

CHAPTER FIFTY-NINE

"UP?" I SAID, LOOKING AT THE ROOF. THERE WAS A skylight there, partially obstructed by the towering stacks of food boxes.

"Up," Aaliyah said. She tucked her pistol back in her jacket and took off her high heels. She stood for a moment, eyeing them regretfully. "Do you know how hard it is to find a good pair of heels?" she asked me, then tossed them aside. With a nimble leap, she was up and wiggling over the stack of boxes. She held out a hand to help me up after her. I was still so shaken up by what I'd just seen—Sorensen dying, the bullets coming at us—that I forgot to get flustered by the fact that I was holding Aaliyah's hand.

We moved around behind the next stack to give us more cover, and kept climbing. The ceiling was one more pallet-height away. I glanced over the edge. Two black-clad SWAT-looking guys were creeping through the stacks, automatic rifles held at the ready. They were going for where we had been, but when they discovered we weren't there anymore, they would be able to sneak up on Dane. I looked around for something to drop on them, then realized I was standing on what I needed. *Boxes.* Boxes and boxes of frozen food. I pushed at one with my feet, but the boxes were wrapped in a thick plastic, like industrial-strength plastic wrap, and wouldn't budge.

"*Kamran,*" Aaliyah whispered. "*Kamran, come on!*"

I signaled for her to wait and ripped and tore at the plastic wrap. I barely made a dent in it. I wished I had a knife. I managed to yank a V-shaped slit in the plastic wrap at last, put my sneakers to the box at the top, and pushed with all my strength. The box tore free of the plastic wrap and tumbled down between the stacks, slamming into the head of one of the black-clad guys with a satisfying crunch and knocking him flat on the ground. The other guy flinched, looked up, saw me, and opened fire. My stomach went to my throat, and I scrambled back as bullets shredded the boxes and plastic wrap. The guy below me stopped shooting long enough to shout something that sounded like Arabic. I kicked at another box, sending it toppling over the side, and took Aaliyah's outstretched hand. I didn't look back to see if the second box had hit the guy below us.

We climbed onto the last pallet, and Aaliyah stood on her toes to reach the skylight. She unlatched the window. It gave a rusty groan as she pushed it open, but there was just enough room for us to slither out. I hefted her up until most of her weight was on the roof and her feet left my hands.

I turned just in time to see a guy in all-black body armor stand up behind me. He had just climbed up over the side. We stared at each other for half a second, both of us surprised, and then suddenly, there was a gun in his hand. I grabbed for it, twisting, pushing down and away, doing everything Dane had taught me, but the guy was strong. Stronger than me. He twisted the gun back toward me, and then—*bang!*—it was all over.

CHAPTER SIXTY

I FLINCHED, BUT THE SOLDIER HADN'T SHOT ME. Blood trickled from his mouth and the tension in his arm went slack, and then he was falling into me. I caught his body out of instinct, and just as quickly pushed him away, heaving him over the side. I tried to ignore the sound of him hitting the boxes as he fell, and then the *thud* of his body as it hit the concrete floor.

I shook uncontrollably. I had almost been shot. Point-blank. And I hadn't been able to do anything about it.

Dane stood on the stack of pallets straight across the aisle, his pistol in both hands. I looked up at him, still dazed.

"Move," he said.

Dully, I understood that he needed me out of the way, and I moved aside as much as I could. Dane got a running start and leaped across the chasm between the pallets, landing with so much momentum he almost went over the other side. He saw me standing there blinking like an idiot and grabbed my arm. Not hard, but rough enough to shake me out of my stupor.

"You all right?" he asked me, his brown eyes finding mine and bringing me back.

"Yeah," I said. "I'm okay."

He put his hands on my waist and lifted me to the window like he was picking up a toddler. I grabbed on, pulled myself up, and there was Aaliyah to help me the rest of the way. We both reached down and helped Dane up.

We were on the roof of a warehouse in the middle of the night with no one else around but terrorists, who were probably at that moment swarming up the pallets and out the exits, meaning to trap us.

"Now what?" I asked.

We ran to the edge of the roof. It was too far to jump. We'd break our legs, or worse. The sound of the man hitting the floor from the top of the pallets came back to me suddenly, unbidden. I stepped back, feeling sick.

"There has to be a ladder down somewhere," Aaliyah said.

"Which they'll be taking up," Dane said. Behind us, another black-clad man had hauled himself halfway out the same window we'd crawled out of. Dane shot twice, and the man went limp and slid back through the window.

Dane put a finger to his ear. "Jimmy, you there?"

"Yeah. Yeah!" Jimmy said. Jimmy! In all the excitement, I'd forgotten about him.

"Where you at?" Dane asked.

"Uh, in the van. In the parking lot," Jimmy said.

"South wall of the warehouse," Dane said. "Now."

"On it!" Jimmy said. We heard tires squeal, and in what seemed like an eternity but was probably only seconds, the white van was parked right beneath us.

"You here?" Jimmy asked. "Dane? Where are you?"

"Don't move," Dane said. "We're coming to you."

Before I could even ask what Dane planned to do, he jumped. He landed with as much grace as he could, slamming into the metal roof of the van and landing on his butt.

"Holy frak!" Jimmy yelled in our ears. "*What was that?*"

"Don't move, Jimmy," Aaliyah said. "We're coming down."

"A little warning would be nice, is all!" Jimmy cried.

Dane got to his feet, apparently none the worse for having fallen twelve feet onto the roof of a van. He signaled to Aaliyah, and she jumped. She half landed, was half caught by Dane, and she slithered down the windshield. Dane waved for me to follow.

I looked down, seeing the twenty feet to the ground, not the twelve feet to the top of the van. Twelve feet was still a lot of feet to drop, and if I missed . . .

A gunshot behind me made me duck. One of the guys was half out the window, his gun pointed at me. He was struggling to aim and keep his balance, but soon enough he was going to get one of them right enough to shoot me.

"Come on, Kamran! You can do this!" Dane yelled. "Your brother jumps out of airplanes!"

My brother had a parachute, I thought.

The soldier fired again, and I jumped.

CHAPTER SIXTY-ONE

FOR A HORRIFYING MOMENT I WAS FALLING, MY body numb and weightless, and then Dane's big hands caught me and my feet crashed into the metal roof, my legs crumpling underneath me.

"Down the windshield," Dane told me before I'd even caught my breath. He rolled off the side of the van while I struggled down the windshield, which is a lot harder to do smoothly than you'd think. Dane pushed me inside the van, and we took off. Bullets hit the back of the van as we peeled out of the parking lot, and I flattened myself against the floor again, praying a bullet didn't catch me. The van swerved, the bullets stopped, and we were away.

Sirens wailed in the distance. The fire department. Jimmy had set off the alarm.

"Those guys back there—they'll kill the firefighters!" I said.

"The firemen ain't going to find anyone back there," Dane said. "Just a really big fire." He pulled a little black box out of his pocket, extended an antenna out the top of it, and pressed buttons on it with both thumbs.

I've never been in an earthquake before. Or a tornado. Or a hurricane. But I have to think that the explosion Dane set off was worse than all of them combined. We were already minutes away at high speed, but the shock wave lifted the van onto two wheels and shook my insides so much I thought I was going to rattle to pieces. Jimmy slammed on the brakes and swerved, and when the van's wheels hit the ground again and it rocked to a stop, we could see the place that used to be Kendall Food Services.

It was now a flaming volcano of fire and ash.

"Left a little C-4 of my own back there," Dane said. "Only, mine had a detonator."

Fire engines roared by. Three, four, five. It wouldn't be enough. It would never be enough.

And all I could think about as I watched the flames was all those explosives leveling University of Phoenix Stadium during the Super Bowl.

"That was almost us," Aaliyah said. "After those terrorists killed us, they would have blown it up to cover their tracks."

"Yeah. The *small army of terrorists*, if you'll remember," Jimmy said from the front seat. "You know what this means?"

"We just saved a hundred thousand people?" I said.

"No," Jimmy said. He turned to look at us, the bright yellow and orange flames of the burning warehouse silhouetting him. "It means one of us ratted out the team to the terrorists. One of us is a *traitor*."

CHAPTER SIXTY-TWO

"DON'T BE RIDICULOUS," AALIYAH SAID. "NOBODY IN this van is a traitor."

"Oh no?" Jimmy shot back. "Then tell me why exactly there was a *strike team* waiting on us back there."

We were on the move again, speeding away from the explosion. We couldn't stop, not even to argue. Not until we were far, far away from Nashville and the swarm of government agents that were about to descend on the Kendall Food Services distribution center. Jimmy was driving, and the rest of us sat in the back, on the benches.

"They were guarding the C-4," Aaliyah said. "They were there in case somebody like us *did* come along, that's all."

Dane shook his head. "Jimmy's right. There were too many of them. You don't leave twelve armed and armored terrorists in a warehouse to guard hidden boxes of C-4. They would be easier to spot than the explosives."

"And they were lying in wait for us," Jimmy said. "Because they *knew*. I'm telling you, man, they knew we were coming."

Jimmy's opinion I could discount, but not Dane's. I looked at him, but he just sat there like a statue.

"And just which one of us do you think told them?" Aaliyah said.

"Oh, I don't know," Jimmy said. "How about the ex–Green Beret who got drummed out of the service on an other-than-honorable discharge and still holds a grudge?"

Other-than-honorable discharge? Dane? I knew that if you retired from the military after your full tour of duty with a good or excellent rating, you got an honorable discharge. If you weren't around long enough and had to leave for something like medical reasons, you got a general discharge. That was still fine. But to get an "other-than-honorable conditions" discharge meant you did something wrong and got kicked out of the army. Sometimes something really wrong. Like fighting, or doing drugs, or stealing. It was worse than never joining the military in the first place. It was a black mark on your life you never got rid of. You were stripped of your rank, you lost all your veteran's benefits, and it made it way harder to get a job.

Had that really happened to Dane? Had he done something bad and been thrown out of the army? I couldn't believe it. Dane was a rock.

But if he was so good, why wasn't he a Green Beret anymore?

"That's right," Jimmy said. "You think I didn't hack into all your files before I took this gig? I know everybody's dirty little secrets."

The air in the van felt like it had just gotten ten degrees colder. Dane turned his head as slow as an owl watching a mouse crawl by.

"Don't," he told Jimmy.

"What about *you*?" Aaliyah said to Jimmy. "You're the one of us who's only in this for the money."

"Yeah," Jimmy said. "Which begs the question: why are *you* really in it? That was a very touching story you told back there about loving America and Justin Timberlake." Jimmy looked at me in the rearview mirror. "What Aaliyah neglected to mention is that she's Jordanian. That's why she can only be an independent contractor for the CIA. She's not an American citizen. She grew up in the Middle East. She's an Arab princess."

"I am *not* a princess," Aaliyah said. "Yes, I am *distantly* related to the Jordanian royal family. *Very* distantly. But I'm doing this for exactly the reasons I told Kamran. I'm doing it to make the world better."

"Just because she's from the Middle East doesn't mean anything," I said, bristling. "My mom's from Iran. You think that makes me a traitor, too?"

"I don't know," Jimmy said. "For all we know, your brother's jerking us all around and you're in on it with him, like those brothers up in Boston."

I scrambled for the front seat. To do what, I didn't know. Punch him, hurt him, strangle him. I was blind with rage. I thought of my classmates, the people in my neighborhood, the media—right at that moment Jimmy was a stand-in for everybody who'd ever called me a name or thought I was a terrorist just because I was Persian. If I'd done anything to Jimmy, he would have lost control of the van and we'd all have been killed, but Dane held me back.

Jimmy's phone beeped in the cup holder beside him. He snatched it up angrily to read a text.

"It's Mickey," he said. "He wants to talk."

"Pull over somewhere," Dane said. I still struggled in his arms, but we both knew I wasn't going anywhere. "Make the call," he told Jimmy.

CHAPTER SIXTY-THREE

WE ALL STOOD APART FROM EACH OTHER ON THE quiet dirt road, each of us breathing out hot jets of air in the cold Tennessee night while Jimmy established the secure connection to Mickey on the hood of the van.

I didn't have a coat, so I kept my arms wrapped tight around myself. The cold helped calm me down a little, but I was still mad. I knew I wasn't a traitor. But what about Aaliyah? I hated myself for even wondering. But *had* she really committed to fighting the good fight after September 11, or had the way the other students treated her turned her against them and their country? The way the DHS said that same prejudice had turned Darius into a terrorist?

And Dane—what had he done to get an other-than-honorable discharge from the US Army?

"I got him," Jimmy said at last.

We stood close to one another so Mickey could see us on the computer, but not too close.

"We're getting reports of a massive explosion just outside Nashville," Mickey said. "A ten-alarm fire, by all accounts. I take it you found something?"

Dane told him all about the explosives—and the force that had been there to intercept us.

Mickey whistled. "Sounds like a near thing you got out of there alive, then," he said. "So it's taken care of?"

"It's taken care of," said Dane.

"Then good work, all of you. It would seem Darius had one last good clue for us—and that the Women's World Cup was just a diversion after all. You saved a lot of lives today."

We ought to be celebrating that, I knew. Everything that we'd done, from the escape in DC to the thundering explosion at the warehouse, had all been worth it. We were heroes, even if nobody ever knew it. But none of us felt like celebrating then. Not with the lingering suspicion that one of us had sold the others out.

"There's only one thing left to do now," Mickey said. "Go after Darius."

"Now that their big double-secret plan is busted, they don't need him anymore," I said, my stomach sinking. "What if they kill him before we get there?"

"It's a possibility," Mickey said. "I'm sorry, Kamran, but that's the truth of it. We just have to hope Ansari still sees some use for him. I doubt the Lion will sacrifice such a useful pawn so easily. But he may do it anyway. You should be prepared for either eventuality."

I nodded, but there was no way I was going to come to grips with the idea of Darius being dead. Not now, and not ever. There were three days until the Super Bowl. Three days until Haydar Ansari knew for sure that his plans had been foiled, if he didn't know already. Three days until Darius Smith was expendable.

We had to find my brother before then.

Mickey told us to call again when we got to Arizona, and said his good-byes.

"You'll notice he didn't say anything about the size of the

strike force that intercepted us at the warehouse," Jimmy said when the call was finished.

"So what?" I said.

"So there was only one other person who knew we were going to be at that warehouse tonight and could have tipped off the bad guys," Jimmy said. *"Mickey Hagan."*

CHAPTER SIXTY-FOUR

MICKEY? THE TRAITOR? IT MADE NO SENSE. WHY would he be in contact with Haydar Ansari? Why would he betray us? The man I knew wouldn't do that. But of course I'd only known Mickey for a couple of months. Yes, he'd arranged for me to break out of the DHS facility, but what if he had some other reason for doing it? What if this was all some elaborate setup to make it look like Darius and I had been in on it all along?

I frowned as I climbed back into the van. Maybe Mickey and Ansari being in contact *did* make sense. Who better for a terrorist to have on his side than someone inside the halls of the DHS and the CIA, someone whom nobody listened to, but who heard everything? Somebody to warn him when the authorities were getting too close. Was that how Haydar Ansari had stayed two steps ahead of the United States at every turn? When it came right down to it, I realized, I didn't know anything about Mickey Hagan. Not really. Even the story about his brother might have been made up.

For all I knew, he could be sending me, Jimmy, Aaliyah, Dane, all of us, into a trap.

We rode together in the van, each of us alone with our thoughts. Aaliyah drove and Jimmy sat up front beside her. Dane and I eventually went to sleep. In the morning, Aaliyah and Jimmy slept while Dane drove and I sat beside him. Never, I noticed, did three of us sleep while only one of us was awake. I guess we were all too suspicious of each other now. And I hated that.

Jimmy saw my unhappiness on my face when we traded places in Oklahoma City. "All part of the game, kid," he said with a humorless smile.

CHAPTER SIXTY-FIVE

TWENTY-FOUR HOURS LATER, WE STOPPED AT A GAS station just outside Albuquerque and stretched our legs. We'd driven all night and into the next afternoon. It was less than two days until the Super Bowl, and we were seven hours away from Phoenix by major roads. But we weren't taking major roads. It was going to take us at least another eleven hours, Jimmy figured, taking the back roads that kept us away from the authorities.

Eleven hours until we could begin our hunt for Darius.

I was restless. I wanted to be there already. Dane must have noticed, because he offered to work with me on some standing self-defense moves while Jimmy and Aaliyah were inside buying food. He showed me the most vulnerable parts of the body to attack, and we practiced attacking each other in the dusty, late-afternoon glow of New Mexico.

Dane blocked a kick at his knees, and I paused, catching my breath.

"I couldn't take that gun from that guy in the warehouse," I said.

"No," Dane said. "I told you. It's hard to do it on somebody stronger than you."

"He would have killed me," I said, blocking one of Dane's slow-motion punches.

"You bought yourself time," he said.

"Enough time for you to save me," I said. "Thank you."

Dane shrugged. "Sometimes it's all about who's got your back." He blocked another of my attacks. Even though I did mine at full strength and full speed—at Dane's insistence—he always stopped me.

"What about you, Kamran?" Dane asked. "You got my back?"

"Of course," I said.

"So you weren't the one who ratted us out?" Dane asked.

I dropped my fists. "Seriously? *Seriously?*"

"Your mom is Iranian. Maybe she raised you and your brother to be terrorists."

I couldn't believe what I was hearing, from Dane of all people. "My mom raised us to love America," I spat, growing angry. Dane threw a punch, and I batted it away. "Darius and I have a *code*. A code of *honor.*"

"This code have anything to do with becoming a martyr?"

"No!" I said. "It's about being strong, and brave, and helping people."

"Helping people die at the hands of your terrorist buddies?" Dane said.

I threw myself at him, fist pulled back to punch him in the face. Before I could even take a swing, he spun me around, twisted one arm behind my back, and used his other arm to put me in a choke hold. I fought uselessly to get free as he forced me to the ground.

"Stop. Calm down," he said quietly in my ear. "*Kamran,* listen to me. I don't believe you or your brother are terrorists, and I know you didn't sell us out back there."

I stopped struggling. "But—then why—?"

"I've seen you lose your cool before, and I wanted to show you what it gets you. You just made some bad decisions. Really bad decisions. Because you let your anger blind you. Do you see that?"

I was on my knees, arm pinned painfully back, with an ex–Green Beret about to strangle me. I could see that I had maybe made some bad decisions right then.

I nodded, and Dane let me go and helped me to my feet.

"You're angry," Dane said. "Anger can be good. It can keep you focused. Alive. If you control it. When it controls you, you're dead. Trust me, I know." He paused, and I saw something more in his usually stonelike face. Was it sadness? Regret?

"What were you angry about?" I asked. "Does it have something to with your other-than-honorable discharge?"

I regretted it almost as soon as I'd said it. Dane's eyes flashed like he might put me back in that headlock and actually choke me, but then the fire went away and he was cool, collected Dane again.

"It has everything to do with my other-than-honorable discharge," he said, and then he told me why.

CHAPTER SIXTY-SIX

"YOU KNOW ANYTHING ABOUT PTSD?" DANE ASKED.

I nodded. You couldn't be a part of a military family without knowing about it. PTSD stood for post-traumatic stress disorder. People who'd been in really scary situations got it. Soldiers who'd seen active duty especially. You might get it even if you weren't physically hurt yourself—just seeing other people get all shot up and blown up could do it. Once you had PTSD, any kind of stressful situation could set you off. Maybe you'd have flashbacks, or nightmares. Maybe you'd lose the ability to connect with people, or feel depressed. Or maybe you'd get angry real easily and lash out at people for no reason. Hurt people.

"Got it good after the Battle of Khafji," Dane said. "The army, they teach you to suck it up. Deal with stuff on your own. Soldiers generally aren't 'talk it out' kind of guys, you know? So when I started to get the shakes, when I started to jump at every explosion, when I started to get angry at every little thing, I didn't tell anybody about it. I chose to self-medicate. With pills. I knew how to find the right drugs in the med tent."

"They caught you stealing medicine," I said.

Dane shook his head. "I got away with it. Then one day we were on patrol, and I was so out of it from the meds I was on that I missed something. Buddy of mine almost got killed. Didn't, but almost. Because I wasn't *there*, you know? I was there, but I wasn't there in the head. I didn't have my buddy's back."

"Sometimes it's all about who's got your back," I said, repeating Dane's words back to him.

"Exactly. And out there, it was life and death, every minute of every day. I didn't care if I flushed my own life down the toilet, but I couldn't be a danger to my team. 'I will not fail those with whom I serve.' It's part of the Special Forces Creed. I couldn't let that one slide. So I turned myself in."

Dane sat on a bench, his arms on his knees.

"For my honesty, I was given an other-than-honorable discharge—just one step above dishonorable discharge. Cut loose. Sent home—wherever that is for a soldier with no family. I took up residence on a bar stool in a dive bar in Fayetteville, North Carolina, and paid a year's rent, one drink at a time. That's where Mick found me."

"Mickey Hagan?"

"He needed a man to do a job for him. Told me I was that man. But I had to get cleaned up first. He got me into rehab. Therapy. He was the only one to ever give me a second chance. I thought my life was over at twenty-four, but Mick changed all that. I mean, every day is still a challenge. I still get jumpy. Tense. Angry sometimes. But I control it; it doesn't control me." Dane paused. "So tell me about this code you and your brother have. This Code of Honor."

I shrugged. "It's just something we made up when we were kids."

Dane looked off into the distance. "Jimmy calls all this a game. The spy business. It's a sick game, if it is one. You play long enough, every part of you that ain't bolted down gets stripped away. Friends, family, ideals—they come loose. They fly away, and one day you look down and you're all that's left. You and whatever code you live by. Call it a code of ethics or code of honor or whatever. It's who you are inside. It's how you live your life. How you, Kamran Smith, are gonna deal with everything the game throws at you today, tomorrow, and the rest of your life. If you really do have a code, you hang on to it. You lock it up tight, deep inside, and you live by it. 'Cause in the end, it's all you're really ever going to have."

CHAPTER SIXTY-SEVEN

A BLUE ROAD SIGN SAID "THE GRAND CANYON STATE Welcomes You" as we crossed the border from New Mexico. On the sign were the star and sunburst of the Arizona state flag, the yellow and orange colors matching the sky as the sun rose behind us.

It was cool in the van, but not cold—the temperature was supposed to hit seventy-five degrees today. Late January in Arizona. I was glad to be back. The warmer weather as we'd driven west made me feel like I was coming out of hibernation. I was ready to wake up.

It took us another four hours to get to Apache Junction, on the outskirts of Phoenix, but we used the time to talk strategy.

"Show 'em the map," Dane said from the driver's seat.

Jimmy called up a detailed 3-D map of the Tonto National Forest on his laptop.

"Here's the mountain you think you saw in the video," Jimmy said.

"I *know* I saw," I corrected him. "Superstition Mountain."

"All right, all right," Jimmy said, not wanting a fight. "I took still shots from the video and ran them through a graphic plotter." On the screen, the image of the silhouetted mountain I'd seen in the video appeared, and then a 3-D map materialized on top of it, spun, reoriented itself on the horizon line, and settled in along the same contours of the shadowy mountain. "If this is the same mountain, this is where it was seen from." The map swept down and away from us, the mountain growing smaller but more defined in the background, and there was a red pin stuck in the map in a small valley in the foothills. Jimmy clicked a button, and a pie-shaped wedge of a lighter color stretched out from the mountain to the foreground, encompassing the little red pin. "Best I can calculate based on the angle and location of that mountain compared to the sun," he said, "that video was shot somewhere in this region. I figure their camp can't be too far away."

"There are caves in these mountains," I said. "That's where I'd be hiding, if it were me."

"Right," Jimmy said. "*If* it were you."

He was back to the traitor business again, like I was leading them into a trap. I was about to tell him, *again*, that I wasn't the one to betray us, but Dane interrupted.

"Enough, Jimmy. We need to get up into those mountains, but we can't take the van. There are no roads. Not near enough."

"We can go on horseback," I said. "It's easiest that way. I know where we can rent some."

I didn't take them to the horse ranch where my mom works. *Worked.* They would recognize me there. But there was another horse ranch I knew about a few miles away. I waited in the van with Jimmy while Dane and Aaliyah went inside to arrange our ride.

"I'm not a traitor," I told Jimmy. He was packing electronic equipment into a backpack to take with him. "I didn't betray us. I wouldn't do that."

"So you say," Jimmy said.

I felt myself getting mad again. "*I wouldn't.*"

"Look, kid," Jimmy said. "For what it's worth, I don't think it's you. But somebody ratted us out back there in Nashville, and I know it wasn't me. That doesn't leave a whole lot of suspects."

No, I thought. *It leaves Dane and Aaliyah. And Mickey.*

"Just watch your back out there, is all I'm saying," Jimmy told me. He zipped up his backpack as Dane opened the sliding door.

"We're good to go," Dane said. "Tell Mickey we're going in."

"You sure I should?" Jimmy said.

Dane gave him a tired look. "Do it," he said. "Then saddle up, cowboys. It's time to ride."

CHAPTER SIXTY-EIGHT

"WOW. I THINK I CAN SEE MY HOUSE FROM HERE," I said.

We were crouching low on a mesa that had a commanding view of the canyons all around. The sky was high and cloudless and azure blue, and the desert air felt warm and dry on my skin. Saguaro cacti, the kind with the tall treelike trunks and arms that curved up like a ref signaling a touchdown, dotted the rocky foothills of the Superstition Mountains ahead of us. In the other direction, through the afternoon haze, we could see the urban sprawl of Phoenix.

And right beside us, tied up and gagged among the desert sand verbena the horses were nibbling on, lay the guard Dane had taken out.

The guard who'd been waiting to shoot us with a sniper rifle as we trotted, on horseback, along the trail into the canyon. Dane had caught the hint of a boot print and told us to wait in one of the little caves that littered the park while he investigated.

Aaliyah whistled now as she checked out the sniper's gun. "IDF M24 SWS with a Leupold scope and bipod," she said.

"You know your guns," said Dane.

"You mean that guy could have shot us coming up over that ridge?" Jimmy said.

"If he was any good he could have shot us *two* ridges ago. This thing's got a range of eight hundred meters," Dane said.

My stomach twisted into a knot. I could have been killed before I even knew what hit me. Dane had saved my life. Saved all our lives. Again. But the sniper even being here meant there was a good chance that Darius and Haydar Ansari might really be hiding out somewhere in the park.

The rest of the guard's gear sat on a dusty woven blanket spread out on top of the ridge—a pair of binoculars, a canteen, a walkie-talkie, and two long duffel bags.

Aaliyah unzipped one of the bags. "Ooh. He's got an Israeli-made nine-millimeter submachine gun," Aaliyah said, pulling out the gun. It was a small black Uzi, the kind of compact, single-hand machine gun bad guys are always using in movies and on TV. "There's more ammo in here, too," Aaliyah said.

"Take it and the gun both," Dane said. He looked down at the unconscious sniper. Dane had tied a wound-up bandana around the man's mouth so he couldn't yell when he came to. "We won't have much time now," Dane said. "When he doesn't report in soon, they'll know something's wrong."

"Why don't we ask him where they are?" I asked.

We had just a day and a half until the Super Bowl. I knew the deadline didn't mean much—Haydar Ansari had no doubt already heard that we'd uncovered his plot to ship explosives to Phoenix in food trucks. He'd probably long since decided what to do with Darius. But to me, the Super Bowl marked a sort of last-gasp moment. The last chance to save Darius before the Lion devoured him. We didn't have any time to waste wandering around the national forest, hoping we'd find some hidden cave.

"He won't talk," Jimmy said, nudging the unconscious guy with the toe of his sneaker. "If he does, he'll just give us the runaround."

Dane turned the long sniper rifle around and set it on the ground pointing the other way. He stretched out behind it, sighting through the scope.

"We don't need to ask him," he said. He rolled out of the way for Aaliyah to take a look. "Cave. Far side of the next canyon."

Jimmy snatched up the binoculars to look, then handed them to me. The cave was a dark slit like a grimacing mouth in the base of the mesa. There were no people in sight, but with a little focus I could make out tire tracks in the dirt around it. ATV tracks.

I'd been right all along. Haydar Ansari was in America. Here in my own backyard. And if Darius was still alive, he was right there inside that cave with him.

CHAPTER SIXTY-NINE

AALIYAH SWUNG THE UZI AROUND AT THE SOUND OF footsteps, but it was only Dane. He slid down behind the clump of verbena where we were hiding. It was getting on toward late afternoon, but there still hadn't been any signs of life from the slitlike entrance to the terrorists' cave.

"I took care of the rest of the snipers," he whispered.

"How many more were there?" Aaliyah asked.

"Three. Two more watching away, but one watching the cave."

If we had just gone right for the entrance, the sniper could have taken us out before we'd ever set foot inside.

"Are you sure there aren't more?" I asked.

"No," Dane said.

"Very reassuring," Jimmy said.

"There's very little in this life anyone can really be sure of," Dane said.

Like whether or not Dane was a traitor? Or Jimmy? Or Aaliyah? Or Mickey? Had the same person tipped the terrorists off that we were about to storm their cave?

Dane handed me a pistol, and Jimmy an Uzi like Aaliyah's. Taken, no doubt, from the other snipers he'd subdued. Dane kept another small machine gun for himself. Jimmy looked impressed at his new firepower, sliding the bolt back and letting it go with a practiced click. I felt distinctly inexperienced and outclassed holding my little handgun.

"You tell Mick we're going in?" Dane asked Jimmy.

"Message sent," Jimmy confirmed.

"All right. Stay close to the ATV tracks and the footpaths," Dane told us. "They might have mined the other approaches."

Mines? As if carrying a gun wasn't scary enough. Now I'd be sweating out every step I took. Unless the plan was to leave me out here, which I was *not* going to let happen.

"I'm going with you," I told Dane. "I won't let you leave me behind."

"Never considered it," Dane said. "There's only four of us, and who knows how many of them. We need every hand on deck. And I'll want you there when we find your brother."

I was stunned. I had expected to have to argue. But no argument was necessary: I was in.

And now that I was in, I was scared all over again.

"There will probably be guards just inside the cave," Aaliyah said. She sketched a rough picture of the cave opening in the orange dirt and marked Xs where the guards would be hiding. "Here, in the shadows. You won't see them before they see you."

"Want to bet?" Dane said. "Stay here, *everybody*," he added, I supposed for my benefit. "I'll signal when I've taken out the guards."

Dane slithered off through the scrub brush, and I stared at the gun in my hands, thinking about what was about to happen. My heart thumped wildly in my chest.

Aaliyah put a hand on my shoulder. "You're going to be all right, Kamran. Just stay behind Dane and follow his lead."

"Only don't shoot him from behind," Jimmy said. "Or us."

I closed my eyes. I did *not* want to accidentally shoot Dane, Jimmy, or Aaliyah. And if my experience in the DHS mail room was any indication, I was more likely to hit one of them than a terrorist if I pulled the trigger. Watch my back, watch my step, watch out for friendly fire—I was going to be so busy watching out for things I would be frozen stiff.

Aaliyah could see my hesitation. "Kamran, you need to answer something for yourself right now," she said. "Could you shoot him if you have to?"

"Shoot who?" I asked.

"Your brother, Darius," she said.

I was shocked. "Shoot Darius? No. Of course not. I won't have to. He's not a traitor."

Aaliyah and Jimmy exchanged a look. Before we could say anything more, Danc whistled from below. The signal. The guards were taken care of. It was time to go into the cave.

CHAPTER SEVENTY

THE TWO SENTRIES AALIYAH HAD PREDICTED would be guarding the entrance were unconscious, and Dane was just finishing hog-tying them with plastic cables. He nodded toward a little camera up on the cave wall, and Jimmy ran over with his computer. Dane stood and held out his hands, and Aaliyah tossed him the duffel bag filled with explosives she'd brought along when we left the van. They worked quickly and quietly like a well-designed play from scrimmage, weaving in and out and around each other.

I stood on the sidelines, watching. Simultaneously hoping and dreading that the coach would put me in the game.

There were three four-wheeled ATVs just inside the cave entrance, in the shadows where they couldn't be seen from outside. Dane taped the duffel bag full of explosives onto the handlebars of the ATV with duct tape and pointed it straight back into the cave. Then he duct-taped the throttle so that when he turned the thing on, it would shoot forward.

"Cameras looped," Jimmy whispered. He fished in the backpack he'd brought with him and handed out night-vision goggles. We could still see here in the mouth of the cave, where the light filtered in, but soon we'd be deep in the cave, and the plan was to knock out their lights so we'd have the upper hand. I pulled on the night-vision goggles but kept them up on my forehead.

"Lights out in three, two, one—" Jimmy said. He pushed a button on a handheld controller, and the lights just beyond the cave entrance shorted out. Someone shouted in alarm farther in the cave. Dane started the ATV and threw it into gear. The front end came up off the ground in a wheelie and almost flipped backward, but it bounced back down and zoomed off into the darkness of the cave.

"*Wait*," I said. "What about Darius—?"

"Down," Dane told us.

I hit the rocky floor of the cave as the explosives went off. People screamed, and rock and dust fell from the ceiling. I struggled to pick myself up, still shaking from the blast. Darius! What if the blast had killed him?

"He'll be deeper inside the cave," Aaliyah told me.

Dane was already on his feet and disappearing into the darkness. Gunshots rang out in the darkness. More screams. Aaliyah flipped down her night-vision goggles and ran in after him, her Uzi at the ready.

I stared at the darkness, afraid to go in. Some soldier I was turning out to be! I tried to think of our Code of Honor.

Be the strongest of the strong, I told myself. *Be the bravest of the brave.*

More gunshots rang out—an automatic rifle—and I flinched.

Jimmy clapped me on the shoulder, scaring the bejeezus out of me.

"You only live once, right?" he said, pulling me in with him.

Yeah, I thought. *That's what I'm worried about.*

CHAPTER SEVENTY-ONE

WE PASSED THE SMOKING, BURNING REMAINS OF the ATV, stepping over dead bodies. None of them were Dane or Aaliyah, I was relieved to see. Or Darius.

We found Dane and Aaliyah a little farther in, hunkered down behind a barricade of crates. Machine-gun fire tore into the wooden boxes, showering the cave with splinters.

"The cave turns left just beyond here," Dane told us over the gunfire. "That's where they're shooting from. Two of them. We need to move on them before reinforcements get here."

"Al-Qaeda likes to leave bolt-holes in corners," Aaliyah told us. "That way one man can hide there with a good view in both directions. I'll bet there's a bolt-hole somewhere between here and there."

Dane nodded. "Aaliyah and I will go in. Jimmy, you and Kamran hold back and watch for somebody to come in behind us."

I gripped the butt of my gun. It was slick and sweaty in my hands.

Dane pulled a grenade from the utility belt he wore, pulled the pin, and chucked it. Seconds later the cave resounded with a thudding *POOM*, and the area was filled with smoke. Even with the night-vision goggles on, it was impossible to see what was just ahead of us.

Dane charged ahead anyway, Uzi firing. Aaliyah ran after him. Jimmy stood, and I did, too, trying to see through the smoke.

"I don't see anybody," I said.

"I don't see any*thing*," Jimmy said.

The night-vision goggles turned everything green, and the smoke was a big green-black blob floating in the air. It might as well have been another wall for all we could see through it.

I thought I heard the scrape of metal on metal, like a heavy door being opened.

Or a bolt being thrown.

"Somebody's coming out!" I said.

"Where? Where?"

"I don't know. I can hear it, but I can't see it!"

Jimmy swore under his breath, and then he surprised me. He ran into the wall of smoke and disappeared.

Seconds passed, and then a single gunshot rang out.

I raised my gun, my hands shaking. The black smoke still clouded my night-vision goggles. "Jimmy?" I called. "*Jimmy?*"

No answer. Had he killed the man in the bolt-hole, or had the terrorist killed him? If Jimmy was dead, the terrorist would be sneaking up behind Dane and Aaliyah. He would shoot them from behind.

Be the strongest of the strong. Be the bravest of the brave, I reminded myself.

Help the helpless.

Dane and Aaliyah weren't exactly helpless, but they didn't know what was coming, and that was close enough. I took a deep breath and stepped out from behind the shattered crates.

I was going to have to go into the darkness alone.

CHAPTER SEVENTY-TWO

DARKNESS SWIRLED AROUND ME AS I INCHED MY way farther into the cave. I sucked in a big lungful of smoke and it burned my nose and throat. I swallowed hard, trying not to cough and give myself away, and reminded myself to keep my mouth closed from now on.

Eyes watering inside my night-vision goggles, I slid my feet forward like I was crossing a room in the dark, trying not to whack my shins on the furniture. But it wasn't really furniture I was worried about. Any second now, I expected a terrorist to come screaming out of the darkness and attack me. I was so scared I could barely summon the courage to keep moving, but I just kept repeating my Code of Honor, like a mantra.

Be the strongest of the strong.

Be the bravest of the brave.

Help the helpless.

Always tell the truth.

The truth was, all I wanted to do was turn and run back out of the cave, to the safety and security of daylight. I didn't want to get shot, and I didn't want to die. Watching soldiers do this in movies was always cool. You always saw the bad guys coming, and when the heroes shot the bad guys, they dropped like bowling pins. This was messy. Scary. *Dark.*

I inched forward. The smoke was clearing. The cave began to take shape again, and I saw a body sprawled out on the floor. I hurried toward it, afraid it was Jimmy, but it was a terrorist, wearing all-black body armor like the team back at the warehouse.

I heard a grunt and I hurried on, my fear replaced by the urgent need to help. *Be loyal*, I told myself. *Never give up.*

Then I saw Jimmy. He was wrestling with a second man in black, trying to keep the terrorist from lowering his gun enough to shoot him. Jimmy's gun was on the ground beside him.

"Little . . . help?" Jimmy called.

I raised my pistol to shoot the terrorist, but they were struggling so much I was afraid if I pulled the trigger I'd hit Jimmy. Visions of missing the bright red fire extinguisher filled my head.

I ran at the man instead and brought the butt of the gun down on his head. In the movies, that always sent bad guys crashing to the ground. But this wasn't a movie. The butt of my gun bounced right off the helmet he wore, and he didn't go down. He did turn, though, surprised, and Jimmy was able to wrench the man's rifle away. The terrorist kneed Jimmy in the stomach and Jimmy went down, moaning in pain.

The terrorist spun on me, and I raised my gun to shoot. But I didn't. Couldn't. I took a step back, and the terrorist understood at once. He lunged for me, grabbing the gun. We struggled, and the gun went flying. I kicked him in the shin, trying to remember what Dane had taught me. The terrorist ripped my night-vision goggles away. The sudden change from green light to no light was disorienting, and my punch at his neck missed entirely. He hit me in the chest and I staggered back, slamming into the rock wall. I put my hands up, expecting another blow, but all that came was the sound of him choking. As my eyes adjusted, I saw a big shape behind him. *Dane.* The ex–Green Beret had his arm around the terrorist's neck, and as my attacker passed out, Dane lowered him to the floor.

Dane picked up my fallen pistol and handed it back to me.

"You know, at some point you're actually going to have to shoot somebody with that thing," he told me.

A shot exploded right behind us, making even Dane flinch, and another terrorist fell face-first to the floor. He'd been sneaking up on Dane with a knife.

Jimmy was still on the floor, his Uzi in his hand. "You're welcome," Jimmy said.

Dane gave Jimmy his hand to help him up. "Come on. We found a locked door. We think Darius is inside."

Darius! My fear and disorientation were immediately replaced with a desperate hope.

Aaliyah stood against the wall beside the door, her Uzi at the ready in case anyone came at her out of the darkness. She tensed as we came running around the corner, swinging her weapon up at us, but she quickly lowered it when she saw who it was.

"Jimmy, the door," Dane said.

The hacker dropped to a knee in front of the metal door, pulled a lockpick set out of his backpack, and went to work. While he worked, we examined the room. Half a dozen bodies littered the floor, and two folding tables along a side wall held bullet-ridden laptops and TV monitors. Along another wall were stacked plastic bins and wooden crates.

"Food, water, guns, gear," Aaliyah said, going through them. "But no explosives."

"Maybe that's what's behind this door, not Darius," Jimmy said. Something in the door clicked, and Jimmy stood back.

We were about to find out.

CHAPTER SEVENTY-THREE

"JIMMY, KAMRAN, BEHIND THE DOOR. AALIYAH, take the wall," Dane said. He clearly meant to be the one to stand in the doorway and face whatever was behind there first. None of us argued with him. When everyone was in position, he nodded to Jimmy.

Jimmy threw open the door and I ducked, waiting for the bullets to fly. But there was nothing.

"Hands on your head!" Dane yelled into the room. "Hands on your head, and don't move."

Dane went inside, his weapon held high, at eye level.

"Kamran," Dane called. "You better get in here."

My heart stopped.

I came around the door and hurried inside.

The small rock-walled room was lit by a hanging kerosene lamp. Standing right below it, his back to a small wooden table, his hands on his head, was my brother, Darius.

Darius looked like he had in the videos, but it still blew my mind to see him like this in real life. Completely different from the Darius I had grown up with. He was still young and strong, but he was scrawnier. Dirtier. He had a woolly black beard that swallowed his face, and his hair was long and stringy. He looked like a crazy old hermit.

No, I realized. *He looks like Rostam. He looks like the drawings of the ancient Persian hero in our storybooks!*

I felt a lump in my throat.

Darius lowered his arms. "Kamran?" he said, his voice coming out in a croak.

"Darius!" I said. I didn't think. I just threw myself at my brother. We hugged. He was *alive.* Darius was alive, and here. I had really found him.

Darius held me at arm's length to look at me, tears in his eyes. "Kamran, what are you doing here?"

"I came to rescue you!" I looked around at Dane and Jimmy, who'd followed me into the room. Aaliyah must have still been outside. "We all did!"

Darius shook his head. "You shouldn't have come, Kamran. I'm so sorry."

"Why?" I said.

Before I could even blink, Darius had the gun out of my hand and pointed it at me.

CHAPTER SEVENTY-FOUR

I STARED STUPIDLY DOWN THE BARREL OF THE GUN.
"Darius, what are you doing?" I said.

"Put the gun down!" Dane yelled, pointing his weapon at my brother. "Put it down!"

Darius spun me around and pulled me close, holding the cold gun to my head. I couldn't believe what was happening. No. *No!* My brother was not a terrorist!

Suddenly everybody in the room was screaming and pointing guns at each other.

"Put the gun down!"

"Step away from Kamran!"

"Get back!"

"Let him go!"

"I'll do it!"

Dane inched forward, and Darius pushed the gun harder into the side of my head.

"No! Don't! Stop!" I yelled.

A gun fired and I flinched, terrified suddenly that Dane had shot Darius. But Darius was still beside me, holding the gun against my head.

Dane was the one who slumped to the floor, blood running from a hole in his forehead.

"*No!*" I screamed. I tried to tear myself away from Darius, but he held me tight.

I didn't understand. Darius hadn't shot him. So who had? *Jimmy?*

No. Standing in the doorway was a woman wearing a black full-body robe, with only her eyes showing. She had a pistol in her hand, pointed at Dane's body. *She* was the one who'd shot him.

A woman who was the same size and build as Aaliyah.

No. No, it couldn't be! Was it her? Was Aaliyah the traitor after all? Aaliyah hadn't come into the room with us, and she wasn't here now, unless she was the woman underneath the robe.

More masked terrorists came into the room and took Jimmy's gun away from him. I jumped as the woman shot Dane again and again in the back to make sure he was dead.

"Aaliyah?" I said through my tears. I hadn't even realized I was crying. "Aaliyah, is that you?"

The woman pointed her pistol at me. "You were expecting the Lion, perhaps? Haydar Ansari?" she said. It wasn't Aaliyah's voice, I realized at once, relieved. But it still was familiar. I knew I'd heard it somewhere before, but it was masked by the veil she wore. I tried to keep her talking to hear more.

"Where is he?" I asked.

"Haydar Ansari is dead," she told me. "You killed him."

"Me? I—I didn't kill anybody," I said. I hadn't even fired my pistol.

"Your government did," the woman said darkly. "Three years ago in a drone strike."

I remembered now—back in the motel room, Aaliyah had said the government was sure they'd killed Ansari in a drone strike. I guess they really had. Somebody had just been pretending to be him ever since then, plotting terrorist strikes against the United States in his name.

"The United States government killed Haydar Ansari, which means *you* did it," the woman said. "How does your constitution begin? 'We the people'? As far as I am concerned, any man, woman, or child who calls themselves 'American' is responsible for what their government does. Which means every one of you killed him."

I kept my eyes on her, trying to figure out who was under the robe and veil. Her voice was *so familiar*, but I couldn't quite place it. Couldn't be sure. How could I be sure of anything when Darius held a gun to my head?

My brother, Darius.

Darius the terrorist.

I struggled in Darius's grip, but he held me tight.

"But why pretend to be Haydar Ansari if he's dead?" I asked the woman. "Why do any of this unless—" Then I remembered something from Ansari's file. The wife he'd had in Syria. What if she hadn't hated her husband for becoming a terrorist? What if that's why she'd married him in the first place?

"Unless you're Bashira Ansari," I said. "Haydar Ansari's *wife*."

"I prefer," said Bashira Ansari, " 'the Black Widow.' "

CHAPTER SEVENTY-FIVE

THEY PUT ME IN THE LITTLE BOLT-HOLE IN THE COR-ner, the one Jimmy and I had been assigned to watch. I didn't know where they put Jimmy, or if he was still alive. I didn't see him again after Bashira Ansari killed Dane.

Dane. I couldn't believe he was gone. *Dead.* Even though a part of me ached with grief, the part of me wounded by Darius's betrayal hurt worse. I felt like there was an empty hole the size of that cave where my heart used to be. I was so shocked, so blown away by everything, that I hadn't even been able to cry. I was like one of those people you see on the side of the road after a massive car wreck, sitting there staring off into space. Distant. Detached. Disconnected.

All those interrogators back at the DHS building in Washington must have been right. About 9/11 turning Darius against his friends, his neighbors. His family. His country. About America being the big white demon, and him vowing to kill all monsters.

All these years, and I'd never really known my brother at all.

So it wasn't me and Darius against the world anymore. And now I didn't have Dane, either. Jimmy and Aaliyah were out of it, too. They were captured or dead. Our only hope was Mickey Hagan—unless he was the traitor. At this point, anything seemed possible.

Which meant it was down to me. Me and our Code of Honor. *My* Code of Honor. Because whatever code Darius was living by now, it wasn't the same as mine.

There was a light knock on the big metal door to my cell, so soft I almost didn't hear it. Then the big metal bolt on the door slid open slowly, quietly. I stood. I had no idea what was coming next, what the Black Widow had in mind for me, but whatever it was, I didn't want to take it sitting down.

The door cracked open, and Darius slid inside holding a gun.

I put my hands up in mock surrender.

"You got me," I told my brother the traitor. "You got me good, Darius."

"Cut it out, Kamran," Darius said. He took a step toward me, and that's when I struck. I did everything Dane had taught me. I stepped to the side, grabbed for the gun, pushed down and away. I used all that pent-up anger inside me, and the pistol came free in my hand.

Before Darius could react, I had it pointed back at him.

"Kamran—"

"*Don't*," I said, my voice low and mean. "We had a *code*, Darius. You and me. Be the strongest of the strong. The bravest of the brave. Help the helpless. Always tell the truth. Be loyal. Never give up." I pointed the barrel of the gun straight at Darius's forehead. My hands shook but I managed to keep the gun steady. *"Kill all monsters."*

Darius realized I was deadly serious and put his hands up.

"Kamran, don't," he said quickly. "I believe in the Code, too. I always have. I'm not a monster."

"Really?" I said. "I *believed* in you, Darius. When nobody else would. I fought for you. I came to *rescue* you. And then you betrayed me!"

The tears came now, the tears I hadn't cried alone in the dark. The world was just me and Darius now, me and the brother I'd loved. Emulated. Worshipped. The brother who'd taken my affection for him and twisted it. Used it. Crushed it under his boot. Now that Darius and I were alone together, every emotion I'd kept dammed up inside me came flooding out at once: anguish, fear, pain.

Even as I cried, I kept the gun trained on Darius.

"Could you shoot your brother if you have to?" Aaliyah had asked me.

"Of course not," I'd told her. *"I won't have to. He's not a traitor."*

But he was. I pressed the gun against Darius's forehead and curled my finger around the trigger.

CHAPTER SEVENTY-SIX

"KAMRAN, PLEASE, WAIT! IT WAS ALL A TRICK!"
Darius said. "I'm not a traitor! You have to listen to me—it was
all a trick!"

I blinked through my tears. I thought my heart had been
torn out before. But no. There was enough of it still left that
Darius's words stuck in my chest like a dagger. Why did he
keep lying to me?

"You're not a traitor?" I said through my tears. "Then explain
to me why I'm trapped here in this cell and you're not. Explain to
me why Dane, a *real* American soldier, is dead and you're not."

"Kamran, I got captured in Afghanistan," Darius said,
quick and quiet. "I was going to escape or die trying, but then
I heard them planning attacks on US targets. Big attacks. And I
realized I could do more good alive than dead. I knew if I could
just convince them I was on their side, I could get word back to
America about their plans. Word back to *you*." His eyes wid-
ened as he looked right at me. "And it worked, Kamran! You
got my messages!"

"No," I said, refusing to be tricked again. "You used me.
You used me to distract the government from the real target.
They said you'd hated America since 9/11, that you went
to Washington when you were in high school to scout for
al-Qaeda. That you joined the Rangers and went to Afghanistan
so you could join al-Qaeda and train them to attack America."

"I—no," Darius said. He looked shocked. "I was *fighting*
al-Qaeda, Kamran. I still am. God, if you knew how hard it was
for me to say those awful words on camera. To just *stand there*

while they beheaded that poor journalist. How much I wanted to jump in there and try to stop them . . . But you got my messages! You knew what I was saying! Wasn't I right about the museum? The Women's World Cup? The Super Bowl? *We saved lives,* Kamran! Together. You and me! You have to trust me now."

I was starting to doubt myself. I'd been on such a roller coaster—believing Darius, not believing him, believing him again. I was so confused, so mad.

"I can't," I told him. "I can't." I steadied the gun against his temple.

"Kamran," Darius said. "Kamran, wait. Don't. Please. I'm sorry. I know this hasn't been easy for you. But I always knew that if there was *one* person who would never stop believing in me, it was you."

Tears streamed down my face. I didn't know what to think.

"I'm sorry about grabbing you and holding you at gunpoint," Darius went on, his own eyes filling with tears. "I was afraid if I didn't, somebody else would shoot you."

I shook my head, trying to deny what he was saying. But deep down, I still wanted to believe.

"And I'm sorry about the soldier—the man who died." Darius sagged. "Kamran, you've got to believe me. I came here just now to break you out! I know where they're holding the woman you came with. We can get her, too, and then we can get out of here."

"Aaliyah? She's okay? What about Jimmy?"

"That guy with the numbers tattooed all over him? He's gone. The Black Widow gave him a suitcase full of money and he left."

My mind reeled. "She—she gave money to Jimmy?" I didn't understand. The only reason Bashira Ansari would pay Jimmy was—

Because Jimmy was the traitor.

Suddenly, it all fit: Jimmy could have sent information about us to the Black Widow the whole time on his computer, and we'd never have known it. And he hadn't been with us in the warehouse in Nashville when we were attacked. He'd come to our rescue, but he'd had to—what if he'd left us to die and we'd survived? We would have known he was the traitor, and then Mickey Hagan would have had the DHS, the CIA, and the FBI on his tail. And if we did escape, he'd want to be with us so he could keep selling our secrets to Bashira Ansari.

But if Jimmy was a traitor, why had he tried to protect Dane in the cave? Was it some shred of loyalty, after all?

I guess it was all part of the game, as Jimmy liked to say.

If Jimmy really *was* the traitor, I realized in horror, that meant he had never sent a message to Mickey Hagan letting him know we were going into the cave. The CIA had no idea where we were or what we were doing. Nobody was coming to save us.

"Kamran, we have to move," Darius said. I still had the gun pointed at him, lost in thought. "We're in Arizona, aren't we? In the Tonto National Forest somewhere. We can get out of here and go straight to the authorities. Catch these terrorists once and for all. But we have to hurry." He stepped away.

"Don't," I told him, aiming the gun again.

Darius lowered his hands in defeat. "Kamran, if you don't believe me, if you think all that stuff about me being a terrorist is true, then you should just shoot me right now," Darius said. "Otherwise I'm going to free that woman you came with and get out of here."

Darius opened the door and backed out into the corridor.

"Darius, no!" I said, and I pulled the trigger.

CHAPTER SEVENTY-SEVEN

THE PISTOL SOUNDED LIKE A THUNDERCLAP IN THE small space.

Darius flinched. The terrorist raising an automatic rifle behind him fell down dead.

Darius turned at the sound of the man hitting the ground, then looked back at me, stunned. "Kamran! I thought you'd really shot me!"

When it came down to it, I couldn't do it. Whether Darius really was a terrorist or not, I could never kill my brother. I knew I'd always have an Achilles' heel when it came to Darius, the same way Mickey Hagan had for his brother.

I stared down at the man I'd shot. He'd been raising his rifle at Darius like he was going to shoot him, so I'd shot first. *"You know, at some point you're actually going to have to shoot somebody with that thing,"* Dane had told me. And now I had. I had killed a man. When I'd applied to West Point, I figured this might happen some day far in the future. You go to West Point to become a soldier, and I knew what soldiers did. I just hadn't known what it would feel like to be responsible for another man's death. It left me hollow and cold inside, like I'd died a little, too.

Darius picked up the dead terrorist's automatic rifle. He saw me staring in shock and horror at the dead man, and he put his hand on my shoulder.

"Kamran. Kamran, you've got to put it away right now. You've got to deal with it later. Understand? I don't know how many of them are left, but somebody had to hear that gunshot. We have to move."

I nodded dully and let Darius lead me along. I still didn't know if he was a traitor or not, if he was taking me right to the Black Widow, but I didn't care anymore. My life was his to protect or throw away. I couldn't hurt my own brother, even if he could.

Darius led me farther back into the cave. I thought it was strange we never ran into another guard, but I didn't have much time to think about it. In less than a minute, Darius stopped in front of another bolt-hole.

"Here, hold this," he said, handing me his automatic rifle. I held it and the pistol awkwardly while he pulled the bolt on the door free. "I saw them put your friend in here."

Darius pulled the door open. Aaliyah sat bound and gagged in a chair in the center of the room. I felt a rush of relief. Darius hadn't been lying after all! I hurried to untie her, but Aaliyah's wide eyes and shaking head made me stop.

Automatic rifles cocked behind me, and I turned. The veiled Black Widow and five of her soldiers stood in the doorway, pointing guns right at us.

CHAPTER SEVENTY-EIGHT

ONE OF THE BLACK WIDOW'S MEN TOOK THE GUNS from me.

"Kamran, I didn't know, I swear," Darius said. He moved like he was going to try and fight his way out of the little cell, but one of the terrorists pointed a gun at his face.

"It's quite true," the Black Widow said. "Darius is more a dupe than you are. I've known all along he was faking his allegiance to us, ever since he was captured in Afghanistan. He was so eager to join our ranks. *Too* eager. We were just going to use him in a terrorist attack at first, sacrifice him to the cause. But then it became convenient to use him to feed false information to the United States government. We have you to thank for that, too, Kamran Smith."

That voice. Even muffled by her veil, I knew it from somewhere. But how? And where?

"But it wasn't false information," Darius argued, sounding firm even with the gun trained on him. "Everything was true. The museum, the Women's World Cup, the Super Bowl. And the US government stopped them all."

"Yes, they did," the Black Widow said. "And now that they are confident the threat has been neutralized—twice over—they will let down their guard. We let you hear only what we wanted you to hear. The rest is still proceeding exactly as we wish it to."

"False clues and misdirection, just like your husband was famous for," I said. "You still plan to attack, don't you?"

"But of course," said the Black Widow.

"Where? When? What are you planning?" Darius demanded.

"Don't worry, Darius. You and your brother will have a front-row seat," the Black Widow assured him. "An angry nation will have to have someone to blame. Why not two young Iranian brothers?"

The Black Widow's men pushed forward to grab us. Darius and I fought back, but there were too many of them, leaving us too little room. The butt of a rifle cracked against my skull, and everything went black.

CHAPTER SEVENTY-NINE

I WOKE UP IN THE DARK. I WAS GROGGY. MY HEAD thumped.

BOOM-BOOM-CHA. BOOM-BOOM-CHA.

I was lying on my side, my hands tied behind my back. My feet were bound, too. My eyes fluttered, threatening to close and take me back to sleep again, but the thundering wouldn't stop.

BOOM-BOOM-CHA. BOOM-BOOM-CHA.

My mouth was dry. I tried to lick my lips and found a cloth tied across my mouth. I was gagged.

Gagged and bound.

BOOM-BOOM-CHA. BOOM-BOOM-CHA.

I was gagged and bound, and I needed to know why. Where I was. I fought to stay awake, letting my panic fill me. The adrenaline pushed away the grogginess, and as my eyes adjusted to the dark, I saw that I was in a low room.

BOOM-BOOM-CHA. BOOM-BOOM-CHA.

No, room wasn't right. A box? A coffin? But that wasn't right, either. It was too wide to be either one. I felt like I was under the bleachers in the gym back at school. There was wood just above me and just below me, and inside, where I was, there were metal struts everywhere.

And plastic explosives.

BOOM-BOOM-CHA. BOOM-BOOM-CHA.

Explosives. C-4. The same stuff we'd found at the warehouse in Nashville. And lots more of it, too.

BOOM-BOOM-CHA. BOOM-BOOM-CHA.

I felt a hand grab mine, and I gave a start. I'd thought I was alone. I couldn't see behind me, so I rolled over, thudding into the plastic explosives. I winced, waiting for the boom, then remembered that it took a massive explosion to set off plastic explosives.

Either that or one tiny electric blasting cap.

BOOM-BOOM-CHA. BOOM-BOOM-CHA.

I inched back to where I was, and saw who'd reached out to touch me. It was Darius! He was bound and gagged, too, and just like me he'd rolled over to see who was behind him. His eyes were wide with panic.

Wherever we were, whatever this was, the Black Widow had made good on her promise. We were right in the middle of something that was meant to go boom. We were going to be sacrificed and blamed all at the same time.

The thundering sound shifted to a rising roar like a wave crashing into the shore. I realized for the first time that the thudding sound wasn't in my head. The floor vibrated as the sound washed over us, and something blew like a foghorn or a basketball buzzer.

Words came floating toward us, pieces of sentences. Big, deep words magnified by stadium speakers: *". . . two-minute warning! . . . halftime show!"*

Darius and I locked eyes. In the same moment, we both knew where we were.

We were at the Super Bowl.

The thing we were inside jerked. Rumbled. Started to move. And then I understood—we were inside a giant stage. One of those enormous platforms they wheel out during the Super Bowl halftime.

And *we* were the halftime show.

CHAPTER EIGHTY

DARIUS'S EXPRESSION TOLD ME THAT HE UNDER-
stood the same thing: we were underneath a stage rigged with
enough C-4 to blow a crater in the football field at University
of Phoenix Stadium, killing untold numbers of people in the
stands. And we were already moving.

I struggled against the ropes that bound me, trying to get
free. I could see Darius trying to do the same thing. But I could
barely feel my fingers, the ropes were so tight.

Music boomed through the stadium—*the new Beyoncé
song*, I thought randomly. Of all the things to think about when
you were tied up and strapped to a pile of plastic explosives.

Another horn sounded, and the halftime float rumbled to a
stop. Of course! That was just the two-minute warning. We
had two minutes of clock time—lots more if they kept running
the ball out of bounds and took a thousand commercial breaks
like they usually do during the Super Bowl. That would buy us
ten, fifteen minutes tops. But as little as two minutes if they
stayed in bounds and called no time-outs.

We had to get out of here.

I could see in Darius's eyes that he'd thought of something.
He tried to say it through the bandana tied around his mouth,
but I couldn't hear a thing over the roar of the crowd and I
couldn't see enough of his mouth move to read his lips. After a
second, he rolled over so his back was to me and started tapping
his bound hands against the floor.

Our code! Not the Code of Honor. The secret code we'd
used on the walls between our rooms at night. I watched his

hands tapping away, but I had as much trouble reading them now as I had when I'd watched him on the al-Qaeda video. I remembered Mickey rapping out the sounds as I closed my eyes. I did the same thing now. I closed my eyes and put my ear to the wooden floor of the float. *Tap. Tap-tap. Tap-tap-tap.*

I frowned. Darius was tapping out the code for pretending to go to sleep. Was he seriously suggesting we just close our eyes and wait for the inevitable? I opened my eyes and shook my head angrily at him. He gave me the tap again, then rolled back over.

Then I got it. The way we always pretended to sleep when our parents checked our rooms at night was to *roll over*. Darius just wanted me to roll over!

I rocked and rolled over again. Moments later, I felt Darius's hands on the ropes that bound me. Our wrists were bound so we couldn't untie ourselves, but our hands were free enough to untie each other. As he loosened the ropes, I pulled and twisted my hands and at last they came free. I quickly rolled back over and untied the ropes that bound Darius's hands. Then we bent over sideways in the short crawl space to untie our feet, and ripped the gags from our mouths. We were free!

The crowd roared—something big had just happened in the game. We didn't have much time.

"I'll look for the timer!" Darius yelled in my ear. "You find the way out!"

CHAPTER EIGHTY-ONE

MY HEART WAS RACING. I CRAWLED AROUND UNTIL I found an access panel in the bottom. It was barred, but not too strongly. I kicked at it with my heels until the outside latch snapped and the trapdoor swung open. I could see a well-lit gray concrete floor below.

More music boomed from the field. Something by U2. A TV time-out? I hoped so. I waved to Darius, and he crawled over to me.

"I found the timer!" he yelled in my ear. "There's no off switch, and I don't know if I can pull out the wires without setting it off! We have to clear the area first!" He pointed to the hole. "Security guard!"

I nodded, understanding. This was no time for heroics. We needed to get word to the stadium authorities, and pronto. I climbed down through the trapdoor and slithered out from under the wheeled float. Darius followed me.

I helped Darius to his feet beside the float. We were in a concrete staging area below the stands. The corner of one of the end zones was visible a hundred yards away through two big open doors. Adam was out there, I suddenly realized. He and his mom and dad and somebody else they had decided to take with them instead of me.

What do you know, Adam, you were right, I thought. *I made it to the Super Bowl after all.*

The space where we stood was packed with people. Gaudily dressed dancers, kids with flags and banners, five different college marching bands, people in puppetlike animal costumes, tech guys and roadies, cameramen, people with headsets and clipboards shouting positions at the performers.

And then there was me and Darius, dusty and rumpled, blinking in the light. But at least I was in jeans and a T-shirt. Darius wore dirty white robes, and was scrawny and bearded, looking like the terrorist everyone believed he was.

"All right, people, twenty seconds to showtime!" a woman announced through a bullhorn.

Twenty seconds!

I spied a security guard among the sequined masses, and Darius and I pushed our way toward him. His eyes raked over us with a deeply suspicious look.

"Who are you?" he demanded. "Where are your access passes?"

"There's a bomb on the float," Darius said without preamble. "You have to get all these people out of here!"

The security guard looked panicked. We'd used the *b*-word, and you never used the *b*-word unless you really meant it.

"You—you're that soldier," the guard said, recognizing Darius. "From TV! And you're his brother!" He fumbled for his gun, drew it, and aimed it at us. "Don't move! Don't you move! I'm calling this in!"

Frustration overwhelmed me. *No!* We were trying to save people! "You don't get it—!" I started to say, but Darius put a hand to my chest and stepped in front of me.

"Yes! Good! Call it in!" Darius said. "Tell them there's a bomb in the float! Tell them to clear the stadium!"

Darius was right. It didn't matter what they thought of us right now. It didn't matter if they zip-tied our hands and feet and strung us up on a pole. We could explain everything later. All that mattered right now was getting everyone out of the way of the bomb.

The security guard kept the gun pointed at us with one hand and reached for his walkie-talkie with the other.

"1-5-1 to dispatch. 1-5-1 to dispatch," he said.

A shot boomed behind us, and a red bullet hole appeared in the middle of the security guard's forehead. With a stunned look, he fell down dead on the floor.

CHAPTER EIGHTY-TWO

SCREAMS. PANIC. SHOUTS. THE STAGING AREA became absolute pandemonium as the performers and stage crew pushed every which way to get out. Darius pushed me to the ground right before another shot rang out, the bullet hitting a woman in front of us in a marching band uniform. More screams. More panic.

I turned, trying to see where the shots were coming from. There—on the float. A roadie with a gun.

Darius saw him, too. He grabbed the fallen security guard's gun. "Stay down!" he told me, and he threw himself into the mayhem, going for the shooter.

I stayed down. The timer on the explosives had to be set to go off some time during the halftime show, which was supposed to start any second now. I could crawl back inside the float and try to disarm the timer, but how? If Darius, a trained Army Ranger, couldn't do it, neither could I. Not alone. I needed help.

Help. Mickey Hagan was just a phone call away! I dug through the dead security guard's pockets, trying to ignore for the moment that *I was digging through a dead security guard's pockets*.

He had to have one . . . yes! A cell phone! And there was no password code to enter. A trusting security guard. What were the odds?

My thumb hung in space over the phone's screen as I tried to remember the phone number Mickey had given me. I'd memorized it. But the chaos, the gunshots, the screams . . . Was the first part 359 or 395?

I couldn't—I didn't—

I reared back to hurl the phone against the wall in frustration.

No. Relax. Breathe, I told myself. *This is what Dane warned you about. The anger. You can control it.* I let the sound of my own pounding heart rise in my ears, let it push out all the screams and yelling and shooting. No distractions. No doubts. No second guesses.

I punched in the number and brought the phone to my ear.

"Consolidated Services," a woman answered.

No! I'd dialed the wrong number! I hung up, my hands shaking. Any second now, I expected the C-4 behind me to explode, blowing me and everyone else to smithereens. I tried to clear my head again, block out all the distractions, and punched in the number I thought I'd memorized.

"Consolidated Services," the same woman answered.

Damn it! I pulled the phone away from my ear and almost mashed the end-call button, but suddenly I had a thought. I brought the phone back to my ear.

"I need to talk to Mickey Hagan," I told the woman.

"One moment," she said.

CHAPTER EIGHTY-THREE

SHE WAS TRANSFERRING ME! EITHER I WAS ABOUT to get some other Mickey Hagan who was vice president of Consolidated Services's marketing division or something, or Consolidated Services was a front number for a CIA operator.

"Hagan," said that familiar Irish voice.

"Mickey! It's Kamran. Listen. We don't have a lot of time."

I hurriedly explained about the Super Bowl and the bomb. If I got out of this alive, there would be time to tell him about everything else.

"Find cover and stay on the line," Mickey told me, all business. "I'm going to make some calls."

I looked around for a place to hide. There were more floats, more stage equipment, but none of those was going to survive that blast. I needed to be out of this area, out of the *stadium*, far, far away.

Another shot exploded, and another security guard went down. The room was finally clearing, and in the wake of the stampeding performers, I saw three more security guards down on the floor, all shot dead. But where was Darius? I ran through the maze of floats and fallen band instruments, looking for him, worried I'd find him bleeding on the floor like the rest. But there he was on a big float designed to look like a football helmet. He was spinning, turning every which way to try and find the shooter.

Who was climbing up behind him.

"Darius! Look out!" I called. Which was stupid, because the shooter heard me, too. The roadie turned and shot at me. He missed, and I dove for cover behind a giant speaker. More shots. I felt the bullets hit the speaker behind me, heard them smashing the vinyl and wood. Then there was a cry and a thud, and I peeked out to see Darius wrestling with the shooter on the bottom of the float. He had leaped onto the shooter from above.

I had to help. I stuffed the phone in my pocket, snatched up the first weapon I could find—a trumpet, which hardly qualified as a weapon, but I had no choice—and ran for the platform like a safety homing in on a wide receiver. The shooter still had his gun, and Darius had the shooter's arm stretched out wide, protecting himself the same way Dane had taught me. But it wasn't protecting *me*. The gun went off in my direction and I ducked stupidly, like I could actually dodge a speeding bullet. I kept moving, though, bobbing and weaving, trying to avoid the swaying barrel of his gun. When I was finally close enough, I hit the shooter in the head with the business end of the trumpet. The blow knocked him out cold, and he dropped his gun over the side.

"Thanks—but we still have a bomb to worry about!" Darius said.

Right. The bomb. *Mickey!*

I pulled the phone back out. "Mickey! Mickey, are you there?"

"Kamran! Yes," Mickey said. "I need you to get out of there. I've got a bomb squad on the way."

"There won't be time!" I told him.

"All right," Mickey said. "I've got someone on the line to help defuse the bomb. Is anyone else—"

"Hands in the air!" someone shouted, and I nearly jumped out of my skin. Half a dozen stadium security guards wearing flak jackets and black ball caps had just run in the room and were pointing their pistols at me. They couldn't see Darius. He was around the other side of the float, and he ducked down to stay hidden.

"Put your hands in the air, now!" the guard shouted again.

"*Kamran*," Darius whispered, meaning I should do what he said.

I groaned and raised my hands, the bomb ticking away steadily behind me.

CHAPTER EIGHTY-FOUR

THE SECURITY GUARDS ADVANCED, GUNS POINTED straight at us.

"You Kamran Smith?" the lead guard asked.

"I—yes," I said. I'd forgotten that people knew me, that my face had been on TV, on the Internet, all this time.

The security guard lowered his weapon and signaled the others to do the same. "CIA says he's good," he told his men. "Make sure everybody else is out of this area. Now!"

I couldn't believe it. The guards ignored me and ran off, some checking the people on the ground, others making sure there was no one left in the surrounding rooms and corridors. I glanced at Darius, still hiding behind the float. We didn't know if the CIA had cleared him or not.

The lead guard climbed up on the float shaped like a football helmet. "This the shooter?" the lead guard asked me as he pointed to the unconscious guy.

"Yeah," I said. "I, uh, knocked him out with a trumpet."

The security guard bound the man's wrists with a zip tie and hauled him away, and I remembered that Mickey was still on the phone.

"Hey," I said. "Sorry. Guards showed up. But they knew who I was. That was fast."

"Told you, I made some calls," Mickey said. "Kamran, who else is with you? Dane? Aaliyah? Jimmy?"

He still didn't know that Dane was dead. Or that Jimmy had sold us out. And Aaliyah—was she dead, too?

"No," I said. "Just Darius."

Mickey was silent for a moment. "Kamran, I need you to tell me straight now: were you right about him? Do you trust him? Is Darius one of the good guys?"

I glanced at Darius, still crouching behind the float to hide from the guards.

"Yes," I was able to say at last. It was an amazing relief, even here, in the midst of all this madness.

"All right, then," Mickey said. "I want you to put Darius on the phone, and then I want you to get out of there."

"But—"

"You're to do anything and everything I tell you. Do you remember me saying that, lo these many moons ago? And you nodded, which I took to mean, 'Yes, Mr. Hagan, I will, under penalty of death, do every last thing you tell me to without question or argument.' *Now give the phone to Darius and get yourself clear.* He's an Army Ranger. He signed on for this. And if worse comes to worst, I'd like to send at least one of the Smith boys home to your parents in one piece."

I wanted to argue, but I knew he was right. And precious seconds were ticking away.

"It's for you," I said, handing Darius the phone.

"Yes?" Darius said. He listened for a moment and stood up straight. "Yes, sir," he said. If Mickey could have seen him salute, Darius would have. Through the beard and dirty robes, I could finally see the soldier underneath again. Darius ran for the float we'd crawled out of. "Yes, sir," he said into the phone. "Yes, sir."

Darius disappeared underneath the float. Mickey had told me to get out of there, and every cell in my body was screaming for me to do just that. But I couldn't leave Darius there without trying to help. But what could I do? If I crawled up inside the float I'd only be in his way.

I spun around, looking desperately for anything I could do to help, and saw the truck attached to the float. Of course! I could drive the float out onto the field. Get it out from under the bleachers. If the bomb did go off, it wouldn't take a quarter of the stadium with it.

I jumped inside the open cab. It wasn't a regular truck—it was a special car for hauling stadium sets around, like a bigger, beefier golf cart. I flipped the on switch and pressed the gas pedal, and the truck started to move. *Slowly.* Very, very slowly. It was like driving one of those cars at an amusement park that have a rail down the middle so you can't drive off the course. I kept nudging forward in my seat, urging the thing on like a horse, trying to get it to move faster. *Come on come on come on.*

The truck emerged from the tunnel and into the giant stadium. I'd been to University of Phoenix Stadium for Cardinals games before, but I'd never been down at field level. From the ground, the placed looked enormous. Five levels of seats swept up and away from the field, and two hundred feet above me the giant white trusses that held the retractable roof stretched from one end of the building to the other. Straight ahead of me on the other side of the stadium was the five-story-tall scoreboard, the giant Cardinal mural above it replaced with the Super Bowl logo.

The timer on the scoreboard said there were only five minutes left in the halftime break. If the Black Widow had timed the explosion for right when the halftime show was ending, right when the fireworks went off and the confetti shot into the air and everybody was standing and cheering, Darius had less than five minutes to defuse that bomb or we were finished.

CHAPTER EIGHTY-FIVE

LESS THAN FIVE MINUTES. I DIDN'T KNOW HOW MUCH of the explosion was supposed to reach the stands, but all those performers and bands and all the fans who would have been on the field to dance around during the halftime show would have been dead. It would have been horrible—and a hundred million people would have watched it on TV.

But even if the bomb exploded now, we had already foiled the Black Widow. The game had been postponed, the halftime show was canceled, and fans were streaming toward the exits. The scoreboard was asking people to leave in a slow and orderly fashion due to a gas leak in the stadium. A gas leak! Well, I supposed that was better than telling them there was a truckload of plastic explosives driving out onto the field.

The tow truck attached to the float moved achingly slow, but I had at least hit the grass of the field. *Come on come on come on*, I told it. I glanced at the scoreboard again. Less than four minutes!

Out of the corner of my eye I saw somebody coming down the aisle in the lower stands, not going up. It was a camera crew! Some TV crew was trying to get closer for a story.

"No! Get back!" I yelled, waving my arms. "Get back!"

But they kept coming. I glanced at the scoreboard. Three and a half minutes. If they got too close, the blast would kill them.

"Get back! Go away!" I shouted, but they couldn't hear me. They were closer, though, and I recognized the reporter leading the cameraman down the steps. It was Emily Reed, the pretty

ESPN commentator, wearing a knee-length red skirt and a white blouse.

Emily Reed.

When I was little, my parents took us on a vacation to the beach at Rocky Point, a resort town in Mexico. I was so little I wasn't supposed to go into the water by myself, but I saw Darius doing it and charged in on my own. The waves weren't very big, but I was tiny, and the seawater swept over me, tumbling me end over end, filling my eyes and ears and lungs and dumping me back on the beach a spluttering, wailing mess.

I felt like that now, images, movements, voices washing over me, drowning me like seawater.

Emily Reed interviewing football players on the sidelines. The Black Widow standing in the doorway, her gun still pointed at Dane's dead body. Emily Reed sharing a joke with another announcer in the studio. The Black Widow laughing at Darius for being such a dupe. Emily Reed talking about the Super Bowl on the TV in the motel room. Bashira Ansari's name in the report on Aaliyah's computer in the motel room.

The wave passed over me, leaving me dazed and breathless, and I suddenly knew where I'd heard Bashira Ansari's voice before.

Emily Reed was the Black Widow.

CHAPTER EIGHTY-SIX

I DIDN'T KNOW HOW OR WHY BASHIRA ANSARI would be working for ESPN, but I was dead sure it was her.

Emily Reed was the Black Widow, and I was the only person who knew it.

My first thought was to call Mickey Hagan and tell him. But Darius had the phone with him, trying to disable the explosives in the float.

I stared at Emily Reed as the truck churned slowly toward the center of the field. She had her back to me now, talking to the camera. Reporting on the sudden, alarming interruption to the most-watched sporting event in America. The interruption she herself had planned.

I had to do something. Tell someone. *Stop her.* The Black Widow was right there, in the lower section of the stadium, not a hundred feet from me!

I leaped out of the truck and ran for the stands. The float shuddered to a stop behind me, with Darius and all those explosives still inside. He would disarm the bomb in time, I was sure. He had to. I glanced at the scoreboard. Two minutes.

Two-minute warning, I thought. *No time-outs left. Six points down. Forty yards to the end zone.*

No distractions. No doubts. No second guesses.

I put my head down like I was running the hundred-yard dash. I hurdled over the abandoned benches and equipment on the sidelines. I jumped the wall into the stands. One minute, fifty seconds. I raced up the concrete steps toward Emily Reed. The cameraman finally saw me coming behind her and pulled his head away from the camera, trying to figure out who I was and what I was doing. Emily Reed noticed, and she turned. I practically ran into her, trying to stop.

"Emily Reed . . . isn't Emily Reed," I said to the camera, panting from my sprint. "Her real name's . . . Bashira Ansari. She's the widow of . . . terrorist Haydar Ansari. And she's a terrorist herself. She put plastic explosives on that halftime float!"

The cameraman looked over his viewfinder at me like I was crazy.

Emily Reed—Bashira Ansari—looked startled, but only momentarily. Then she regained her calm. We must have been live.

She laughed humorlessly. "I'm sorry, Bill," she said to whoever was back in the studio. "There's a young man here with a crazy story about explosives—"

"She put them there," I told the camera, talking quickly. "Her name is Bashira Ansari, not Emily Reed. Her husband was an al-Qaeda terrorist killed in a drone strike. She planned to blow up the Super Bowl halftime show as revenge."

I must have looked as crazy as I sounded. The cameraman shook his head, and Emily Reed gave me a pitying look.

"I'm sorry, Bill," Emily said to the camera. "We'll have to get back to you with more on this situation once we have less interruption. Security obviously has greater concerns right now."

"I'm telling you," I said, moving between Emily Reed and the camera, "she's a terrorist! She put a bomb on—"

The stage behind us exploded, knocking us all to the ground.

CHAPTER EIGHTY-SEVEN

PIECES OF TORN, TWISTED METAL AND CHUNKS OF sod rained down all around me, and I curled up into a ball. My brain was pounding and my ears rang with a constant hum, like a house security system warning you to put in your code before the alarm goes off. I shook my head, trying to remember who I was, where I was, and what I was doing. I pulled myself up on one of the red stadium chairs beside me.

And then I saw the hole.

The middle of the football field, from one forty-yard line to the other, was one giant, gaping hole. But it wasn't just a big dirt crater. I had forgotten: the University of Phoenix Stadium was unique in all the world for having a *retractable field*. It was too hot in Arizona to play outside, and natural grass wouldn't grow in a dome. The architects who designed the stadium made it so the natural grass field slid out on a huge two-acre tray. On game days it slid back in. So underneath that retractable green grass field inside the stadium wasn't more dirt—underneath were 546 steel wheels, sixteen metal rails, an irrigation system and drainage ditch, and seventy-six motors to move the whole thing back and forth.

All of which had been blown up when the float exploded.

The float—the float with Darius inside it!

"Darius!" I yelled. *"Darius! No!"*

I hauled myself to my feet and almost went tumbling down the concrete steps. I was still dizzy from the blast, and I could feel blood trickling down my forehead. I stumbled downhill and had to catch myself on one of the stadium seats. The seat was loose, wobbly, and I almost fell down again. I frowned at the seat, and then I saw it was almost ripped in half. A piece of metal shrapnel from the exploded machinery underneath the field had split it almost in two. It was the same all over the lower stands, too. Metal debris was everywhere, and dozens, *hundreds*, of those hard, seemingly indestructible plastic stadium seats were torn to shreds throughout the lower sections. The Black Widow hadn't needed enough plastic explosives to take down the stadium. With all that gear under the field, and all the equipment that was supposed to be on top of it during the halftime show, the explosion would have killed thousands of people.

Instead it had killed only one.

"Darius!" I screamed, staggering down the steps toward the smoking crater. *"Darius!"*

Behind me, over the ringing sound still in my ears, I heard a security guard yelling out as he ran down the steps. I turned to see the guard checking on the cameraman, who lay on his back, his face bloody.

Emily Reed lifted herself up on hands and knees behind the security guard, still wobbly, and pulled the pistol from his holster. Before he could turn around, she shot him in the back, and he fell across the wounded cameraman.

I took a step up toward her, but she wheeled on me. I was a few rows away from her now, but close enough to be staring down the barrel of that pistol. I put my hands up to show her I wasn't going to do anything stupid. I was so upset and disoriented that anything I did at this point *would* be stupid.

"I should have killed you and your brother before I put you inside that float," Bashira Ansari said. She *was* Bashira Ansari, the Black Widow. Emily Reed had just been her cover. "I worked for years to avenge the murder of my husband. *Years!* And you and your brother ruined it all."

"Your husband was a terrorist!" I told her.

"Haydar Ansari was a *hero!*" she yelled. She raised the gun and shot at me. I flinched, ducking again like that would do any good. But she was obviously still shaken up from the blast, and had missed. When I looked up again, she was running up the steps, her back bloody and her blouse shredded from the explosion. It was stupid, but I ran after her. She had killed Darius and I wasn't going to let her get away.

The cameraman was still pinned under the dead security guard, but he was conscious, and I realized he had been pointing his camera at us the whole time. He looked at me differently now as I ran toward him, shocked but no longer skeptical. I didn't care. I had to stop the Black Widow. I leaped over him, taking the stairs two at a time. Ansari heard me coming and turned to shoot at me over her shoulder, but I was ready this time. I tackled her from behind like I was blindsiding a quarterback, slamming us both down onto the concrete steps. Her gun went flying, clattering down through the shredded stadium seats.

I was stunned by the fall, and the Black Widow was too fast for me. She kicked me in the head, dazing me, and scrambled to her feet.

I tried to pull myself up, but I was too slow. She was going to get away! Then suddenly, there was someone standing in her way, waiting to intercept her.

Darius!

CHAPTER EIGHTY-EIGHT

DARIUS WAS ALIVE!

I didn't have time to ask how. He and the Black Widow began to fight. Darius was good, but Bashira Ansari was better. She fought with a fury born of rage and desperation. She got a punch in to Darius's stomach, and when he bent double she kneed him in the head. He staggered back, almost tripping over the stair behind him, and just managed to right himself before a half-blocked punch sent him down on his butt.

"Kamran! Lex Luthor on the Hoover Dam!" Darius cried.

The story from one of our childhood games in the backyard came flashing back to me, and I remembered how we'd dealt with the evil genius Lex Luthor. I crawled up behind Bashira Ansari on my hands and knees, and Darius kicked at her with both legs. She stumbled back, tripped over me, and went tumbling backward down the stairs.

Darius helped me up. "Lex Luthor always was a pushover," he said.

"Darius! How are you alive? The stage—"

"I couldn't defuse it," he said. "Too complicated. Too many fail-safes. She really was an evil genius. Come on."

I looked down, to where Bashira Ansari lay on the concrete. She wasn't moving, but we had to make sure she didn't get away.

"But when did you get out?" I asked, hurrying behind him down the stairs.

"When it was obvious I wasn't going to be able to disarm it, Mickey told me to get out. I had already felt the stage moving, so I knew you had driven it out onto the field, where it wouldn't do as much damage." He looked around at the busted stadium seats. "Or so I thought. Anyway, the stage had just stopped moving when I climbed out. I was going to grab you and run, but you were already running for the stands, so I just took off in the other direction. It took me forever to get back over here and help you out. I'm sorry. I had no idea *she* was here."

We stood over the body of Bashira Ansari, aka Emily Reed, aka the Black Widow. One of her arms was badly twisted, and she had a painful-looking broken leg, but her chest was still moving up and down. She was unconscious, but alive.

Police—actual police, not just stadium security guards—rushed down toward us, guns pointed at us.

"Hold it! Darius and Kamran Smith, you're under arrest! Hands in the air!" one of them cried.

I'd forgotten. We were both still wanted terrorists, and there was a bomb hole the size of the Grand Canyon in the floor of the stadium behind us. No call from Mickey Hagan was going to get us out of this one, not until we'd been able to tell our side of the story. And maybe not even then, for Darius.

We put our hands up, and the officers moved in to hand-cuff us.

"Be the strongest of the strong," I said.

Darius managed a smile. "Be the bravest of the brave," he replied.

"Help the helpless."

"Always tell the truth."

"Be loyal," I said.

"Never give up," he said.

"And kill all monsters," we said together as we stepped over the unconscious Bashira Ansari and were taken away.

We *were* in this together, me and Darius. Just like always. The Smith brothers against the world. And we'd lived by the Code, both of us. All the way until the end.

CHAPTER EIGHTY-NINE

I TOLD MY STORY TO THE CIA, THE FBI, AND THE DHS. And then I told it again. And again. And again. They poked and prodded and questioned every little detail, but in the end, they were satisfied. They might not have been happy about the means, but they were happy about the ends. But I didn't know if everything I said would help Darius. Or Mickey. And nothing I said could ever help Dane again.

In return for my story, I got Bashira Ansari's. The CIA had quickly put the pieces together. When her husband died in an American drone strike, she swore to get revenge. She left her children with a sister in Syria, came to America on a forged passport, and started a new life for herself. A very different one from her life as a Muslim extremist. She shed her veil for Western clothes and went to school to become a sports reporter, all with the idea of bringing America to its knees with a vicious, unexpected terrorist attack on a major sporting event. She worked patiently for years, establishing her credibility and waiting for the perfect opportunity to do the utmost damage. She was playing the long game, one she'd learned from her husband, a game of intricate plots, false clues, and misdirection. The Super Bowl had been her magnum opus. But we had taken the poison out of the Black Widow's bite.

They called in a doctor to examine me. I was fine, except for some cuts from flying shrapnel and mild dehydration. They gave me water and bandaged my forehead. Then I was free to go. Free. To go. My parents were, too. They were waiting for me in the lobby of the government building in Arizona I'd been brought to.

"Kamran joon," my mother said with relief, wrapping me in her arms. I hugged her and Dad like I would never let them go. They both looked haggard, and older somehow. But also relieved. At least they knew now I was okay. And that Darius was alive and innocent.

My parents had been detained by the Department of Homeland Security the entire time, each in their own cells while I was in mine. When I escaped, they'd been put under even stricter security. The DHS hadn't told them anything more than that I'd run away, and I had to tell them the whole story all over again as we were driven home. Telling the story to federal agents in a debriefing room was one thing. Telling my parents, who gasped and interjected and looked terrified the whole time, was another experience altogether. It made me realize just how surreal the whole thing had been. It was like I had lived a spy thriller movie.

And now what? Would I really just go back to being Kamran Smith, high school senior? That seemed even more surreal.

And what about Darius? His absence felt so profound as I sat between my parents in the backseat of the government car, their arms still around me. He was still being detained and questioned, and no one would tell us when he was going to be released. *If* he was going to be released. No matter what, I hoped we'd be able to see him soon.

We reached our street, where TV vans and camera crews waited for us, just like before. I sagged in my seat. This again? Still the media attention? Still the accusations, the doubt, the insinuations? After everything Darius and I had done?

The mob of TV reporters parted for the government car to pull into our driveway, filming everything. My parents and I sat in the car for a long moment, staring at the house we hadn't been back to in months. The word TERRORISTS was still spray-painted on the front.

"Are we ready to do this?" Dad asked. He reached out and squeezed my hand. Mom took my other hand. Slowly, the three of us stepped outside.

The questions hit us instantly.

"Kamran, what's it like to be vindicated?"

"Are you bringing legal action against the government for your wrongful incarceration?"

"Will Darius be released soon? Have you spoken to him?"

"How did you know Darius wasn't a traitor?"

"What's it like to be a hero, Kamran?"

I stumbled on the walkway to our front door and stopped to look back at the camera crews. They weren't calling me and Darius terrorists anymore—they were on our side! But how did they know? The federal agents had grilled me like Darius was public enemy number one and I was public enemy number two, like they didn't believe a word I'd said.

"Kamran," Dad called. He'd unlocked the front door, and I followed him inside.

The phone was ringing again, but Dad went straight to it and unhooked it. Mom stood in the middle of the living room, looking around at the house like it was some place she'd never been before. Dad went to her and hugged her.

I thought about going to my room, or maybe taking a long-overdue shower, but I turned the TV on instead. It was all me and Darius and the Super Bowl all the time. The ESPN camera-man had caught the whole thing—me confronting Bashira

Ansari, the explosion, her shooting the security guard, her ranting about her husband's murder and shooting at me. So that was how they knew. How everyone knew. The feds had made me tell them the story again and again, even though they'd had video evidence.

It was bizarre, watching myself, seeing the whole thing from the outside. Mom and Dad watched with me, my mom putting a hand on my arm in concern every time there was danger, as if this time I might actually get shot or killed.

All anybody on TV could talk about was the terrorist attack on the Super Bowl.

The terrorist attack foiled by the brothers Smith.

Another station had interviews with kids from my school. They never doubted me, they said. They knew I wasn't a terrorist the whole time. I was so humble. So friendly. Julia Gary called me her boyfriend. Adam Collier explained how I was supposed to have been in the audience at the Super Bowl with him. It was a different song and dance now that I was a national hero.

I decided to go have that shower after all.

CHAPTER NINETY

A FEW DAYS LATER, I SAT ALONE IN MY ROOM, STAR-
ing at the stack of textbooks on my desk. I was supposed to go
back to school tomorrow. Life goes on, and all that. The pep
squad had probably already hung a banner over the front door,
welcoming me back. The principal would call a special assem-
bly to honor the senior who saved everybody from a terrorist
attack at the Super Bowl. Adam would be waiting to clap me
on the back, and Julia would be waiting to parade me around on
her arm. They would all treat me differently than they had the
last time I'd seen them.

That was the problem.

Mom knocked on my door and opened it. "Kamran? You
have a visitor," she said.

"If it's Adam, tell him I don't want to talk to him," I said
without turning around. Adam had called the house at least
once every day, and I always told my mom to tell him I
wasn't home.

"Well, I don't know if you'll know me from Adam," said
Mickey Hagan, "but I'd like to say hello nonetheless."

Mickey! I ran over to him and we hugged. Mom smiled and
left us alone.

"I hope you've been on your best behavior," Mickey said,
glancing around my room. "I daresay your home is still bugged
from before you were detained."

My house had been bugged! But of course it had been
bugged. But why was Mickey telling me now? Then I realized—
Mickey was telling me to be careful about what I said to him,

in case someone was still listening. And we had a lot to talk about.

"Are you still with the CIA?" I asked him, choosing my words carefully. "Did you get in trouble?"

"It's a funny thing, that," Mickey said. "The CIA appears to be under the impression that I had nothing to do with your escape and subsequent adventures until you called the CIA hotline looking for a friendly voice to help you out of a jam. Someone told them that an ex–Green Beret named Dane Redmond was entirely responsible for putting the team together that extricated you from DHS headquarters in Washington, blew up a stash of plastic explosives in Nashville, and confronted the Black Widow in the mountains of Arizona."

"You don't say."

"I do say," said Mickey. He motioned for me to sit on the bed, and took a seat in my desk chair. "Now, where could they have heard such a wild story as all that?"

"I have no idea," I said. But I did know: it was exactly the same story I'd told the FBI and the CIA and the DHS over and over again.

"And of course, Dane Redmond isn't alive to confirm or deny any of this."

"He died a hero," I said, meaning it.

"And your country agrees," Mickey said. "They have posthumously upgraded Dane Redmond's discharge status from 'other than honorable' to a 'general discharge,' which he would have much appreciated, I know. The upgrade has the added advantage of restoring his benefits, including his veteran's pension, which will come as a great comfort to his ex-wife and young daughter."

"He—he has a daughter? I didn't know." I'd made up all that stuff about Dane being the brains behind everything just to get Mickey out of trouble. I had no idea it would fix Dane's discharge status, or actually help the family I didn't know he had.

"And Aaliyah?" I asked. Mickey knew what I meant. I hadn't had a chance to tell this version of events to Aaliyah. If she went into her debriefing and told the truth—

"She corroborated the whole thing," Hagan said. "Thankfully, she has been well trained to receive and analyze information rather than volunteer it."

I felt like Mickey was scolding me, but only slightly. I deserved it some, too. If I hadn't been careful, the government could easily have caught me out in the lie, and then it would have been worse for everyone. But it sounded like it had all worked out—even better than I had hoped.

"All's well that ends well, as the Bard once said," Mickey said with a smile, letting me know all was forgiven.

"What about Jimmy?" I asked.

"Ah. That's one that didn't end so well. Jimmy got away. We're still after him, but he's very good at not being found, as you might guess."

"All part of the game," I said, repeating Jimmy's favorite phrase.

"That it is, I suppose," Mickey said. "That it is."

CHAPTER NINETY-ONE

MICKEY TAPPED THE BIG STACK OF TEXTBOOKS ON my desk. "Back to school for you, then, I see. No rest for the weary."

"I don't care about the schoolwork part," I said.

"But the non-schoolwork part?" he asked, picking up on my tone.

I looked at my hands. "You're the only one who ever had faith in me, Mickey," I said. "The only one who believed me right from the start and never gave up on me."

"Ah, I see," Mickey said. "Your friends at school, they weren't so . . . faithful. And now they're back on the Kamran Smith bandwagon, trumpets and cymbals in hand."

"I'm not sure I want anybody as a friend who wasn't there for me when things got bad."

"I can understand that," Mickey said. "But tell me true, Kamran: How many times did you doubt your brother in all this? How many times did you give up on him, only to come 'round again when you found out you were wrong?"

That stung. Mickey knew better than anybody what it was like to believe wholly and completely in a person and then have him break your heart. But unlike Mickey, I had given up on Darius more than once before I'd finally learned the truth. Mickey had believed and been burned; I'd believed, and disbelieved, and believed again, and disbelieved again, and Darius had been innocent after all.

"I don't mean to punish you," Mickey said. "Heaven knows I've punished myself plenty enough that I don't need someone else to help me. Nor do you. I'm only after pointing out that you doubted your brother once or twice even when you were closer to him than any other person on God's green earth. Now think about your friends at school. They're not nearly so close to you as you are to your brother. Think about what they heard, and what they saw, and how they felt. Can you really blame them for not believing in you when they barely know you? The *real you*, I mean?"

"Yes," I said, just to be perverse. I sighed. "Adam knew the real me. He's been my best friend since we were kids."

"And he knows you even better now," Mickey said. "The real you he's maybe never seen before. The real you maybe *you've* never seen before."

There was something to that. Something I hadn't been able to talk about with anybody since I'd gotten back. I'd been relieved to finally come home, to be normal again, but at the same time . . . At the same time, I missed it. The excitement. The way I was valued by the team, and not treated like a kid. The feeling that I was doing something important. I didn't like the thought of good people dying. Of *me* dying. But the rest of it—the rest of it I found myself longing for.

"Don't let these fair-weather friends of yours off the hook," Mickey said. "I'm not saying to do that. They need to know they hurt you. That's what'll keep them from hurting you the same way next time. But don't push them away either, Kamran. What good will that do? Yes, you'll graduate in a few months' time, and then you could blow them all a big fat kiss good-bye. But in the meantime, you'll just be friendless and alone—not to mention missing out on all those beautiful young lassies who will surely want to date the hero of the Super Bowl."

I blushed and laughed.

"Aha," Mickey said. "You begin to see the wisdom in it, I think." He smiled.

"It's just so hard," I said.

"And it always will be," Mickey said wearily. "Some people will always think the less of you for the color of your skin, for the country of your mother's birth, or for the despicable actions of someone who kind of, maybe, on a good day in the right light looks a bit like you. Which means you always have to be the better man. You go back to school and be all broody and mean and push people away, and they'll turn on you again just as fast. 'He's just what we thought he was all along,' they'll say. The best thing for you to do is to keep living by that Code of Honor of yours and proving the haters wrong. You going to West Point will go a long way toward helping do that."

"But I'm not going to West Point," I said. "Congresswoman Barnes withdrew her nomination."

"And yet, like the young lassies lining up to date you, so too are America's politicians falling all over themselves to recommend you for West Point again," Mickey said. He took a letter out of his jacket pocket. "Including this recommendation from the vice president of the United States, with whom I happened to put in a good word."

I took the letter from him in disbelief. Sure enough, it was a glowing letter of recommendation right below the vice presidential seal, signed by the vice president himself.

"If you still want it, that is," Mickey said. "Do you?"

"Yes," I said, still mesmerized by the vice president's signature. "Yes. It's what I've always wanted."

"It's not going to be easy for you there, either," Mickey said. "You'll have even more haters and doubters than before."

"I know," I said. Maybe nothing was ever going to be easy for me again. Not now that I'd had my eyes opened. But that didn't mean I wanted to stick my head under my pillow and hide.

"Good, then," Mickey said. "There's good news for me as well. Seems my work in all this business has earned me a bit more respect at the Company, as befits my pay grade. I've been put in charge of my own counterintelligence team at the CIA."

"That's terrific, Mickey!" I told him.

"It is. I've already recruited a couple of people for it, too," he said, "including Ms. Aaliyah Sayid. Now I'm wondering if I might not entice you to join us."

My mouth hung open so far, it must have brushed the floor. "*What? Me?*"

"You'd have to keep up with your studies at West Point at the same time, of course. And that won't be easy. They keep you busy there, believe you me."

"Yes! I mean, yes, I'll join! I'll do whatever it takes," I said. I still couldn't believe it.

"Good, then. That's settled. First things first, I want you to start training to fight. Pick up where you left off with Dane." Mickey slapped his knees and stood. "Let's go meet your new trainer."

"What, now?" I asked. I had school tomorrow.

"No time like the present," Mickey said, beckoning me down the hall.

CHAPTER NINETY-TWO

"KAMRAN SMITH, MEET OUR TEAM'S NEW TACTICAL specialist," Mickey said. "Darius Smith."

My brother sat on the couch between Mom and Dad, Mom's hand holding his. Darius's dress uniform looked five sizes too big on his emaciated body, but he'd bathed and shaved and had a haircut and was starting to look like his old self again. He got up from the couch, and we hugged for a long time.

"Hello, Cadet!" he said, holding me out at arm's length. "Good to see you again."

"Good to see you, too," I told him, which was a major understatement.

There was so much I wanted to say to Darius, so much I wanted to talk about, and I could tell he felt the same way. But it wasn't a conversation either of us wanted to have with an audience.

"Come on, let's go outside," Darius said, nodding toward the backyard.

I looked at Mickey Hagan. "Go on, then," he said. "I'll stay here and tell your parents all about our little arrangement."

I followed Darius outside. It was almost the beginning of February, but it was still sixty-five degrees and sunny. Arizona weather.

"Are you staying for a while?" I asked. "Here?"

Darius nodded. "Until I move to DC to work with Mickey. I'll still be in the army, just attached to the CIA. Did Mickey sign you up, too?" Darius asked.

"Yeah."

"Good."

There were chairs on the patio, but we stood looking out over the small plot of green grass wedged in between brown gravel paths.

"You remember when we used to play Rostam and Siyavash out here?" Darius asked.

"Of course," I said. "You do, too, or else you wouldn't have been able to give me all those clues."

We were quiet again for a while. Maybe Darius was remembering all our silly adventures. I was remembering putting a gun to his head.

"I'm sorry," we both said at the same time.

Darius laughed softly, and I smiled despite myself.

"You first," Darius said.

"Oh, me first?" I said, half kidding. "How's that work?"

"Mine's going to take longer," Darius said.

I took a deep breath. "I'm sorry I didn't believe you."

"But you did," Darius said.

I shook my head. "Not all the time. They told me things. Told me you hated the government for the way you were treated after 9/11. That you went to Washington senior year to spy for al-Qaeda. That you were a Muslim—"

Darius closed his eyes and sighed. "Well, obviously I didn't go to Washington to spy for al-Qaeda. I went because Sofia Ramirez was going, and she was totally hot."

I laughed.

"And of course I don't hate the government," Darius said. "I mean, yes, I hated the way people treated me after 9/11. You don't know how it was. You were so young."

"I think I know a little bit how it was now," I told him. He nodded at that.

"But what about the prayer beads?" I asked. "The Internet searches?"

Darius looked off into the distance. "I need something more in life, you know? Something spiritual. It's really tough, as a soldier. The things you see. The things you do. I needed to find some kind of meaning in everything. And I wanted to reconnect with where Mom came from. Who we are. So I started looking into Islam. Other stuff, too. Nonreligious stuff. But they probably didn't mention my poetry books by Rumi or Hafez."

"No, they didn't." I couldn't believe it. My brother? Reading *poetry*?

"But why didn't you tell us that you were starting to become more religious?"

Darius shrugged. "I felt like it was something I needed to do on my own. I was doing this for me, not for anybody else. And what was I supposed to say? I was still seeking. I still am. I don't feel like I have all the answers, but I feel like I'm on the right path. Does that make any sense?" He kicked a pebble off the porch. "Anyway, I'm not going to apologize for being Muslim. And I shouldn't have to just because some terrorists somewhere twist Islam to fit their own awful agenda."

I nodded. He was right. It was the same thing I'd told the DHS when they'd asked me about our mom.

"Now can I say *I'm* sorry?" my brother said, giving me a small smile. "I came out here to tell you I'm sorry for dragging you into all this. I knew it would be hard for you, but I didn't know how hard. The alienation, the TV crews, the DHS taking you away in the night and interrogating you for months. And then you having to go on the run, getting shot at just to save me.

If I'd known it was going to hurt you like that, put you in that kind of danger, I would have just let them kill me in Afghanistan."

That hit me like a punch to the gut. I remembered how I'd once wished that Darius *had* died in Afghanistan, just so I could have my old comfy life back again. I felt sick all over again for having ever doubted him.

"No," I told him. "No. I'm just sorry I wasn't strong enough from the start."

"Are you kidding? Kamran, you risked your life to save me when you didn't have a single good reason to do it."

"Yes, I did," I told him. "You're my brother."

Darius clapped my hand and pulled me into a hug.

"It's you and me against the world, huh?" Darius said, and I nodded. "How are you doing?" he asked, eyeing me seriously. "I mean, just with—everything. Are you sleeping okay? Nightmares? After what happened in the cave—"

I looked down. I knew Darius was talking about that horrifying moment when I had shot the terrorist. Killed him. It was something I still thought of constantly. Every night before I went to sleep, I saw his face. Heard the gunshot. Saw the blood. As terrifying as everything else I'd experienced had been—especially those last moments with the bomb and the explosion—the death of that man haunted me the most.

"I'm not doing great with it," I told my brother truthfully, but I didn't like to talk about it. "What about you?" I asked my brother. "You must be worse off."

"It's tough," Darius admitted. "But I'm seeing a counselor. She specializes in this kind of stuff, and it's really been helping me deal with what happened to me. She's really good." He put a hand on my shoulder. "You could talk to her, too."

My first thought was *No way. I can handle this by myself.* But then I remembered what Dane had said, about how soldiers didn't like to talk about stuff, didn't get help when they needed it. And how it eventually ate them up inside. As much as I didn't want to talk about what happened with someone else, I promised myself I would. For Dane's sake.

"Yeah," I said. "Okay."

The sliding door to the patio opened and Mom leaned out, her hand covering the receiver on the phone.

"Kamran, I'm sorry to interrupt," she said. "It's Adam calling again. Are you home?"

Behind her, I saw Mickey Hagan give me a questioning look. I glanced at my brother, and back at my mother.

"Yeah," I told her. "I am."

ACKNOWLEDGMENTS

Thanks to everyone at Scholastic for all their enthusiasm and hard work: to David Levithan for saying "yes," to Emellia Zamani for reading the first draft, to Emily Cullings and Dan Letchworth for reading the final drafts with such eagle eyes, to Nina Goffi for designing such a beautiful book, and to Antonio Gonzalez for helping me get the word out about it. Very special thanks to Aimee Friedman for being such a terrific editor (again), and of course to Grace Kendall for bringing me on board in the first place! Many thanks to my great friend Bob, and to my early readers at Bat Cave: Gwenda Bond, Alexandra Duncan, Rebecca Petruck, Carrie Ryan, Megan Shepherd, Courtney Stevens, and especially Gabrielle Charbonnet and Megan Miranda. I'd also like to thank reader and fan Nick Toosi for answering my questions about growing up Persian American, and Hossein Kamaly, assistant professor of Asian and Middle Eastern cultures at Barnard College, for reading the manuscript and helping me get my facts right. Any errors that remain are my own. And last but never least, thanks again to Wendi and Jo.

ABOUT THE AUTHOR

Alan Gratz is the author of several books, including *Samurai Shortstop*, which was named one of the ALA's 2007 Top Ten Best Books for Young Adults; *The Brooklyn Nine*, which was among *Booklist*'s Top Ten Sports Books; and *Prisoner B-3087*, which was named to YALSA's 2014 Best Fiction for Young Adults list. Alan lives in North Carolina with his wife and daughter. Look for him online at www.alangratz.com